MODEL GHOST
THE BACKYARD MODEL MYSTERIES

TK SHEFFIELD

MAKING HAY PRODUCTIONS, LLC

ALSO BY TK SHEFFIELD

Model Suspect, a holiday cozy, a humorous small-town mystery served with a brandy old-fashioned and cheese curds. (Named Top 100 Notable Indie, among other awards.)

Model Wave, romance, boats, and bad business in the Wisconsin Northwoods (A Killer Nashville Winner for Best Cozy, among others.)

Identifiers: ISBN: 979-8-9905631-2-4 (ebook) | ISBN: 979-8-9905631-3-1 (paperback)

Title: *Model Ghost* : the backyard model mysteries, book three / T.K. Sheffield.

Description: Genesee Depot, WI : Making Hay Press, 2024. | Series: Backyard model mystery, bk. 3.

Subjects: LCSH: Murder--Fiction. | Models (Persons)--Fiction. | Internet personalities--Fiction. | Wisconsin--Fiction. | Cozy mysteries. | Mystery fiction. | BISAC: FICTION / Mystery & Detective / Cozy / General. | FICTION / Mystery & Detective / Amateur Sleuth. | FICTION / Mystery & Detective / Women Sleuths. | GSAFD: Mystery fiction.

LCC applied for.

This is a work of fiction. Any resemblance to actual persons or specific location is pure coincidence.

Other books by T.K. Sheffield

Model Suspect

Model Wave

Making Hay Press, d.b.a. Making Hay Productions, LLC

I

TUESDAY, THE GHOSTLY GALA REHEARSAL

I'D HEARD OF BEING FASHIONABLY LATE, BUT BEING FASHIONABLY DEAD WAS quite … unfashionable, was it not?

I thought so.

However, things had changed since Mel Tower (that's me) retired from the modeling industry. At my feet in the ballroom of The Golden Promenade, Cinnamon's premier senior living complex, was a ghastly sight.

Not a ripped sleeve or broken heel. Mishaps *snagging* a show of muumuu dresses, models, and a quartet. Well, not a quartet. A lively polka combo.

We were in Wisconsin, after all.

Lying on the glossy runway was Ichabod Hall, designer, age sixty —*and we were conducting his new fashion line's rehearsal in a few hours!*

His mouth gaped. His eyes were open in a blank stare.

"Ichabod, can you hear me?" I asked. "What happened?"

I touched his wrist. Near his hand was a small book. Probably slipped from a pocket.

His skin felt cold, and he didn't have a pulse. *Egads.* I looked around—had anyone seen what happened?

The room was gilded for a Halloween fashion show: Gold-framed chairs lined a runway snaking through the space, the catwalk installed just yesterday.

Free-standing candelabras laced with fake spider webs decorated corners. Inflatable pumpkins with leering eyes hung from the ceiling.

I'd protested those ghastly gourds when they'd been hung. *Overkill*, I'd said. Now I wished the pumpkins could speak because they'd seen how Ichabod died.

"Is someone here—help!" I yelled.

Ichabod's trench ensnared his gangly legs. The cravat he wore appeared tight. Strangulation tight, like he'd clawed at the orange silk and choked himself.

The inhaler he always carried was beside his clenched hand, cracked as though squeezed in desperation.

"Help, someone! Please, come quickly!" I yelled.

This couldn't be happening—how could this be real?

Ichabod and I were supposed to be finalizing his show. Confirming the rundown of models, music, and order of flowy dresses that announced the re-emergence of his womenswear line.

I stared at the end of the runway, where Cinnamon's one paparazzo, a stringer from the local newspaper, would take photographs. In the corner was a podium where the journo would ask questions for a post-event interview.

Unless Hall's ghost spoke for him, everything was canceled.

My cousin Lou Jingle banged out of the kitchen adjacent to the ballroom. Lou always banged. She was a firecracker in a forty-five-year-old cowgirl's body.

She wore an apron—"Cowgirls Give a Ship"—and set a platter on the buffet. "I finished makin' snacks for the crew," she said. "What'd you do to Ichabod?"

"Call nine-one-one!"

She stared at the form on the runway. "Is this a weird fashion thing? That guy has squirrelly ideas—"

"Call an ambulance!"

"Mel, we're in a senior center that thinks it's a cruise ship. There's no need to call. Doc Graves has a walk-in clinic on the Lido Deck."

"Get him. Run, Lou—hurry!"

I noted clues while waiting for help.

I wasn't a professional gumshoe but had moonlighted as an amateur.

Ichabod's head veered at an angle, his skin shockingly pale, as bright as the final element of his fashion show, a ghost-like muumuu of delightfully light satin.

Had he fallen and injured himself? Had he choked?

Near him was a shattered plate. Crumbs covered his slacks. Fried cheese curds greased the runway. It was as though Hall caught a heel on the slick surface and crashed down.

I squinted at the book near Hall's hand and gasped—*The Tempest! The same book had tumbled from its shelf in my bookstore mere hours ago!*

Crystal Broadway, my shopkeep at The Bell, Book & Melville was on vacation. Last evening, I'd taken a shift behind the counter. At the witching hour, six o'clock, I'd closed the place. (Cinnamon was an older community and residents tucked in early.)

I doused the fire in the hearth, donned a jacket. Before I reached the exit, *The Tempest* flew from its shelf like a sprite fleeing a ghoul.

I investigated but found nothing. *A Midsummer Night's Dream* had been the book adjacent to *The Tempest*—perhaps Puck had something to do with the shenanigans?

I'd restored *The Tempest* to its place and locked up, anxious to get home to my rescue collie, Max.

In the ballroom, I stared at the book on the runway, unsure if it was the same volume that bewitched me.

I wouldn't touch it for fear of contaminating a crime scene.

I shivered despite the garment I wore, a vintage black dress. Cozy cashmere, warm as a campfire on a Wisconsin fall evening.

It had been a favorite during my twenty-year gig in New York City, a security blanket of sorts. It was like wearing a hug while experiencing the pressure of a fashion career.

Where was Doc Graves—I wish he'd hurry!

Lighting flashed through the ballroom's tall windows. Thunder followed—*boom!*

Storms were predicted for the week of Boo Bash, Cinnamon's annual celebration of everything spooky.

The Cinnamon Roll, the local paper, had warned of spooky shenanigans—if a storm struck during the fest, disaster followed.

In an editorial, Wooly Gallagher, publisher, advised diligence at every party: During The Golden Cheesehead senior dating event, be wary of fake personalities. At Reader's Theater, watch for suspicious characters.

At the Ghostly Gala Fashion Show, Wooly wrote to break a leg—but it was tongue in cheek, meaning good luck.

I stared at lifeless Ichabod Hall. He was broken, all right. In his all-black clothing, with his limbs bent at odd angles, he looked like a haute couture scarecrow.

What happened?

Thunder *boomed!* again.

What disaster had befallen my beloved village of Cinnamon?

MY COUSIN LOU HELD A ROLLING PIN, STARING AT THE RUNWAY.

"Well, if this doesn't beat my beer batter. Looks like Ichabod got knocked in the noggin." She stepped closer. "No, he was breaded. Crumbs everywhere." She swung the pin as though practicing for pickleball, a sport she'd begun learning. "This changes everythin' this week."

Doc Graves and Pauline Pickle, his nurse, had burst into the ballroom with a stretcher and First Aid kit.

She was a pickleball instructor with health supplements and sportswear clothing line.

I wasn't sure if her real last name was Pickle. People started calling her that, and it stuck.

She set up a triage station. "Mr. Hall won't be a long-term guest in sickbay, obviously." She glared at me. "Stand back."

Pauline—never Paula—had joined the doc a year ago, if I recalled. She was fit, tan. About sixty, give or take a century. She seemed ageless, like someone who'd made a deal with a no-nonsense underworld fellow to never grow old.

I'd met a few folks like that in NYC.

She and Doc were crazy-successful pickleball players. I always saw their pictures in *The Cinnamon Roll* posing with cucumber-shaped trophies. Their team was the ones to beat 'round these parts.

She handed shoe covers and gloves to Doc Graves. "Don't touch anything. Put these on."

He ripped ribbon cordoning off the first row of gold chairs, then plunked down in a seat to put on the protective gear.

So much for not touching anything.

The front-row throne Doc occupied was reserved for an editor. One so important that I, the fashion show's second, no third, banana, hadn't been told her name.

The woman's attendance was top secret, need-to-know basis only.

I suspected her name rhymed with "Janna Sintour," but that could be wrong.

White lighting flashed through the ballroom's windows. I jumped before thunder crashed—*BOOM!*

The pumpkins hanging from the ceiling shook like we'd hit an iceberg.

Lou looked at the swaying orange globes. "Batten down the hatches. Goose drownder comin'."

"How long have you been here, Lou?" Pauline asked.

"Got here at oh-nine-hundred. Worked by myself."

"Did anyone see you?"

"Lou, don't talk—" I began.

"No, tell me everything, Louella," Pauline said, glaring *again*. "I need to know!"

Why was she so hostile?

Lou ignored my warning, as usual. "It's fine, Mel. You're so uptight lately." She took another swing with the rolling pin. "I made batter for curds. Started the fryers for donuts, apple fritters. You know, food that says ya live in Wisconsin."

"There are other ways to indulge without so many calories," Pauline said. "Go on."

"Trudy from the Cinnamon Spices called sayin' her gals are hot over Ichabod." Lou looked down. "Wait 'til they find out he's passed on to the great runway in the sky."

"How did you speak with Trudy?" Pauline asked.

"FaceTimed 'til our phones froze up. Then I called her 'til the line dropped. Bad weather always messes with the service here. It's like we really are out to sea."

Doc Graves stepped to Ichabod, observing the scene.

I didn't hear sirens, surprisingly. "Are the police on their way?"

"They are, but our policy is to arrive silently," Pauline said. "Negative sound energy affects the cruise experience."

"Lou, why were the Spices hot about Ichabod?" I asked.

"Cuz of the Golden Cheesehead! The single gals wanted time with him before the competition started. They were aiming to get the First Wedge." She pointed to the buffet. "It's over there, a gold cheddar triangle on a stick. He was gonna hand it out."

"But it's for charity," I protested. "They were that competitive?"

"The entire week of Boo Bash is for charity, but gals wanted it."

I felt my face flush. "This fashion show was serious business. Mr. Hall shouldn't have been distracted—"

"Whoa, Mel," Lou said. "I'm not one to call out attitudes, but you've been high-strung since elbowin' in to run this hoedown." She looked skyward. "Like that gal up in the suite, I imagine."

"What 'gal' in the suite?"

"The editor up on the Gold Level."

"*The one no one knows about?*" I asked.

She rolled her eyes. "Kitchen staff knows everythin'. We're the heartbeat of a place. No offense, Doc."

"No problem, Louella," he said.

"Who's the editor?" I demanded.

"Didn't see her. Just talked through the door." Lou pointed to the broken dish near Ichabod. "I took up appetizers on a plate just like that: curds, fritters. Veggies, and a side of ranch. Midwest hospitality, you know."

Pauline rolled her eyes. She stood by the runway, hands on hips. The woman always seemed irritated around me.

Or, *because* of me.

Lou continued, "I figured that fancy New 'Yawk' editor was a sourpuss, but she sounded okay. Not sure why it she was kept secret."

Suddenly, I heard sirens—were they in my head?

I wasn't sure, but they definitely were distress signals.

2

THE GALLEY

I needed water and dragged Lou into the galley, the kitchen adjacent to the ballroom. There was a beverage dispenser on the stainless steel counter. Cucumbers, lemons, and ice floated in the crystal clear water.

Lou grabbed a goblet, filled it, and set it in front of me. "Drink up. It's good for your skin, accordin' to Pauline." She nodded at the dispenser. "She made it."

"Thanks."

Lou sighed. "What's wrong?"

"You're kidding, right?"

"Yeah, Ichabod, I know, but what *else*?"

"Nothing—our guest of honor has taken an early bow. It's terrible."

I gulped water. Lou waited to speak until I drained the glass.

"When you wanted to run the fashion show, I shoulda refused," she said.

"*You* submitted my name to the committee. I didn't ask for this."

She slammed a hand on the counter. "You needed it! It was your chance for revenge. Get even with those folks that treated ya like a mannequin, a side of beef, when ya worked in New York."

I shook my head. "I retired five years ago. I made a decent income that allowed me to move home and buy the craft mall. The bookstore, too. I'm grateful for it."

"Grateful, schmateful. You got a chip on your shoulder the size of Lambeau Field. That career squished your personality like a cow in a chute. Forced to stand still, be silent." Lou's nostrils flared. "If someone said that to Louella Jingle, I'd hook 'em with a horn, toss 'em in the Hudson River." She grinned. "I love that bull by the stock exchange. He's my spirit animal."

"Things were different when I started. It's better now."

"There's no time limit on revenge!" she yelled. "Every gal knows that—"

The door swung open. An older gentleman walked in, his wingtips tapping the tile—*click, click, click*. He wore an overcoat and a hat with a feather tucked in the brim.

I recognized him: Detective Bruce DuWayne, Dane County law enforcement. He'd investigated a murder in my mall last year.

"Hello, ladies," he said. "It's a pleasure to see you again. My condolences on the loss of Mr. Hall."

Lou, being Lou, served DuWayne coffee and a cinnamon roll as though customary to have an investigator in her kitchen.

She pulled out a stool at the counter. "Sit, make yourself at home, Bruce. How long's it been? Almost a year since that set-to in Mel's mall?"

He nodded. "Correct."

"Glad that murder was solved. No hard feelin's that Mel solved it before you did?"

"None at all."

"What are we gonna do 'bout that rodeo in the ballroom, The Grand Saloon?" Lou nudged him. "More fun to call it a saloon, eh? What brought ya here from Dane County? Fresh air? Reality check?" She laughed.

"I'm here in an official capacity, Louella. I'm filling in for your police chief who is on a hunting trip in Canada." He took a bite of roll. "These are delicious."

"Detective," I began, "we can reveal what we saw, but nothing —"

"Mel found the body," Lou interrupted. "She's a suspect, right? That's how it works?"

"I'm here to ask a few questions. That's all." He smiled.

Lou nodded. "We got nothin' to hide. Shoot."

"No—" I said.

"Mel, you got the right to clam up, remain silent," she said. "I'll recite the caterer's oath and blab." She held up a hand. "I solemnly swear I won't make my customers barf. Or whack 'em with a meat mallet when they drive me crazy. Nor will I poison 'em." She sighed. "That's a serious oath."

"Amen," DuWayne said.

"More coffee?" Lou asked. "There's more rolls where that one came from, too."

"Yes, please."

They chatted like neighbors gossiping over a fence.

I felt discombobulated. Lou's remark about a chip on my shoulder rattled in my brain like a fashion accessory, a chunky necklace or bracelet.

She talked. I listened—especially when she described the editor upstairs. Having a mystery VIP attending the show irritated me, someone responsible for the show's success.

Who was she?

LOU REFILLED THE DETECTIVE'S MUG. "I'LL SOLVE THIS RIGHT NOW: The editor did in Ichabod Hall in the ballroom with a scarf. Then she skedaddled back to her suite and ordered room service to make it seem like she was there the whole time."

DuWayne coughed. "H-how do you know this?"

"I took a snack up to her. Spoke to her through the door."

"When did she order room service?"

"'Bout two hours ago." Lou shrugged. "She didn't order, exactly. I ran it up 'cuz I figured she was hungry. Fashion peeps don't eat much."

"Did you speak to her or an assistant?" I asked.

Lou frowned. "Could have been her cowhand, I guess. Door was closed. Want me to zip up and ask?" She looked at DuWayne.

"I prefer not."

A square-jawed fellow in a uniform stuck his head in; he was Tony Giugliano, the Promenade security guard. "Detective, the salon and buffet are secure. Should I do this space, too?"

"No way!" Lou protested. "My kitchen is locked down. Caterer's oath—"

"May I handle this, Lou?" DuWayne asked.

"Sure, but *nobody* messes with this cook's shanty."

"Tony, I'll take care of it."

Lou waved at the guy. "This is my cousin, Mel Tower. She's solved a couple mysteries in case ya need help."

He looked at DuWayne. "Do you need assistance, sir?"

"I do not, thank you."

Lou watched the door swing shut. "Is he a part-timer with the village?"

"He's with a private company."

"He was practicin' for the Golden Cheesehead in the Whoopee Den yesterday." Lou whistled. "Spy-*sea.*"

She slapped her thigh, knocking the water dispenser with an elbow. It rocked back and forth, then tipped to the floor—*crash!*

"Watch out!" I yelled.

Bruce DuWayne swung out of the way, spilling his coffee. I jumped to avoid getting soaked, slamming into Lou—coffee, rolls, water, napkins went flying.

Her "spicy" comment caused all kinds of chaos.

Talk about messing up the cook shanty.

Order was restored to the kitchen, but not logic.

Lou argued, "What's the big deal about 'spicy'? I cook with spices all the time. We live in Cinnamon, everybody's *spicy* here."

"The word has a different meaning now," I said.

She frowned. "Does it mean highfalutin'? Like the fashion crowd? They're *all* spicy."

I gave up.

DuWayne dabbed his tie. "The Whoopee Den is a room on the ship? Er, the senior resort, I mean."

Lou nodded. "It's where they host comedy shows. And The Den of Intrigue is the library. The Fit Republic is the gym." She began counting on her fingers. "The Room of Thrones is admin. And then there's the Board Room."

"Where they play games, I assume?" DuWayne asked.

"No, it's the Board Room. Where big shots meet."

"Thank you, Lou," he said. "I'll try to keep the rooms straight while I investigate."

"You gonna chew the fat with Mel? She didn't do it, by the way." She slugged my bicep. *Ouch.*

He turned to me. "How are you, Ms. Tower? "It's been some time since we've talked?"

"I'm fine, thanks, and that's correct." I rubbed my arm.

"Things are well at your mall, The Bell, Book & Anvil?"

"Yes."

Lou said, "She owns a new bookshop in town, too, 'The Bell, Book & Melville.' Old building on Main Street, just down from her art mall. Brick walls, fireplace. Musty smell. Great vibe."

"Congratulations, Ms. Tower," DuWayne said.

"Thank you."

"Do you mind telling me about discovering Mr. Hall?"

"Sure, but let me ask a few questions first," I said.

"Hold your horses," Lou said. "Bruce, you're okay with Mel askin' questions? It's not typical from what I've seen on *Columbo*."

"I know my boundaries," he replied. "I trust she does, too."

"She scooped ya on that murder in her mall. Proved herself innocent. No hard feelings?"

"None at all."

Lou pounded the counter. The rolling pin she'd held earlier in the salon nearly tumbled off, and she grabbed it. "As judge, I'll allow it. Let the witness proceed."

I wasn't in the keenest head space. I felt like a fashionista without her stilettos, not that I wore those anymore.

I cleared my throat. "The ballroom is closed until further notice?"

DuWayne sighed. "I'm afraid so."

"You'll need statements from us?"

"If you both would make yourselves available later, I would appreciate it."

"I'll tell the stage manager to cancel the rehearsal," I said. "Can we still have the show Saturday night? The Ghostly Gala is for charity. I want to support that."

"Objection." Lou shook her head. "Rescheduling is tough. I have to order fresh curds. Mix up more beer batter." She counted on her fingers. "Make more puppy chow … monster cookies. I'll need help."

I glared at her. "We'll figure it out. I'd like to hear what the detective thinks."

"Bruce, you gotta come," she encouraged. "Food's gonna be great. Fashion's cool, too, if ya need a gown."

"I'm sure I'd enjoy it," he said.

"You still seein' Fern Bubble now and then? She's great with PR for Mel's businesses. Everybody loves her."

He blushed.

I'd heard rumors and wanted to ask. Lou did my work for me. DuWayne's reaction revealed what I needed to know.

He pulled a handkerchief from his pocket and dabbed his lip. "I see Ms. Bubble from time to time."

"She's in the show," Lou said. "The First Look model that opens it. That spot is a big deal, right, Mel?"

I nodded. "That's correct."

"I promise to be expeditious," DuWayne said. "I'll release the ballroom as quickly as possible. I wish to support charitable causes."

"Cool. Sustained," Lou ordered.

I paused. "There was a book lying next to Mr. Hall—"

"Lemme guess," Lou interrupted. "*The Devil Wears Prada*—"

"Let me finish the question." I glanced at the swinging door. "If the book is still on the runway, I'd like to see it."

"I have it with me." DuWayne pulled a narrow volume wrapped in plastic from his coat pocket. "Is this the one?"

I nodded, studying it.

The book was smaller and dogeared—not *the one from my shop.*

"Is this book familiar to you?" he asked.

"No, not that volume," I said.

"But you are familiar with the book?"

"Objection," Lou said. "Counselor, Mel owns a bookstore. She's gonna know the book!"

"I've read the play," I said, nodding. "I'm familiar with its themes. Power, revenge. Exploitation."

Lou whistled. "Holy smokes, Shakespeare wrote about the fashion biz?"

"Mr. DuWayne asks the questions," I said.

"No, I thought *you* were!" she complained.

DuWayne slipped the book back into his pocket. "I'm finished for now. You'll be available in the coming days, Ms. Tower?"

"Yes—"

"Hold up," Lou demanded. "Mel, you gonna tell him about Nate the Grate? Or should I?"

DuWayne looked between us. "Pardon me?"

"Nate Gould is the honcho with guys that bought the House of Hall when it went belly up," Lou said. "Nate thinks he's a big cheese, but grates like a rasp."

"Mr. Gould is with White Owl Holdings, a private equity firm," I explained. "He's orchestrating the relaunch of Ichabod Hall, a heritage American brand."

"Ya sound just like him, Mel." Lou looked at DuWayne. "If ya need a translator for fashion speak, talk to her."

He smiled. "I will."

"Nate's not all bad, though," Lou said. "Loves my chicken pot pie. See what he was up to when Ichabod met his maker."

"I'll check into it."

Lou stood. "I'll start puttin' things away."

He stopped her. "Will you leave things as they are? I wish to observe the kitchen space."

She picked up the rolling pin. "Sure enough, but my recipes are off-limits—this isn't a scam to heist my secrets?" She jabbed him with the rolling pin as though it was a weapon.

DuWayne stared at it.

Uh, oh.

"Will you please place that on the counter?" he asked.

Lou held it up. "This? It's my favorite. Pure hardwood. Tapered handles. Had it forever."

He pulled a plastic evidence bag from his pocket, the same type that protected the book.

Lou turned red. "If you're looking for DNA, all you're gonna find is dough, nuts, and apricots. Last thing I made was apricot bread—"

"If you don't mind, Louella, I need to run that for prints."

Lou handed it over without bopping DuWayne on the head with it, a miracle.

Thunder rumbled, and the lights flickered when she gave it to him, quite a tempest.

Lou grimaced. "Bruce, the only thing you'll find on that rolling pin is apricot bread. And if you ever wanna taste it, I'll get it back—and you'll find the bad guy—or the gal." She pointed upward. "Check into that editor in that suite."

"Please do not worry. We have not confirmed a crime occurred in the unfortunate demise of Mr. Hall."

"Remember, we're in international waters," Lou scolded. "It's like the Old West. Laws are different out here."

"You always have an interesting point of view, Louella."

"Fern Bubble and I are partners in pickleball." She wagged a finger. "Just sayin'."

Gently, he said, "The ballroom is cordoned off for now. Please leave a different way. I'm sorry for the inconvenience." He grabbed his hat. Then, *whoosh*, disappeared through the swinging door to the ballroom.

"I'm gonna need an attorney," Lou said. "Call Hank Leigel."

"No, he's a real estate lawyer," I said.

"He's *real*, right? Hank's a *real* attorney?"

"He doesn't practice criminal law—"

She yanked off the apron protecting her outfit, a sparkly sweater and flared jeans, then marched to the closet. "I got frozen muffins and rolls in my freezer at the ranch. I'll give 'em to Hank as a retainer."

"That won't do it."

"I'm caterin' his birthday party. It'll do. Believe me."

She pulled a tote bag, a purse patterned with pumpkins wearing cowboy hats. She wrangled herself into an orange jacket, then asked another question—*one I knew was coming.*

"When are you gonna call Cole? Right now, or eight seconds from now?"

"Who?"

She slapped the counter. Bowls clanged. "Cole Lawrence, the sheriff you're seein' but not talkin' about!"

"He lives five hours away."

"You got a phone in your office down on the crew level, right?"

"It hardly works." I glanced around. "Too much metal in this place."

She pinched her nose. "I get it. A cowgirl needs space when it comes to datin', but tell him what happened. What if *you're* a suspect?"

"Cole's out of town."

"He lives up north. He's always '*out of*' town."

"He's in Green Bay this week at the Pistol Packers Conference," I said. "I doubt we'll speak until after it ends."

Lou softened. "I know ya don't like talkin' about your personal life, not even to your cousin and best friend—"

"Because I don't want it to be the lead story at the Tool & Rye. Or with your volunteer groups: the Book Trouts or the Cinnamon Spice Bakers' Club."

"Naw, just the Trouts. I don't get along with the Spices—especially Trudy, the leader. She's so competitive."

"That's why I keep my personal life *personal.*"

She hooked an arm through mine. With our height difference, the top of her head came to my shoulder.

She towed me toward the exit. "Call Cole. Tell him the guest of honor at your fashion show got breaded, and you need his help. He'll want to know you found another body."

Technically, this was the first one *I'd* found. The other two were on someone else's watch.

Lou was right, though.

I needed to speak with Cole.

3

THE GOLDEN PROMENADE, LATER

It wouldn't take much on her part. In a competition between a ship's horn and Lou, she'd win.

"Nathan Gould is in charge of official announcements," I said. "He and the stage manager will let the backstage crew and models know."

"You want me to herd him to your office—does he even know where it is? He ever been down there, or has he been up in that Fantasy Suite the whole time?"

I shook my head. "It's the Golden Stateroom, not the Fantasy Suite."

"Tomayto, tomahto. Poseidon, or poisoned 'em. I'll find Nate."

"Thanks."

I escaped the kitchen and took the crew passage down to my closet-sized office among the barnacles.

The Golden Promenade was a luxurious "ship" for its passengers, a.k.a. residents.

Seniors enjoyed morning yoga, afternoon tea, and evening

concerts in its glass-ceiling atrium. Gardens, hiking trails, and a pool decorated the exterior landscape.

Their apartments, or cabins, were spacious, and included patios to enjoy fresh air and sunshine.

The crew side of the "vessel" was less luxurious, economical and efficient. After a voyage down back hallways, I arrived at my temporary closet.

My cell phone was useless in my little room in the hull; too much metal.

I watched storm clouds—fat, gray, and boiling—through the tiny portal window. I wanted to contact Cole, my special guy. He and I were having issues, though. Finding another body would make things worse.

Using the landline, I called Wooly Gallagher, editor and publisher of *The Cinnamon Roll.*

Wooly volunteered to mind my bookstore while I worked the fashion show. Crystal Broadway, fashion student and store manager, was on vacation with her fella; she'd return in a few days.

Wooly answered cheerfully, "The Bell, Book & Melville, local authors and lore."

"Hi, Wool, it's me."

"Mel, great to hear from you," he chirped. "How goes it at the Promenade?"

"Under water, actually."

"I've got a joke: What did the fashion photographer say to the Wisconsinite?"

"Cheese?"

He laughed. "Too obvious?"

"It's delightful, but I have bad news."

"Oh, no—what's up?"

"It's who's down. Ichabod Hall."

He gasped. "Hold on, I'll get a pen."

I heard footsteps as he traveled the bookstore's creaky wood floor. Then, the clap of a notepad slapping on the counter.

"What happened?" he asked.

"Has a reporter from the paper called you? Did anything about the fashion show come across the scanner?"

"Not yet, but we closed early for the start of Boo Bash. Staff are volunteering everywhere. The Pickleball tournament at the high school, and the—"

"The Ghostly Gala rehearsal is cancelled for now," I interrupted.

"Why?"

I filled him in. "Detective DuWayne isn't saying if it was natural causes or foul play. I couldn't tell by looking at him."

"Terrible to hear, Mel. I'm so sorry."

The newspaper had published a feature story about the fashion show. I had a copy on my desk and asked Wooly about it. "How much research did you do for that article?"

"It was Cozette, actually. My dear wife assisted. She may have sources to share."

"I know Nathan Gould, but that's it."

"Any clue about what happened to the guy?"

"Nothing yet. Doc Graves and Pauline are here along with private security. Detective Bruce DuWayne, too."

Wooly paused. "He's filling in for the chief, I heard. I'll get a stringer over. See what we can get posted online ASAP."

"Will you keep me in the loop?"

"Sure, but watch your step. If you found the body and it was a homicide, you're a suspect. Not to mention there's a killer on the loose."

I groaned. "Thanks."

"Any cameras?"

"Yes, but no. None in the backstage area. There was one in the ballroom, but Ichabod insisted it be turned off. He didn't want anyone leaking his spring designs until they'd officially been released."

"Fall designs, you mean. It's October."

"No, fashion exists on its own schedule. Fall means spring. Spring is fall. Pre-fall is early summer. Winter is—"

"When Midwesterners reserve summer camping spots." Wooly sighed. "I get it. To each their own."

I heard rustling like he'd covered the receiver. Then, the line went silent.

"Wool?" I asked. "Are you there?"

No answer.

"Wool?"

I started at the receiver in my hand. "Wooly?"

Where'd he go?

Had another book sprung from a shelf?

"Wooly!"

I HEARD A GRUNT. "ARE YOU OKAY?"

"Ow."

"Stay on the line," I said. "I'll get help—"

"No ... I dropped my pen." Wooly exhaled. "Then I clunked my head on the counter. Gee whiz, when carpenters describe something as hardwood, they mean it. *Ouch.*"

"Okay. Good."

"Are *you* okay?"

"No, definitely not." I rubbed my neck.

"You sound like you saw a ghost."

"No, did you?"

He paused. "It sounds odd to admit it. I did see an apparition on the staircase."

"What?"

"I'm kidding, Mel. Wrong time for humor, sorry."

"Nobody said anything about ghosts when I bought that building last fall."

"Like with the storm curse on the Boo Bash, there've been rumors—"

"*What rumors?*"

He chuckled. "Sorry, Mel. Please, take a breath."

I changed the subject. "Have you heard about the fashion editor in town?"

"Sure, she's rooming in a suite out there."

"Who is she?"

"No idea. Her arrival was hush-hush."

"How'd you know?"

He paused. "Cinnamon has limited methods of arrival. When a public works employee must cut the grass at the airstrip in preparation for a VIP's private plane, word gets out."

I thought of something. "If she wanted to leave unnoticed, how—"

"The village tow truck is kept at the airstrip. It's been used to transport visitors anonymously."

"Why couldn't she use an SUV and leave from O'Hare?"

"She could, but a luxury SUV with blacked-out windows would draw attention." He cleared his throat. "Do you have ice packs here?"

"Yes, in the kitchen in the apartment upstairs. I'm still remodeling, but the fridge works."

"Oh, never mind."

"*Wooly.*"

"Sorry, Mel." He sighed. "I hate to say this, my friend. But you've been jumpy lately as an adverb in front of an editor. Please be careful."

"Really?"

He laughed. "That's the Mel Tower I know. Watch your back. I'm *not* joking. I've heard of crimes of fashion—but this sounds like the real thing."

THE PHONE WHISTLED AS SOON AS I PUT IT DOWN. THE BOATSWAIN'S CALL indicated an internal line. "Hello?"

"Mel, it's Nathan Gould. How are you?"

"As well as can be expected. How are you?"

He sighed. "Remember that campaign a few years ago by the House of Granite? 'Dead Man Walking?' It was black on black, with black satin ribbons accenting every piece."

"No, that was after my time in the industry."

"Well, I'm experiencing it." He coughed. "A d-detective named Bruce DuWayne was just here. Will you come up?"

Gould sounded frazzled. I'd known him only a few weeks, but in that time he'd been a confident, high-energy fellow.

"I'll be right there," I said. "Can I bring you something?"

"Tarantula cookies and black tea from the Moon Cafe."

I grabbed my phone, locked my office door, and began the climb via hidden passages up to the Moon Deck, the location of the Moon Cafe.

I walked back corridors to avoid questions about what happened in the ballroom, thinking about Nathan Gould.

As spokesperson for House of Hall, he would responsible for releasing news of the death of an important, but forgotten, American fashion designer.

Two years ago, White Owl Holdings private equity firm purchased HOH out of bankruptcy. Nathan Gould was the fablicity—fab plus publicity—officer reviving the brand known for comfortable, stylish caftans.

Gould knew Fern Bubble, the woman who did PR for my art mall and bookstore. That's how my involvement in this disaster, er, event came about.

Chicago had been the original location for the pre-show, but strings (threads?) were pulled, and the mini-launch ended up in Cinnamon.

Few fashionistas knew because it was a dress rehearsal for charity. The show was like a band embarking on a concert tour that had to tighten loose threads (strings?) before embarking on the real thing.

I'd been asked to model in the show, but refused.

Mel Tower was content with being a worker bee.

I climbed the metal steps—*clack, clack*—exited via a door near the Moon Cafe. It had taken me days to learn the network of staircases and passages of the Promenade.

I still got lost.

The cafe was empty except for Lou and Cozette Gallagher, the part-timer who worked in the cafe and Wooly's better half.

Lou leaned against the counter chatting with Cozette, who was putting fresh bakery in the case. Both women wore aprons and walkie-talkies on their hips.

The lack of patrons in the cafe wasn't surprising. It was an after-dinner haunt, and it was only three o'clock.

"Word's out that rehearsal's off," Lou said. She leaned toward Cozette and stage-whispered, "What do ya know about the editor on the Gold Deck? She order anything weird? A strawberry strangler? Or a Chicago Bear massacre?"

"Lou, don't put Cozette on the spot." I said. "I'd like tarantula cookies and black tea, please. They're for Nathan Gould."

"Right away," Cozette said, turning a computer screen to me.

I pressed a code to charge it to his room. "I'm headed up to his suite."

"You're not goin' up alone," Lou said. "I'll be your butler and carry 'em. Before we go, let's find out what that editor has been orderin' from the Moon Cafe."

Cozette, Lou, and I sat at a table, a plate of cookies among us.

"Cozette, please don't reveal anything you shouldn't," I said.

Her eyes lit up. "I won't—but I *adore* mysteries. On Sundays during the season, the Packer Party Murder Club meets here. Before the game starts, we solve the disappearance of the opposing coach."

"Sounds like unnecessary roughness," Lou said. "Offsides, at least."

She smiled. "It's all in good fun. The crime usually involves a banana peel or a foam football." Cozette stood up. "You ladies wait here. I'll do some checking in the computer."

She quick-stepped to the register, then began scanning the screen.

I heard the *tap, tap, tap* of raindrops and glanced at the glass doors opening to the observation deck. The Moon Cafe overlooked the resort's picturesque meadow. An occasional white flash revealed a tempest still brewed outside.

Lou glanced around as though taking in the planet wallpaper and white-orb sconces. She rocked side-to-side in her chair. "How'd they add waves to this place? It's like I'm on a ship in a storm." She winked.

Shoppers strolled in, and Cozette greeted them. "Hi folks, be with you in a minute."

She jotted on a paper and returned to our table. She handed the paper to me. "The person upstairs orders Sinful Shortbreads every day." She pointed to the slip. "And the room is reserved in that name."

"Thank you," I mouthed silently.

She put a finger to her lips. "You didn't hear any of it from me, but I *adore* solving mysteries."

4

THE GOLD DECK

 "ship."

The ride up was as calm as flat water. Chimes sing-songed as we rose, the elevator's cushioned walls deadening external sound. Halloween music—"Werewolves of London"—pipped from hidden speakers.

Lou held a tray with the cookies and tea. "Before ya fixate on the cowpoke written on that paper Cozette gave ya, let's reduce what we've got so far."

"*Deduce*, you mean." I pinched my nose between my fingers.

"When ya boil somethin', it's *reduced*." She jerked a thumb. "Ironic that we're reducin' while going up, eh?"

I felt a headache coming on.

My parents died in a car wreck when I was eighteen. I was an only child. Lou was my sole relative, bless her heart.

It's said love for one's family is the oil that reduces friction. In Lou's case, friction is the forty-grit sandpaper that reduces love.

Sometimes, when she and I are together, it reminds me of why I didn't return home for years after signing with a New York agency.

"We don't know if a crime occurred," I said. "Before we jump to conclusions, let's wait to hear what Bruce DuWayne says."

"I was gonna say don't jump to *delusions*."

"No, it's—"

"Just kiddin'." She studied me. "You're not yourself."

"Nobody is in fashion."

"*Ouch.* Who's the tall sourpuss standin' in front of me, wearin' Mel Tower's favorite dress?"

"She's an illusion," I said.

THE ELEVATOR GLIDED TO A STOP.

It felt like the cab landed into pillows.

Lou pressed a button to keep the doors closed. "Before ya race out like a horse from a startin' gate, let's get on the same page. Get our rhinestone ducks in a row."

"What we know is a crime may or may not have occurred. Bruce DuWayne is investigating. It's unclear who would have a motive to hurt Mr. Hall."

"And?"

"Nathan Gould is the promotions person for the brand's relaunch."

"Him and Hall get along?"

"No comment."

"C'mon. Spill it."

"I do not want it to become gossip at Tool & Rye."

"What about the editor?"

"She appears to be in residence here, a senior resort that thinks it's a cruise ship." I pointed to the panel of buttons. "Can you let me out now?"

"Not yet—this place is amazin'. They should call it The Cheese Princess, Wisconsin's perpetual boatin' experience."

"Please refer to it as The Golden Promenade."

"Same thing—but how 'bout the hidden passages on board this tub." Lou's eyes widened. "I got it: Someone snuck down to the ballroom, clobbered Ichabod, and slunk out like a Bears fan after a loss."

"Nathan's tea is getting cold."

"I'm the foodie. Let me judge that. You call Sheriff Cole yet?"

"No, but I will."

She nodded toward a gold-framed cabinet on the elevator wall. It was hinged and used to enclose posters and announcements.

"Look in the mirror, Mel. What do you see?"

I examined the cabinet. "I see a ghoul, Lou. A poster promoting Boo Bash. It's a ghost wearing a foam cheese head and holding an ice cream cone."

"Don't be afraid of demons, magic, or *anythin'*. You can buck off the wildcat in your past while solvin' this mystery."

I had zero desire to confront my past—and Lou was a the wildcat.

She blocked my exit from the elevator.

As soon as possible, I wished to return to my office in my craft mall, spend quiet evenings with my rescue collie, and finish restoring my bookstore's apartment—that was *it*.

A bell chimed, reminding us the elevator had stopped.

Lou smiled. "Hear that jingle? That's a fashionista gettin' her wings because she was smart and brave. She busted free from memories holdin' her back. That's *you*, Mel."

In the hallway, I stopped Lou. "I'll take the tray."

She refused. "I'm your butler. I should carry it."

The corridor extended left and right. Thick carpet and framed paintings dampened the sound of our conversation.

"There's Nate's room—I'll go in with ya," Lou whispered. "When Nate's not lookin', I'll snoop in his drawers."

"No, you're backup. Wait out here."

She jerked her head in the opposite direction. "What if I tap on the door of the editor's place? See if she answers—who is it, BTW? What did Cozette write—"

"I'll tell you later."

"Why not now?"

I studied her. "Because you'll fake a disturbance outside her door, call her name, and try to get her to come out. That's why."

"You're no fun."

I set my phone on "record" and put it face down on the tray, then took it from her. "No one knows we're up here. A man has died under mysterious circumstances. Wait here, and *be vigilant.*

She smiled. "*Vigilante.* That's what I like to hear. Now you're talkin'."

I tapped on the door, then entered the suite to see Nathan Gould reclining on a couch.

He wore a black tracksuit with a stripe down the side. His head was pressed back into the plush cushions.

The salon held a sand-colored sofa and matching chairs. Two paintings hung on the walls, one of sun, clouds, and blue sky, and a companion image of the same scene at night.

A sliding door opened to a large balcony. If it hadn't been gray and stormy, the view would be a stunning look at the resort's pool and meadow beyond.

Gould held an ice pack on his forehead. "How many dead fashion designers does it take to ignite a relaunch?"

"None, I hope," I said.

"Wrong. The answer is 'all of them.'"

"Excuse me?"

"That's fashion. When you're alive, they ignore you. When you pass on, they *love* you." He sat up. "Ichabod's death is gonna be so much work for me. This is, like, *so* inconvenient."

I removed my phone from the tray, then set the platter on the coffee table. "I'm sorry about Mr. Hall's death. It's tragic for him and his company."

Gould shook his head. The pack slid to the rug. "Not *his* company. White Owl bought it all. Every dress. Ichabod was a name only—and I needed the guy *alive* for this relaunch. In addition to his original stuff, we were adding moneymakers: fragrance, makeup and wellness."

"Mr. Hall was always kind to me," I said.

"No wonder why he went bankrupt, then." Gould studied the tray. "Cookies. Tea. The only thing missing is black rum. Would you mind, Mel?"

He nodded at a sideboard with liquor bottles and snacks on it. I placed my phone near the booze and selected a bottle. "Should I pour the tea into this? Or the rum into the tea?"

He laughed. "If I were on vacation, it'd be the former. For now, just a shot into the tea." He removed the cover on the ceramic mug.

I poured. "Bruce DuWayne was here earlier?"

"Foghorn Leghorn meets Sherlock Holmes? Yeah, I told him what I knew: Ichabod and I lunched here in my room, then he went down to inspect the ballroom and meet you. He was in good spirits but sounded wheezy. Ichabod's asthma was acting up. No, I didn't kill him."

"Okay, you're innocent. Case closed."

"Thanks." He sipped tea. "How come people in the Midwest are so nice?"

"Because we can't not be nice?" I shrugged. "Unless you kill us. We're not so happy about that."

He bit the leg off a tarantula cookie.

The treats were macabre works of art. Pretzel legs covered in icing and sprinkles. Bodies of truffle brownies coated with a mirror glaze. White chocolate chips for eyes.

The cookies were delicious, and delivered on all flavor sensations if one didn't mind biting a poisonous creature.

"It's the food," Gould said. "Maybe the cheese. Fermentation mellows out a person and affects stress hormones."

Thunder crashed—*BOOM!*

We both jumped.

"I'm not gonna lie, I can't wait to return to New York." He sipped tea. "Your climate is controlled by a spirit so crazy it couldn't even work in fashion." He patted the couch. "Sit. Let's strategize our next steps so I can get on a plane home."

"Sorry, I've got phone calls to make and a store to run—"

"You're kidding, right? What could come before fashion?"

"That's why I don't work in it anymore, Nathan."

"Would you come back? I see a position for you at the company." He raised his eyebrows. "I'll make an offer too good to refuse."

I changed the subject. "Did Lieutenant DuWayne speak with the editor who's here?"

Gould tapped his phone. His cell worked, I noticed. Probably because the suite was so high.

It was like a private island up on the high levels.

"I'm texting her. Asking if she'll stop in before you leave. No sense in keeping her a secret now."

According to what Cozette Gallagher wrote on the paper, the room was registered to White Owl Holdings. That was all I knew. I didn't know the editor's identity.

I glanced at the door. The woman would have to run the gauntlet of Lou. That was like casting a spinnerbait past a hungry muskie, but there was nothing I could do about it.

I stepped to the sideboard and picked up the bottle. "More rum?"

"Sure, put it on the coffee table." He sighed. "Dying is so off-brand for Ichabod Hall."

"Stay positive, Nathan," I said. "'Cheddar' days are coming."

There was a commotion in the corridor: Loud voices followed by thumps. Lou versus a big city editor—what could possibly go wrong?

Someone pounded with a fist on the door.

"Would you get that, please?" Nathan asked. "That's her."

5

THE EDITOR

I opened the door to see Lou.

I should have recognized her knock, which sounded like a clobber with a tire iron.

She pointed behind her. "Look who I found—the tallest, handsomest cowpoke anyone's ever gonna meet: Swannie, Eden Hoff's assistant."

I looked to see a black marble god, Swan, a man I'd worked with in New York.

If one weren't aware such a human could exist, if someone were going about the day and Swan appeared, it would seem like a deity had dropped by; an Italian-African god was paying a visit to provide guidance.

The fellow was perfect, an editorial photoshoot sprung to life.

Swan wore a dark suit, collared shirt, no tie. A scarf draped his neck.

From ten feet away, I could sense the fine wool fabric of his clothes and the scarf's soft cashmere. All that was missing from the man's "fit" was wings. For all I knew, he had a pair and wore them on special occasions.

Lou rubbed her arm. "Did you guys know Swannie used to play hockey?" She winked. "Still can bodycheck, big fella."

He smiled. Outdoors, through the window at the end of the corridor, the storm ceased, and the sun appeared.

Not really, but Swan had that effect.

I didn't know the man's surname. He didn't need one. Though he was called an assistant, he was the brains and brilliance behind editor Eden Hoff's years of success.

Or *former* editor, I should clarify.

The last I'd heard, Eden had slunk away from New York after being fired to start a marketing company in Chicago.

During the holidays last year, Eden and Swan had spent time in Cinnamon. For the record, Eden and I had a history—*a short one*. She hadn't appreciated my look as a model or my sense of humor.

Swan was a different story. He'd always been gracious to me.

I stepped over and gave him a hug. "Swan, nice to see you again."

He kissed me on both cheeks, European style. "It's lovely to see you, Melanie."

Immediately, I noticed a flaw in the man's smile, and a crease in the skin between his eyes.

Something was wrong.

"I've just visited Eden Hoff's suite," he said. "She was here earlier, but now it appears she is missing."

Still in the hallway, Lou slapped a thigh. "I shoulda known the mystery editor was Eden! That cowgal has a habit of hauntin' this town. Haven't seen her since the holidays last year—does she celebrate happy occasions? Or just the spooky ones?"

He nodded, moving his chiseled cheekbones up and down. "She does, Louella. Allow me to say I have missed your humor."

"Same, big guy. I've missed havin' a real, live Thor in town." She jerked her head toward the suite. "Scoot inside and figure out where Eden went. She got here on a broom, right? She musta took off the same way."

I stepped back. "Please, come in."

"I'll guard the threshold. Keep an eye out for mischief," Lou said.

He entered, and Nathan stood up. He offered his hand. "Good to see you, friend. It's been a year, maybe two. Where was it?"

"After a show in Dallas, I believe," Swan said. "Fashion shows are no longer in New York. My sympathies on the death of Ichabod Hall."

"Thank you," Nathan replied. "Have a seat."

Swan gazed at me. "After you, Melanie."

I took a chair facing the sofa, and Swan floated to the seat near me. "You looked stressed, my dear," he said.

"I've felt better, that's for sure. How long have you been here?"

"I just arrived. Ms. Hoff summoned me yesterday." He sighed. "She was ... troubled. Since being removed from her position at the magazine, she has struggled. I am not betraying her confidence to admit that."

"What happened to the marketing agency in Chicago?" I asked.

He paused. "Acquiescing to the demands of others was not her strong suit."

Gould rolled his eyes. "You got that right. Clients can be a nightmare. Or, they drop dead."

Swan studied him. "Was Mr. Hall ill?"

"Not any more than anybody else in this industry." Gould held up his mug, looking at me. "Would you mind?"

"Please, allow me," Swan said. "What may I make, Nathan?"

"More rum, please."

Swan noticed the bottle on the coffee table. "If you wish to enjoy a drink, I shall make a proper one." He turned to me. "May I prepare something for you?"

"Go ahead, Mel," Nate said. "If you don't drink in company, you're either a thief, a spy—or a killer."

"Sparkling water, please," I said.

"I'll create something special," Swan replied.

SWAN WHIPPED UP A BOURBON HOT TODDY WITH HONEY AND CINNAMON. For me, he poured a delightful sparkler with sliced apples and orange juice. For himself, he selected a cabernet so luscious I smelled cherries, chocolate, and cedar from my chair.

I had no idea where the wine or drink ingredients came from; the man had special powers, a magic bartender.

Alongside the cookie tarantulas, he placed bowls of nuts, crackers, and cheese.

If the man's name hadn't been Swan, I'd call him Prospero. Or, *Mr.* Lou Jingle. Like my cousin, he had a gift of feeding people refreshments with frightful ease.

He handed me my phone, which had been on the counter. "Your cell, I assume, Melanie?"

"Yes, thank you."

"Swan, are you looking for a corporate position?" Nathan asked. "White Owl Holdings is expanding into retro. Huge market. As Boomers age, they're looking back—"

"I would enjoy talking about a position. One needs an income, after all." He winked. "To paraphrase, the *lack* of money is the root of all evil. For now, I shall concentrate on Mr. Hall, and the missing person, Eden Hoff, my superior and friend."

"Swan, where could Eden be?" I asked. "Could she have left in her own vehicle?"

"She rarely drives."

"If you're worried about her, we shouldn't be sitting here," I said. "Ichabod may have been murdered. We should contact the police—"

He placed a hand on my chair. "I suspect that Eden is beyond reach by choice, not harm."

That didn't make sense to me. But of all the creative types I'd met during my career—the editors, designers, photographers, models, and moguls—Swan was one I trusted. He had reasons for downplaying Eden's disappearance.

"I saw her this morning for breakfast. Not since." Nathan nodded toward a table with a laptop computer and briefcase. "I've been stuck in my room, working and making calls." The lights flickered, and he looked around the room. "The weather gods are trying to call me out—I swear that's the truth."

Thunder rumbled. Gould laughed, but there was a weird pitch to his voice.

"Swan, why was Eden here?" I asked.

"She wished to return to a position with a magazine. She asked to cover the relaunch of Ichabod Hall. White Owl gave her an exclusive to report on it." He nodded toward Gould. "For which she was grateful."

"No problem. Glad to help out."

"She also heard about a nurse here claiming to possess youth-giving supplements and a sportswear line. Eden wanted to learn more."

"Yeah, she wanted to kill two birds with one cheese curd—" Nathan stopped. "Sorry, poor choice of words."

"Tell me about Ichabod Hall brand relaunch," Swan said. "Were there problems?"

Nathan shook his head. "The purchase of his company went fine. He created perfect designs and met his deadlines. His model-muse was fabulous, a dream to work with."

Swan and I exchanged glances. Nathan watched our reactions, then smirked.

Thunder crashed—*boom!*

"Oops, the gods called me out again." He picked up his drink. "Would you make me another, Swan?"

S WAN MADE ANOTHER HOT TODDY, THEN MOVED TO THE SLIDING GLASS doors and looked out.

It was mid-afternoon, but the storm clouds made it seem darker, later. Flashes of light showed Swan in silhouette. He looked like a god standing on the edge of a mountain.

If I didn't know better, I'd believe he lived on Olympus and possessed superhuman powers.

He sighed. "I take it the acquisition was stormy, for lack of a better word."

"It was *not* smooth sailing," Nathan replied. "But, not terrible. Just a lot of work. Ichabod seemed happy despite the deadlines and schedule. Sourcing materials, lining up production facilities, and marketing four collections a year is a lot."

Fashion's seasons usually were resort, spring, pre-fall, and fall. Others existed, too, including haute couture, bridal, swim, and men's.

Then, after New York, international shows included London, Milan, and Paris. And more cities had joined the tour: Copenhagen, Berlin, Hong Kong, and others.

There were worldwide opportunities to show off a designer's vision of style.

The schedule was relentless if a company had the talent, clothing, and funds to participate—but, the intense production calendar was a major cause of burnout.

"Tell me about Ichabod's muse," Swan said. "What is her name?"

Nathan groaned. "Do I have to? It was a package deal. She came with Ichabod."

I helped out. "Her name is Alicia Cliff and—"

"I would've pushed her off a high one if I'd the chance." Nathan sipped toddy. "Sorry, bad words again. Go on."

"She was the inspiration for the entire collection," I explained. "And she was particular about the runway show. Adamant about its presentation and insisted that she close every one for the season."

"Who has spoken to her about Ichabod?" Swan asked.

"I called her rental," Nathan said. "Alicia has a place off the ship. 'On land,' so to speak. Our conversation went as well as you'd think."

"She was upset," Swan said.

"*Very.*"

Gould sipped, and the lights flickered again. At the same time, there was a clobber on the door.

"Guys, get out here!" Lou cried. "Sounds like we got mutiny downstairs. Models are restless."

Lou, Swan, and I stood in the hallway by the elevators.

"If you two ladies don't mind, I shall remain and search for Eden," Swan said.

"Sure thing. Got the Hercules Suite, do ya?" Lou asked.

Swan smiled. "The Thor—and I promise to keep the lightning bolts to a minimum." He looked at me. "Keep me informed, Melanie?"

"Of course."

Nathan poked his head out saying he'd take the next elevator. Lou and I boarded a car, then doors *whooshed* closed.

She held up her walkie-talkie. "Fern Bubble's in the warm-up pen, that big room off the ballroom. The local models and the big city ones are havin' a set-to. And Ichabod Hall's show pony—Alicia Cliff —is stirrin' 'em up."

Translated, that meant Fern was in the staging area by the ballroom, quelling issues among the models, and Alicia Cliff was making things worse.

Everybody was stressed due to Ichabod's death—including me.

"You guys figure out what happened to him?" Lou asked. "It's obvious."

I looked in the "mirror" cabinet of the elevator. Someone had replaced the cartoon ghost sign with a witch announcing the post-ponement of the fashion show rehearsal.

The witch scowled and held rotten fruit. An orange-red orb, maybe an apple. Hard to tell.

Accurate, though. It was how I felt.

Lou repeated, "You guys figure it out?"

"Not quite," I said.

"Didn't you ever watch *Knot's Landin'*? We got a love triangle. That's always it, what turns a peaceful neighborhood into a fright fest."

"You're saying a jealous lover killed Ichabod?"

Lou held up a hand and began counting, thumb first. "There's Ichabod. And he has a girlfriend, the show pony muse, Alicia. But Eden Hoff wants him, too. That's why she's here. Wants face time to plead her case." She held up three fingers.

I shrugged. "You could be right."

"There's more, though. Ichabod let himself get roped into playin' the Golden Cheesehead datin' game, and there were gals anglin' in like bass to a minnow, wantin' to nab the first date."

"Like who?"

"Trudy from the Spices." She held up four fingers. "A love triangle, like I said."

I pondered. "But if it's Ichabod and three women—"

"A rectangle, then. Close enough. It's a crime of passion. One of 'em got mad and" —she bunched her fingers as though mixing dough— "and breaded Ichabod, turned him into crumbs. That's what happened, I tell ya."

The scary part was if Lou's theory turned out to be true, I'd never hear the end of it.

"Call Sheriff Cole, your silver fox hottie of the Northwoods," she demanded. "Have him run a background check on everybody. Tell him I said so."

"What if I ask Fern Bubble to do it? She has a PR firm and

subscribes to financial and intelligence services. Her sources are better than the police department's."

Half true. Worth a shot.

"Do it," Lou said. "We gotta watch out, Mel. Prepare a defense for ourselves. You know what they say in fashion: one day, you're in. The next day, you're a suspect."

6

THE WARM-UP PEN

We entered the "warm-up pen," the backstage behind the Grand Salon ballroom—and I immediately felt like a murder *victim*, not a suspect.

The frenzy within the space triggered flashbacks. I saw women with my friend and PR person, Fern Bubble, in the middle. Fern stood near a rack of clothes, directing traffic and arguing.

Fern appeared frazzled, unlike her.

Near the ladies were tables with brightly lit mirrors, the area for makeup and hair. Beyond that were dressers' stations, which held shoes, sewing kits, and clips used for adjusting sizes last minute.

There were pipe-metal stalls draped with black curtains for fast changes. A white cardboard sign showed pictures of garments and the models to wear them.

During the past week, while the room was being prepped, I'd avoided it. It had been years since I'd experienced the pressure of a fashion show.

I felt anxious, like a terrified eighteen-year-old again. When staring in the industry, I was a deer-in-the-headlights Midwesterner among gazelles.

I recalled my first show. I'd arrived early, a rarity among the fashion crowd. I'd operated on Lombardi time. Still do. It means if you weren't fifteen minutes early to an appointment, you were late.

The show director at Bryant Park, where shows were held back then, was annoyed. She'd studied my face, then measured my hips, her brows creased in frustration. "What was your agency thinking?" She turned to her assistant and sneered, "Who sent a commercial girl for runway?"

At the time, runway models had to be a strict size. And the biz had ranks, levels that were similar to the decks of a ship.

There were the "It" girls of high-fashion editorial and runway. They were flown around the globe and booked big-money campaigns.

From those lofty heights, the work descended to steerage: catalog, body parts, and fit modeling—guess which class I'd worked in?

There was a secret to my success, though.

That was a story for another day.

Lou nudged me. "You okay? Look like ya saw a ghost."

"Just a glimpse into a land from long ago and far, far away."

"Dubuque? Peoria? You thinkin' about where this fashion show circus goes next?"

"Not exactly."

She pointed. "There's Fern. Looks like she's caught between the Models and the McCoys." She grabbed my arm. "Let's go."

Fern's silky gray hair was wrapped in a pony, but wisps escaped, and her cheeks were red.

Her half-glasses clung to the tip of her nose as though held by a lifeline. She looked wind-lashed, as though battered by the elements while aboard a ship at sea.

Fern's discombobulation was alarming.

I'd seen her maneuver a crisis as quick and nimble as a racing yacht. Stop corporate shenanigans like a locomotive. Leap bigwigs' objections in a single bound.

Fern was a PR superwoman. Seeing her out of control felt strange.

Lou slugged my bicep. I'll take the McCoys. You take the models."

She pushed into the fray, yelling at the local women cast in the show. "Let's hash this out upstairs, cowgirls. It's Vampire Hour in the Moon Cafe. Witches Brews are half-off." She pointed to the door. "Let's ride."

They followed her out.

"It will work out, ladies, I promise," Fern called out to them. She turned to me. "There are disagreements about rescheduling the show, and they want their paychecks for the time spent in fittings and rehearsals." She nodded toward Alicia Cliff, who sat in a chair. "Ms. Cliff is upset."

An understatement.

Alicia Cliff was draped in a chair like a wilted flower. She wore a caftan from the new collection, a flowy muumuu patterned with orange hibiscus. The dress was comfortable, well-made.

The sales strategy was to market it as the sales-leading "Hero" garment, Alicia had said.

"Do you need medical attention, Alicia?" I asked. "There's a doctor on staff."

She blew her nose. "Doctor Graves already prescribed medication, but thank you."

"I'm sorry about Ichabod. I know this is difficult for you."

She dabbed her eyes. "He was my whole world. What do I do?" She waved toward racks of clothes. "This was our future. I'm ... lost without him."

A woman behind her rubbed her shoulder; another patted her arm. They were the professional models flown in from New York.

"The show must go on, right?" Alicia said, sounding desperate. "*We must do this for Ichabod.*"

Fern tried to appease her. "Management is doing their best. The ballroom is off-limits for now." She looked at me. "What's Nathan Gould saying?"

I shrugged. "That the ballroom hasn't been released."

Alicia pounded her thigh with a fist. "That's not good enough—Ichabod would want this show to continue!"

"I'm sorry, but that's the intel I have."

Fern began, "What Mel means is—"

"*That's the information I have,*" I repeated, staring at Alicia. "That *is* what I mean."

She looked away. The models behind her whispered to one another.

It had been years since I'd retired from the fashion biz.

I'd moved home, purchased a building, and remodeled it into an art mall. I'd negotiated contracts with vendors and assisted hundreds, perhaps thousands, of customers to ensure they were happy with their shopping experience.

Something about Alicia brought out my dark side.

As far as I was concerned, Vampire Hour was upon us.

Nathan Gould arrived *looking* like a vampire.

He wore the black tracksuit, but slung a coat over his shoulders like a cloak. He draped a blood-red crossbody bag over his heart.

The combination made him look ominous—*what took him so long to travel five minutes by elevator?*

He'd been right behind Lou and me. If I didn't know better, I'd suspect Nathan stopped at the Moon Cafe for a quick one.

Lou was in there, though. If she spied Nathan, she'd have thrown him out fast as a bronc tossing a city slicker and sent him downstairs.

He beelined to Alicia Cliff. She began jabbering about how hard this was and lamented about what she'd do next. He nodded and listened.

Wow, the fashion world had changed.

There hadn't been much active listening when I'd worked in it. Perhaps I felt sour grapes. No, in fashion terms that would be *Raisin Aigre,* and the grapes would have tiny logos and be insanely expensive.

Alicia's tears seemed phony to me. Crocodile? There were expensive croco belts in the show, I knew. Given my familiarity with the rag trade, I suspected her distress was linked to money, especially if she were tied to the brand's finances.

Models often were the last to get paid for a job, and it took months to wrest the cash from the powers-that-be.

Alicia would know that.

While Ichabod's death was tragic, I'd stand by the women booked in the show. If anyone interfered with the compensation they'd been promised, I'd be a vampire, all right.

Fern nudged me. "Would you like a change of scenery?"

As long as it doesn't involve fashion, accessories, or models!

"How about supper in exchange for help with barn chores?" she asked. "I've got chicken chili in the crockpot and a 'We are All Made of Dreams' white, an excellent pairing."

I nodded. "I'll pick-up Max from my place and meet you at the farm."

My home was a Federal-style fixer-upper. More fixer than upper. I'd updated my businesses before the house. The place needed new everything, including decor.

Establishing a *home* was hard for me.

Yes, it reflected my emotional state.

Fern Bubble and I spend many evenings discussing my commitment issues, whether it was to a house or a relationship. The good news was I'd hung a few pictures, including one of Max; he was on the fireplace mantle, a place of honor.

The house had a huge backyard. Fenced and perfect for a dog. I opened the French doors and stepped out. Max trotted to the grass, and then worked the perimeter, weaving among the shrubs and pines.

The sky was gray soup. Light rain fell, misting my face.

The yard was adjacent to the alley behind my craft mall. My morning commute consisted of a walk across the grass, up a hill, and through a gate. Then it was a quick jog across the street to arrive at work.

Max, a border collie rescue I'd acquired last year, was delighted to hear he'd been invited to Fern's.

I'd like to say his favorite spot was the backyard, but Fern's farm and Cole Lawrence's Northwoods ranch were favorites, too.

Cole Lawrence.

The sheriff and I began dating last summer. It was long distance, and we were having issues.

Or, was *I* the one having issues?

Tonight, he'd be busy with the kick-off to the conference, but he'd want to know what happened to Ichabod.

Tell him, Mel—do not *be stubborn!*

This was the second, no third, dead body I'd encountered in the last year. Awkward when mentioning it to a law enforcement professional.

While keeping an eye on Max, I dialed Cole.

No answer.

That was part of our problem, from my POV. I feared the sheriff and I were too busy with our jobs, and too much alike.

I left a message to call me back, keeping things vague.

Max returned from his perimeter check. I dried his paws, changed my clothes, and then buckled the dog into the backseat of my Saab.

We zipped to Fern's farm out of town. She operated a PR business and rescued horses. I sponsored one, a Draft mare named Tulip. I paid for her room and board, plus hoof trims, which amounted to a lifetime membership at a pedicure spa.

I parked at the house, and Max and I splashed through puddles to the barn. The yard light illuminated the white sliding door.

Fern pulled it open and warm air whooshed out. I smelled hay, horses, and what they make together.

Fern glanced at my casual outfit. "You know what they say in fashion: One day you're in. The next day, you're wearing clothes to muck out a horse barn."

I nodded. "There's no place I'd rather be at the moment."

She moved aside. "C'mon in. I'm glad you're here. I have theories about what happened today."

7

FERN BUBBLE'S FARM

Fern's place was a recombobulated dairy barn with box stalls, a wash rack, and a tack room.

The horses were off-track Thoroughbreds, geriatric mixed breeds, and discarded Draft horses she'd saved from kill pens.

Before talking about the day's tragic turn, Fern and I dove into barn chores. The horses' needs came first. Like my bookstore, the barn was bewitched. A pitchfork leaped from its bracket on a wall and landed in my hands.

Within minutes, I found myself mucking out Tulip's stall. "Honest woman's work," it was called, and I was happy to do it.

There was something about the outside of a horse that *was* good the inside of a person.

Tulip was seventeen hands high, fourteen hundred pounds. About the size of an entire NFL offensive line, and when she walked the barn aisle, her metal-shod hooves rattled *CLOP! CLOP! CLOP!*

The mare had velvety lips, though. And to clean under her plate-sized feet, all it took was a tap and the behemoth stepped aside.

She and Max adored one another. The dog supervised while I cleaned.

He also monitored Fern distributing grain after the animals ate hay. Fern dropped nuggets of sweet feet in front of each stall. I sensed it was on purpose as Max dutifully vacuumed up the morsels.

I finished cleaning while Fern gave medications or treats. All in all, chores took an hour. I wheeled the last cart of dirty shavings to the compost pile and returned.

My arms felt sore.

"Just think," Fern began, "People pay money at a gym for the exercise you just had."

I rubbed a bicep. "I should pay you for the opportunity, come to think of it."

"It's good to see you relax. The fashion show was stressing you out."

I looked at the pitchfork and the wheelbarrow. "There are some things here that remind me of the industry, though."

She nodded. "Soups on. Let's head to the house and chat."

HOW MANY WISCONSINITES DOES IT TAKE TO SOLVE THE MYSTERY OF A THE death of a fashion designer?

Just two. And the crime-solving involved a cozy fire, white chicken chili, and wine.

Pumpkin cheesecake, too, but Fern and I solved the mystery before dessert.

Fern sat opposite me in her living room. We occupied cushy chairs and faced the fireplace. Max snoozed in front of the hearth, his black-and-white chest rising and falling.

The stormy weather had passed. Lightning flickered in the windows, but it was in the distance.

Fern's set her cheesecake plate on the coffee table. "As gruesome as it sounds, I think Ichabod experienced a fatal asthma attack."

She sighed deeply, her mouth forming a frown. *Unusual for her.*

"His breathing was compromised," I said. "His was never without his inhaler. He bedazzled it and wore it like an accessory, had one in every color."

"You saw it?"

"Crushed on the runway. Like he'd squeezed it until it broke, it looked like a squished, sequined butterfly."

"What was he doing before you found him?"

"He'd either been in the 'warm-up pen,' as Lou calls it, with a plate of snacks he'd gotten from the buffet, and then returned to the ballroom. Or, he'd been at the buffet and then stepped straight onto the runway." I shrugged. "I'd just arrived. We were supposed to finalize elements of the show."

"Did you witness anything odd these past few days? Anyone who'd want to hurt him?"

I nodded. "Sure, but that's normal in fashion. People say and do outrageous things. It's like working in a circus without the clowns." I paused. "No, clowns are involved. It's like a rodeo without the bull— no, there's plenty of that, too."

"Fashion shows are theater, aren't they?"

"Exactly." I ate my last bite of dessert. "The designers are the writers. The script is the clothes and theme for the season: Preppy Glam. Urban Couture. Love Letter to the Midwest."

"Never heard of the last one. Was that a real show?"

"No, it was Love Letter to New York." I winked. "I changed it. I'm partial. I'll tell you a secret about the industry, though."

"Oh?'

"A successful line comes down to simple principles. A silhouette is picked, the part of the body a garment will accentuate: shoulders, waist, legs. After that, a designer adds one of two elements: color or texture."

She frowned. "Surely those rules are broken. I've seen outrageous things in magazines—"

"That's just it. The wild-looking pieces get press or editorial photoshoots. After that, what's purchased by store buyers is what will *sell*."

"That's the side of the industry you worked in?"

"For me, catalogue and body parts was where the income was. I had what they called a commercial or lifestyle look. Pleasant but not exotic. I was a fit model, too, where you stand for hours and get fabric pinned on. About as unglamorous as it sounds."

I felt her gaze on me. Fern worked in PR. That meant she was a psychologist, lawyer, financial analyst, and expert communicator.

When she was silent, I worried. That meant her wheels were turning.

"I always wondered where you developed your superpower," she said.

"My ability to stand still and be quiet, you mean? Yes, the industry made me into a super wallflower."

"No, to observe people and their body language. To guess their motivation. Or spot deception."

"It's not much of a superpower." I looked at my empty plate, then at her. I did it again.

"Would you like another slice of cheesecake?" she asked.

"You have the same ability, Fern. You're pretty super, too."

I skipped the cheesecake, saying I'd enjoy it with coffee in the morning.

Due to the wine, Fern asked me to stay in her guest room, and I accepted.

Well, Max accepted on my behalf. He thought another round of barn chores in the morning would be therapy for what ailed me, and I agreed.

I changed into jammies and returned downstairs to help with dishes.

Fern washed. I dried.

She handed me a wine glass. Then another one. And surprisingly, one more. "Three?" I asked. "I thought there'd been only two of us this evening."

"I, ah, had a visitor."

Her eyes watered—was she near tears? The description "cool as a cucumber" described normal folks. "Cool as the Arctic Circle" described Fern.

Seeing her upset made *me* upset. "Are you okay?" I asked.

She changed the subject. "How are things with Cole?"

"Okay, I guess. He's in Green Bay at a conference—but what's wrong with you? And whose glass—"

"The fire hasn't burned itself out yet. Let's go back to the living room and watch the embers die out, shall we?"

FERN MADE TEA, AND WE WATCHED EMBERS WANE IN THE FIREPLACE. They glowed orange-red while we talked.

Fern and I switched chairs. This time, I was in the one nearest the kitchen, and she was in the seat by the window. All I could see was her silhouette in the dim light.

Max didn't flop down by the hearth. He pressed against his aunt's knees, and Fern scritched him behind the ears as we chatted.

I didn't want to pry about the wine glass.

"When was the last time you saw Cole?" she asked.

"Three weeks or so. Max wanted a horseback ride. He picked up the phone, called him. The next thing I knew, we were headed north for the weekend."

She hugged the dog. "If there were a canine smart enough to dial, it'd be Max. Things are going okay?"

"With Max? Yes, he's perfect."

"No, with *Cole*."

"We're great in a long-distance, casual way." I set my tea on the side table.

"Why do you do that?"

I looked at the mug. "It was hot. I'm letting it cool."

"No, have long-distance relationships. Your last one was with a pilot who was always gone—"

"I bought a cottage up north in part to *see Cole*."

"It's closed for the season."

True. My tiny place on Lollygag Lane in the Northwoods was locked tight, its water pipes drained and its dock out of the water.

"It's not like I can shorten the off-season to spend more time there," I said. "Absence makes the heart grow fonder. Shakespeare said if cell phones be the aide to love, text on."

She didn't laugh. An ember popped and landed on the tile by the fireplace. She rose to douse it. She moved slowly, as though a weight was on her shoulders.

I watched her. "What's wrong, Fern? Is this about Mr. Wineglass? Does he live around here?"

"Oh, Mel, stop. You've heard about Bruce and me."

I had, but that was different than hearing it from the source.

"So what's going on?" I asked.

"I don't … think I'm cut out for dating. I wanted to, but I'm good with being alone—it makes me feel sad and weird at the same time. Is it okay to be like this?"

"Yes."

"I don't want to hurt Bruce's feelings."

"Was he here when the call came about Ichabod?" I asked.

"Yes."

"What's his point of view?"

She paused. "Would you like popcorn? *Great*. Before I answer, I'll make us a batch."

I followed Fern to the kitchen. Max came, too, because his fav snack was freshly popped corn.

Fern poured kernels into a pot, then nodded at a cupboard. "Get bowls, would you?"

The kitchen was original. The linoleum floor sloped starboard, and the counters were beat-up laminate. The cabinet doors creaked, and the knobs were worn smooth by decades of hands.

There was a shelf with vintage cookbooks above the sink. I opened a cupboard and saw red-striped bowls with words stenciled on them.

I pulled out funny ones to make her laugh. One said, "Hot." The other, "Stuff."

Fern didn't react. "Bruce and I aren't dating," she said.

"He *is* charming in an old-school way."

"It's like he stepped out of a Fifties film. He's Sam Spade meets," —she pondered— "Bruce Wayne."

There also was a Sheriff Andy Taylor vibe about the man but didn't interrupt. Persuading Fern Bubble to speak about her personal life was like getting me to talk about mine.

The aroma of popcorn filled the kitchen. Max tippy-tapped to Fern's side. "In a minute, fella," she reassured him.

Her cell phone was face down on the butcher block table.

"Has Bruce called with any information?" I asked.

"No."

"It could get weird if Ichabod *didn't* die of natural causes." I scratched my forehead. "I found the body. Lou stocked the buffet, which he ate from. If things went wrong, and one of us were implicated—"

"Mel, you know I'll stand by you no matter what—"

I sniffed. "The popcorn's burning."

Fern yanked the pan from the stove; it was too late. There was the stench of scorched toast meets burned rubber.

When popped corn goes bad, it goes *fast*.

Fern waved a hand past her nose. "Ugh, I hate this smell!"

"I'll open a window."

I reached over the sink and grabbed the window's handles to slide it up, but—*drat it*—the quick jerk shook the bookshelf above me. A razor-thin paperback, one of those books with pages stapled together, dropped down, its spine a stiletto.

It was like the book was pulled down by a string or invisible hand it moved so fast. The book became a mini-missile, and a painful stab ripped my scalp.

I released the window. "Ouch!" I yelled.

I sat at the table, its butcher block top cluttered with alcohol wipes, wrappers, and a blood pressure cuff.

It reminded me of the scene in the ballroom when Doc Graves and Pauline arrived to help Ichabod Hall.

Nurse Fern pressed a sterile bandage to my scalp. "It's just a flesh wound. You'll live," she announced.

"Does it need stitches?"

She paused. "No, it's just a scrape. Head wounds always bleed so much." She pressed my skin. "But I could give it a staple. My gun is in the barn—"

"*What?*"

"I'm joking, Mel."

"Max says you're scaring him."

She applied liquid bandage like an expert. From now on, when describing Fern's skills, I'll add medical practitioner. Rescuing horses for years had been an OTJ degree for her.

"You're not going to colic on me after this trauma, are you?" she asked. "I could give you an injection of muscle relaxant."

"No, thanks. But I might pin my ears back." I glanced at the shelf over the sink. "What book tried to kill me? Please say it wasn't *The Tempest*."

"No, *The Devil Wears Prada*."

"You're kidding."

She nudged me. "Yes, I am."

"What was it? *Attack of the Zombies*? *Moby Dick*?"

I felt a tap on the shoulder. Fern showed me the killer volume, a haunted tome if there ever was: *The Fall of the House of Usher*.

"I propped it there as Halloween decor," she explained. "You know, deaden up the place."

I felt a pinch. "Ouch!"

"Sorry. I had to press the edges together." Fern tossed a bloody bandage on the table. "You'll be fine. Take two aspirin, and call Cole in the morning."

I rubbed my neck. "Why? So he can arrest the books attacking me? Not going to happen. Books have rights."

"What are you talking about?"

I explained what happened in my shop the previous evening. That *The Tempest* launched itself at me like a tennis ace attacking the net. "If I needed a partner for pickleball, I'd consider that book. Heck of a serve."

She crunched wrappers in her palm. "No one ever told you the history of that shop before you bought it?"

"*No.*"

"Wooly Gallagher's been there while you're working the fashion show?"

"Yes. Crystal Broadway is on vacation with Steve. I miss them both."

"You're still remodeling the apartment? Wooly shouldn't go upstairs."

"Fern—"

She giggled. "I'm teasing, Mel."

I rubbed my temples. "Boo Bash lasts how many more days?"

"We've got a week of fun and games ahead, including the Golden Cheesehead, the fashion show, and Reader's Theater."

Bah humbug. I didn't need fun and games.

Famous last words.

8

WEDNESDAY MORNING

The next morning, a pitchfork jumped into my hands. After that, a push broom leaped from the wall and into my arms.

There was something magical about a horse barn.

The tools seemed possessed, but I didn't get the heebie-jeebies.

Fern fed the animals while I cleaned stalls. Max supervised. As the stable's CEO, its Collie Executive Officer, he picked his duties.

I contemplated asking him for a raise, but doing chores was so mind-clearing I'd pay to do them instead.

We splashed through puddles while walking toward the house. The skies had cleared, but more rain was on the way. Temps were about fifty degrees, and orange leaves still clung to trees.

The horses had been let out to pasture. Fern, Max, and I paused to watch them. Most of the animals were furry, brown, and similarly sized. Except for Tulip, she was *huge*. It was like watching a Great Dane cavort among puppies.

Hay was stacked in piles across the field, but the horses preferred the last of the summer grass. They stretched their necks to nibble and then frolicked about, their breath visible in the chilly air.

"Do they ever get stressed by their choices in life?" I asked. "Like they worked too hard and missed out on experiences or relationships?"

Fern nodded. "They do, but I advise them to not dwell on mistakes, and spend time with friends and family. Wisdom comes with winters, after all."

I smiled. "Foghorn Leghorn said that?"

"Close. Oscar Wilde."

A dually pick-up roared into the driveway, shattering the morning peace. The vehicle's custom sparkle paint glittered in the light, and the truck's plate read, "JNGL LOU."

Lou Jingle.

What was she doing at Fern's place at eight o'clock?

She hopped out wearing a fringe jacket, jeans, and a serious expression. "Team, I got word about what's goin' down at the Promenade. We got strategizin' to do." She handed Fern an insulated coffee urn. "I brought breakfast. Mel, grab the picnic basket, would ya?"

She yanked open the door to the backseat. I looked inside to see a wicker basket that gave off the aromas of bacon and cheese.

A pink box was next to it gave off the scent of cinnamon.

"I'm suspect Numero Uno in the murder of Ichabod Hall," Lou announced. "So we're gettin' up a posse. Fern, you're in charge of fundraisin' for my defense. Mel, you'll prove the authorities wrong and investigate. Max will be our sidekick."

Fern gasped. "What have you heard, Lou?"

"Lotsa stuff. My Book Trout gals have their ear to the ground. They've got my back," she answered. "Let's eat first before the food gets cold." She grinned. "If Eden Hoff thinks she's gonna get away with framin' this cowgirl for murder, that's *bull*. She has no idea who she's messin' with."

Lou looked at me. "It's like the ghost of your Christmas past showed up to haunt ya at Halloweentime, Mel. This is your chance to get back at her. Gosh, this is gonna be fun."

It was the best of breakfasts; it was the worst of breakfasts. The food was excellent. The scuttlebutt about the death of Ichabod Hall, not so good.

We sat at the butcher block table in the kitchen. Lou glanced at the cabinets, slanted floor, and large sink. "Keepin' it retro. I like it, Fernie." She carved the quiche. "Who wants a slice of tomato cheddar? I used the last of my summer Romas."

Fern and I opted in. Barn chores stirred one's appetite.

Lou added fruit to our plates, too.

Max got a homemade dog treat, a cut-out cookie shaped like a little diploma. His intelligence impressed everyone, especially his Aunt Lou.

She served the food on plates with green witches on them. "I figured you'd get a kick out of 'em, Mel. Remind ya of Eden, your old boss."

"Eden Hoff was never my boss or agent," I said. "She was an editor at a magazine. That was it."

"But she was a fashionista, right? A bigwig. A *bigwista*."

"As 'bigwista' as they get."

Lou bit into quiche. "Did you two start fightin' out of the gate? Or did ya break bread before ya became like Boss Mares sharin' a stall."

"Eden and I never saw eye to eye."

"Course not!" Lou pounded the table. "Eden's pony-sized. You're tall as Tulip. Probably intimidated the heck out of her."

"That wasn't possible."

"Sure it is. You walk in the door, all wholesome and Midwestern. She was used to Thoroughbreds, and in walks Mel, a friendly Quarter horse. Both critters are beautiful, but they're different. It's like comparin' Max with a Wolfhound."

I wasn't sure which one I was, but didn't ask.

Some mysteries are better left unsolved.

"When did Eden arrive at the Promenade?" Fern asked. "I helped with at fittings. I never knew she was here."

"I didn't either," I answered. "They kept it quiet to give her the exclusive on the show. She's trying to reestablish her career."

"She high-tailed it," Lou said. "No one knows where Eden is. Put the clues together: Eden was canned from the magazine. I heard they ran her off cuz she wouldn't hire more gals like Mel. You know, average." She raised her coffee mug. "Here's to average: If ya don't support it, you're just *mean*." She winked.

Fern looked at me. "Your thoughts?"

"The industry has changed since I started. Twenty-five years ago, social media and selfies didn't exist, and you *never* released an image your agency didn't approve." I shook my head. "Unfortunately, the phrase 'Don't Feed the Models' was a joke repeated constantly."

"I'm glad it's changed," Fern said.

"I got it!" Lou cried. "Eden blames Mel for losin' her job. And for magazines, too. So many of 'em went belly up. Nobody subscribes anymore. I even canceled my subscription to *Gravel & Glam*. Now I just follow 'em on social."

"No," I said. "I'm not perfect, but I didn't cause the demise of an entire industry. I couldn't afford college, and the career provided a decent income. I retired on my terms and bought the craft mall and bookstore. It worked out in the end."

Lou tapped her temple. "What happened to your head? You get a cut?"

"Long story. I could write a book about it." I changed the subject. "About your impending arrest, Lou. Who said it was murder—"

"Eden Hoff wants to put me in jail—yeah, right," she scoffed. "I'm in the county lock-up all the time. The Book Trouts and I volunteer and share positive stories with the inmates. I'm behind bars once a week."

Fern cut to the chase. "What did you hear, exactly?"

"It went down like this—hey, we're like The Thursday Murder Club." Her eyes glowed. "We'll call ourselves The Horse Rescue

Rascals. We can solve murders and raise money to save ponies. Pretty cool."

"*Tell us what happened*," I said.

"All right, here goes: Yesterday, Cozette was dawdlin' by the ballroom, pretendin' to clean. She overheard Bruce DuWayne talkin' to a pooh-bah on a landline, that one on the hostess stand. Bruce starts talkin' about what a good cook Lou Jingle is, and he can't believe I'd poison someone—"

"You're joking."

Lou giggled. "I'm just bein' my own editor like Eden, *hehe*. I can see why she's addicted to writin' about herself. Anyhoo, Cozette overhears Bruce sayin' stuff about the kitchen, cheese curds, and homicide."

Fern's eyes widened. "*He did?*"

Lou nodded. "I don't know for certain who he talked to. Bruce coulda neglected to dial 'nine' for a line out, and he was chattin' with dead air. But Cozette wouldn't lie about a Book Trout gal in trouble. It's against our code."

"How is Eden involved?" I asked.

Lou looked at me. "Can't you see her strategery? Eden sneaks to the kitchen when I'm away. She snatches a curd, sticks it with poison. Somethin' easy to get." Lou nodded at the First Aid kit on the counter. "Fern's probably got poison in that kit. Eden fixes a plate for Ichabod, serves it to him, and frames me for it." She shrugged. "And by doin' it, she's gettin' even with *you*, Mel Tower."

Lou dug into the picnic basket, pulled out a tub of icing and a spatula, and slathered a layer of cream cheese frosting on a cinnamon roll.

She handed one to Fern. "I'm gonna need T-shirts for my defense. Somethin' glitzy. Write 'Free Lou' on the front and 'Mel didn't do it, either,' on the back. We'll gin up a fundraiser, but the cash will go to the rescue." She smiled. "I won't need it. We'll kill two editors with one stone: Proclaim my innocence and raise money for the horses."

Fern shook her head. "That's generous of you, but no—"

"I need an attorney, Hank Leigel." Lou laughed. "He'll get a kick out of it. Last time him and I had a dust-up was with the Chicago folks livin' on Lake Cinnamon, *hehe*. They call it Lake 'Cin' for a reason." She stopped. "Never mind. Need-to-know basis only."

"Hank's a real estate attorney," I objected. "Not a criminal defense lawyer."

"He's *real*. Not a ghost, in other words," Lou declared. "He advised you about buyin' the mall and the bookstore, right?"

"Yes."

"So he's a *real* attorney. I rest my case." She rolled her eyes. "People get caught up in names these days."

Fern sampled the roll. "These are delicious."

"Thanks. I made 'em at the Promenade. I hope Eden didn't poison those, too."

Fern coughed. "*What?*"

Lou grinned. "Gotcha. Sorry, I've never been a suspect before. I'm practicin' makin' up orange herrings."

"*Red* herrings," I said.

"No, it's fall, Halloweentime. The names of stuff switches up with the seasons, like fashion changes spring and fall. You should know of all people."

Lou piled more frosting on a roll. I could smell the sugar from my chair—who was she buttering up?

She handed the treat to me. "As I was sayin' about the Golden Cheese Head competition, I asked a friend of yours to step in. Now that Ichabod's passed on to the cheddar factory in the sky."

I paused. "*Were* we talking about it?"

"I just brought it up. Boo Bash. Golden CheeseHead."

"I don't have any single men friends."

"Sure ya do. Captain Rand Cunningham is single. Cute, too. And funny in a nerdy, pilot-y way. Is he single? I heard he's chattin' with—"

"That better be a red herring, Lou, and you did *not* invite him for a dating show," I said.

Rand was a pilot for Viking Ship Airlines. He was my ex; we were still navigating what that meant.

She shook her head. "Naw, I didn't. I was gonna blackmail ya. Say I would unless ya asked Sheriff Cole to help with my defense. Do police stuff on the sly. Run background checks. You know, inside baseball from a copper." She looked at Fern. "But did you see her hackles go up when I mentioned her old boy toy? What's what that?"

I knifed icing off my roll. "Rand and I are friends. Two people can't date for almost ten years and not stay in contact."

"He won't be a fill-in," Fern said. *"Right, Lou?"*

"Nah, he won't, forgive me" She sighed. "But did ya hear he's talkin' to the pickleball gal—"

"Let's not discuss it," Fern interrupted. "I don't mean to pry, but are you and the sheriff okay, Mel?"

I nodded. "He's at a conference in Green Bay."

"Yeah, the Pistol Packers fall round-up," Lou said. "They meet in a rock quarry every mornin' and—"

"Stop it, Lou."

"What? *Gravel & Glam* covered it on their Instagram. The pistol range *is* in a quarry."

"He and I are fine. He just has a problem with ... staying in contact."

Fern fainted, dropping from her chair like she was clunked by a barbell. Lou's head spun around, Exorcist style, and she started bragging about the Chicago Bears, her favorite team.

No, not really.

But both women were surprised at my confession—I don't have a history of discussing my personal life.

"Lemme see your eyes," Lou demanded. "Did you get a concussion from that head wound?"

"What are you saying?" Fern asked.

"Cole can call me more often," I said. "When I lived in New York, I tolerated distance and non-attention. That's why I dated a pilot. He was always gone." I cleared my throat. "I expect more of my relationship now. Even though I adore him, *he* can call *me* rather than the other way around."

"Fern, you got rescue piggies at this place?" Lou asked. "I just saw a couple fly past the window."

"Cole needs to learn he can't use his job as an excuse," I said. "Put up a wall like *I* used to do. We're alike in some ways, and we need to grow and change in this relationship."

Fern hugged me. "I'm so proud of you."

Lou spoke to Max at her feet. "You didn't see anybody put a spell on your momma, did ya? Everybody says that bookstore of hers is haunted. Maybe there's somethin' in the water over there, and she drank it."

"Cole and I are figuring out our relationship." I said. "That's *all.*"

We cleaned the kitchen. Fern washed, Lou dried, and I cleared the table, avoiding the shelf over the sink and its trickster knick-knacks.

I clarified rumors about my bookstore. "If the Bell, Book & Melville has a ghost, I'll lean into it. Readers love a haunted shop."

Lou wiped a dish. "Good idea. Our earth-movin' machines are possessed. It's a story I tell when sendin' out bids. Folks know we're gonna git 'er done."

Lou and hubby Jason owned an excavating business, Diggers & Dozers, specializing in knockdowns and site restoration. "You build it, we bust it" was its tagline.

They lived on forty acres outside of Cinnamon in a log home with a kitchen big enough to serve Paul Bunyan.

The giant space was where Lou baked for the masses and cooked up mischief for the village, like the Boo Bash.

They also had a barn to store the business's heavy equipment and a workshop for Jason, her high school sweetheart-husband, who miraculously hadn't been driven crazy by his wife's shenanigans over the years. Unlike Mel, her cousin.

"Are you still opening a satellite shop in the Promenade?" Fern asked. "I'll create a marketing plan for it."

"I have a meeting about it today." I looked at the wall clock, one of those black cats with eyes that moved. "Have to be in my conference room in an hour."

A cell phone buzzed. It rested on the counter near Fern. The image that appeared was a cartoon picture of Batman wearing a foam cheese hat.

Detective Bruce DuWayne.

"Lou, we're going outside," I said. "Let's give Fern privacy."

"Wait, that's Bruce—we gotta get the scoop."

I grabbed the towel from her and set it over the dishes. "You established a working theory, remember?"

"Good point. Gotta make it fair."

Fern took the call. We beetled out the door to stand on the porch facing the pasture.

Clouds covered the sun, and the gray ruffles looked like the skirt of a puffy dress. The October air felt cool and sharp.

The scent of horses wafted to my nose, and Max trotted across the gravel drive to observe the animals.

"What do ya think they're talkin' about?" Lou asked.

"The horses? Probably chatting about what tree to snooze under after breakfast and what time lunch will be served."

She smiled. "Yeah, that's right, probably. Hey, I just thought of somethin': Does Fern have a cowhand that could do the Golden

Cheesehead? Also, which guy are you datin', and which one is the friend, again?"

"When we go back inside, stand right under that shelf above the sink."

"Why?"

"It's good luck."

The door rattled open. "Come back in, ladies. It's too chilly to be out here."

I called Max, and we reentered the kitchen.

"That was Bruce." Fern said, still holding her phone. "He couldn't give details, but it appears Ichabod didn't die of natural causes."

Lou slapped her thigh. "Eden got ahold of a concoction. Probably across the border—Illinois where they can get away with it. She did it to get even, Mel."

"We don't even know where she is," I said.

"She's hidin' out." She wagged a finger at us. "Watch where you eat. Maybe she'll use her potion on someone else. You know what they say in fashion: One day you're in; the next, a nutty editor is gettin' revenge."

I showered while Lou and Fern finished in the kitchen. Twenty minutes later, we stood by Lou's pickup. Even under a gray sky, the truck's paint sparkled like light glinting off waves.

Max was given a choice: Come with me to be the greeter in The Bell, Book & Anvil, his day job. Or stay with Aunt Fern and the horses.

He chose the horses. He leaned against Fern's legs, a sign he knew she felt troubled. After the call with Bruce DuWayne, frown lines appeared between her eyes, and her lips narrowed to a tight smile.

I would have stayed if I didn't have meetings, a fashion show to reschedule, and discover why an editor disappeared.

Where could Eden Hoff be?

In Cinnamon, there were few places to hide. We had a village square with a band shell and a statue of John Muir, who'd grown up in Portage, a town an hour to the west.

Main Street was lined with mom-and-pop stores, no vacancies. There was one coffee place, the Tool & Rye, a combination bakery and hardware store. Locals gathered around its potbellied stove to share stories and grab nails, paint, or potting soil.

My three-story art mall, The Bell, Book, & Anvil, anchored one end of the main drag. The mall was a blacksmithy that I'd converted into booth spaces for vendors, keeping the original character of the building: plank floors, huge beams.

The new bookstore, The Bell, Book & Melville was in the center of the street, next to Hank Leigel's law office.

Cinnamon bustled on weekends and during holidays like Boo Bash.

Otherwise, it was a dot on a map, a village tucked into a countryside consisting of cows and the Kettle Moraine hiking trails.

Peaceful and picturesque, the way residents like it.

Lou elbowed me. "Are you listenin'? We need a safe word to know it's okay to talk."

"How about, 'is it okay to talk?'"

"It's gotta be cool. Fashion-y."

"Hermes? Prada?"

"*Cool*, I said. Bell bottoms. No, Wrangler." She extended a clenched hand. "Fist bump."

Max held up his paw at her gesture. A border collie's intelligence should surprise positively no one.

Perhaps Max could find Eden Hoff.

Animals know.

Fern hesitated, and Lou noticed. "We got a PR cowgirl lookin' anti-social. What's up, Fern?"

"Ichabod is dead, and a woman is missing. Both of you, be careful. I'm worried."

"Don't let Eden get to ya. She pulls her designer chaps on one leg at a time, just like us. Right, Mel?"

"Darn tootin'."

"You gonna ring up Cole?" Lou asked. "Spur him a bit? Or let him lallygag 'til ya drop the hammer?"

"I will not be spurring anyone."

"I'd get on the horn and chew him out. Squeaky wheel and all that." Lou glanced between Fern and me. "I'm glad I'm not datin' an older hottie—let's have a girls' night. I'll give ya advice." She winked. "If I'm not in jail by then."

Fern agreed, to my surprise.

"We'll rodeo-vous soon," Lou said.

"Rendezvous, you mean?" I asked.

"Tomato, tomahto. Your New York is showin', Mel."

A breeze swooshed through the trees, rustling the debris scattered about the yard.

Shockingly, a dust devil of pine cones and leaves shape-shifted near us. It was like a ghost twirled, wearing a garment of foliage—it reminded me of a McQueen or Mugler—then it sashayed across the driveway.

"Oh, my, I've never seen that before!" Fern exclaimed.

"That's Eden Hoff showin' magic powers!" Lou said, amazed. "If you gals are drivin' and that thing square-dances from the woods in front of your car, gun it."

"It's the wind," I scoffed. "Eden does *not* have special powers, believe me. The last time she stepped on grass was probably for a tennis tournament in London."

"Not a big off-road gal, eh?" Lou asked.

"Not unless you count driving through Central Park."

I shivered. Temps had dropped in the short time we'd been outside. The next storm was blowing in.

Lou whistled. It sounded loud and sharp. *Fweet.* Like she blasted a warning. "Eden's still hidin' out somewhere—hey, why'd the editor cross the road?"

"No idea," Fern said.

"To get to Mel's apartment above the bookstore. She could come and go by the back door to the alley—"

"The only thing living above my store is a ghost," I said.

Lou's eyes went wide. "Holy cow, you really believe it?"

"Sure, it's Lady Macbeth. Ariel, maybe."

"Mount up and get to your shop! Check out the digs upstairs."

"You'll be okay, Fern?" I asked.

"Yes, I have Max to keep me company." She leaned down to pat his chest.

The breeze swirled again. The pines around the farmhouse swayed in the strong gusts. The trunks bending as though they'd break.

A tempest was on its way.

The trees showed it, and I felt it, too.

9

THE BELL, BOOK & ANVIL

Ghosts haunted the conference room. I arrived to find the place filled with them—*shocking!*

Inga Honeythorne, the mall business manager, pointed to transparent chairs around the table. "They're replicas of Philippe Starck's 'Louis Ghost Chairs.' I *love* how they look. So high fashion. What do you think?"

"I don't know, can't see them." I looked at the clear chairs, then studied her costume. "You look like a Midwest Morticia Addams."

She laughed. Inga wore a shredded black dress and a gruesome clay brooch that looked like moldy cheese. She tapped the brooch. "A vendor up on the third floor makes them. That floor's theme is 'Dinner with the Devil.' Everything is ghoulishly delish."

Inga was seventy, give or take. A Big Cheese in Cinnamon.

Five years ago, I hired her to run the place. It was the best decision I made. She ran the Anvil like a corporate CEO.

No, better because Inga had mind for business and an artist's heart.

A name tag written in a fancy font was pinned by her brooch. Inga was an award-winning calligrapher who claimed beautiful penmanship was vital to civilization. "When the world runs out of money, grace and civility toward one another is all we will have left," she always said.

Inga hugged me. "I heard about what happened at the Promenade. Are you okay?"

"Yes, but do any of our vendors sell beach vacations? I could use one right now."

"Hmm, the closest thing would be a landscape painting. Or a vintage travel book, but you'd get more variety in your bookshop—"

I held up a hand. "Never mind, thanks. Do I have any calls?"

She stepped to a sideboard to read a clipboard, her clogs thunking the plank floor, *clunk, clunk.*

The room had been a storage space for blacksmith tools, but we converted it to a conference and classroom.

A tray on the sideboard held coffee, tea, and shortbread cookies. "Inga's Shortbreads" were legendary. She made the treats for every holiday, decorating them with sanding sugar according to the season. These were round, a half-inch thick, and glistened with orange crystals.

Inga gestured to a chair at the long table. At least, I assumed the seat was there.

I couldn't see anything to sit on, remember.

"We've got problems with the pop-up shop at the Promenade," she said, flipping pages. "You had two phone calls, Wooly Gallagher and Captain Rand. The captain said he tried your cell but didn't get an answer. He's flying from Heathrow later and wanted to bring a Halloween souvenir from the Tower of London." She glanced around the room. "I took the liberty of asking for toy ravens. They'd go perfectly in here."

I nodded. "No problem."

Inga was a sweet as they come, salt of the earth. Her late husband had been in the military.

She adored a man in a uniform and had a *major* soft spot for Rand. She'd love to see the captain and me back together.

After my parent died, Inga stepped in as a mentor and found my first modeling agency in New York City. Back then, casting was conducted by snail mail and phone calls.

Inga hunted down a New Faces agent, bought me a bus ticket to the Big Apple, and the rest was history.

Since I could remember, Inga went off-plumb in October, the spooky season. In calligrapher-speak, her graceful curlicues tangled to snarls.

For every Boo Bash, Inga wore costumes and bedazzled the place.

This year, the conference room was a fashion photoshoot for a Pumpkins & Demons editorial.

Orange gourds were painted with cat-eye makeup and red lips. Old cameras with glued-on wings hung from the ceiling. On a table by the exit to the mall, doll-sized Macbeth's witches were posed not by a cauldron, but a tiny three-way mirror.

Inga had been assisted by the other artists in the mall, obvi. When Mel Tower was away, her employees and vendors liked to play.

A sign on the door, written in blood-red ink, said, "A false face must hide what the false heart doth know."

An interesting phrase given the career I'd worked in—*where was Eden Hoff, anyway?*

Inga handed me a paper with a phone number. "Here's Rand's number at his hotel near Buckingham Palace. If you have a chance, call him before he flies out."

I sighed. "I'm besieged at the moment. I'll try later."

"Don't wait too long."

I studied her. "What's up about Rand?"

"There are rumors … he could be … dating someone."

"That's okay. I'm dating someone else."

She stared at my hair. "You've got a nasty-looking slice on your head. What happened?"

"Would you believe it if I said my crown fell off?"

She perched half-glasses on her nose to look at the wound. "I have honey healing ointment for that. The First Aid kit is in the cabinet."

"The injury is a long way from my heart. I'll live."

"I don't mean to pry about Ichabod Hall ... can you discuss what you saw?"

I hesitated. Whatever was said would be the lead story at the Tool & Rye. Not that Inga would betray my confidence. It's that she'd hear gossip and set the record straight.

Inga and Lou had tangled a few times when chatting about village events.

"Do you remember that runway show called 'Orange You Mad'?" I asked. "It was the last one before I switched to body parts."

"Yes, it's in Wooly's archive at the newspaper." She looked around the room. "I could ask for those images and add them to the decor. They'd fit the theme."

Wooly had documented my career over the years. My parents were gone, and I didn't have siblings. Cousin Lou had been busy with her life. Who else would do it?

"Not what I meant," I said, shaking my head. "That's what seeing Ichabod reminded me of—black, orange, and *frightening*."

"Oh, dear."

"It wasn't just a look or an emotion like fashion strives for—it was the real thing."

"How awful." She paused. "Would you like a hand-drawn sympathy card? I can create one."

"I'd appreciate that, thanks. I'll send it to his business associates from everyone at the mall."

The room's glass door opened to the first floor, where shoppers entered to peruse work by artists and crafters.

Today, for Boo Bash, the place was jam-packed.

People strolled past, looking at jewelry, candles, and painted furniture. After shoppers toured the first floor, there were two more to enjoy.

Inga watched them. "Is the fashion show canceled? So many

people are in town. It would be a shame. You all worked so hard, and it benefits the Dress for Your Dreams program."

"It will be rescheduled," I confirmed. "The charity will get a donation if my life depends on it. The show stops for no one. Not even a legend like Ichabod Hall."

Inga and I discussed mall business over tea and shortbreads. I'd been helping with show and needed to catch up on the news.

Inga had held down the fort.

Well, the anvil to be accurate given where we were meeting, but she seemed distracted. She made notes but kept asking me to repeat myself.

Inga was as beloved in the village as the spice shop with its landmark sign announcing, "Cinnamon is Cinn-amazing." When Inga was having an off day, one took notice.

"What's wrong?" I asked, finally. "Is it that Max isn't here? It's not the same without our official greeter. I miss him, too, but he wanted to stay with Fern."

Inga smiled, wrinkles forming around her eyes. "I always miss my assistant, but the pop-up shop at the Promenade is an issue. Are you familiar with Pauline Pickle? She's been in town for about a year."

"Yes, why?"

"We're testing ideas, as you know. Our vendors want to curate seasonal products and offer them to the residents. For fall, we have Halloween earrings. For those with grandkids, we have stickers to hand out instead of candy." She touched the orange half-glasses she wore. "And we're selling sassy cheaters for autumn."

"Pauline has nothing to do with our inventory. We work with Sally Calico in the sales department."

"Oh, she has *lots* to say. We can't sell what they carry in the clinic." Inga touched the frames again. "Like cheater glasses."

"Pauline doesn't set the rules for our vendors. I'll check it out." I studied Inga. "Is that all that's bothering you?"

Her face flushed immediately. "You've heard about events this week?"

I nodded, listing the major ones. "Yes, reader's theater, the fashion show, and the Golden—*no*."

She gasped. "Why not?"

I'd hurt her. *Not my intention.* I covered her hands with mine. Inga's skin smelled of vanilla and honey. She used a lotion from a skincare seller on the second floor, and I reminded myself to purchase some.

"Forgive me," I said. "You're interested in dating? If I were doing the casting, *you* would be the star, not the bachelor, whoever he'll be."

"Thank you."

"I'd try to get a fellow in a uniform to participate, too." I winked.

"It's been years since Ed died." She reached for a tissue from the box on the table. "I adored him, but I'd like to spend time with someone. I was wondering if ... you would help me with an outfit to wear?"

I looked around to see if Inga spoke to someone else. A ghost or spirit that had shimmered through the wall.

Inga asked *me* for advice about clothes and styling?

I had a closet full of garments. Lovely pieces made of cashmere, wool, and cotton. All vintage, many were runway samples I bought for pennies at long-ago sales. Donna Karan, Ralph Lauren, Tom Ford.

The pieces were gorgeous and all I could afford when I'd lived in New York City.

I'd kept them for years and rarely purchased anything new. But what my wardrobe had in common was it was all *black*. Different shades, but still *noir*. They were dark clothes, lovely fabrics, and simple silhouettes.

"Mel, will you help me?" Inga repeated.

"Yes, but are you sure?" I tipped my head toward the door. "There are so many artists out there—"

She smiled. "No, Mel, you always look put together. I'd appreciate ideas about what to wear."

I glanced at a stack of cards and pens on the table. When I arrived, Inga was drawing Halloween cards. She sketched scary cartoons and penned quotes in her signature, elegant hand.

The top card showed a raven and a revealing phrase. In curlicue letters, Inga wrote,"The underworld is empty this week. All the ghouls are in Cinnamon."

There were talented designers in Wisconsin. Mount Mary University in Milwaukee offered a four-year degree in fashion design. I knew a student with fabulous style, Crystal Broadway—*I wish she was home to ask advice.*

I nodded. "Yes, I can help."

"Fantastic! This will be so much fun." She picked up a card showing a witch posing in a gown and read its quote. "The soul of a woman is her clothes, after all."

Inga and I exited the conference room. Well, flew out was the better verb, given the decor and season. She fluttered to her office, and I breezed to my mine.

My workspace was a closet, basically. Smaller than Inga's because she had a bigger job. I ceded management of the mall's operations to her, and marketing belonged to Fern Bubble.

I paid the bills and stayed out of the way. To stick with the Halloween theme, I was a "Ghost CEO." I kept an eye on the checkbook and made sure customers were satisfied.

Otherwise, this former model faded to the background to let the experts work their magic. Not a bad system.

While I'd been busy at the Promenade, Inga and the Halloween elves paid a visit to my little space. Vintage cameras with wings floated from the ceiling, and a glam pumpkin posed on the bookshelf.

As I was alone, this was my chance to contact Sheriff Cole, who'd responded to my call yesterday with a short text. *Annoying.*

That was why I had problems—my desk phone rang, its receiver having grown a plastic claw. I grabbed it. "The Bell, Book and Anvil, it's Boo Bash week—"

"Good afternoon, Mel. No, you're six hours behind in the Midwest. Good morning from London."

I smiled. "Hello, Rand."

His voice was deep and reassuring, exactly as a pilot's should. It felt comforting to hear him after what happened yesterday.

"I have a Halloween riddle," he said. "Where did the pilot meet the ghost?'

I paused. "No idea. That one's over my head."

He laughed. "On another *plane.*"

"Did you *wing* that joke?"

"Yes, thought it up on the fly. I'm in London for a few more hours. What can I bring you?"

"Hmm ... how about toy ravens?"

"Sorry, Inga has dibs on those."

"Toy crows, then?"

He sighed. "Something for *you*, Mel. You love Shakespeare. How about a collection of his tragedies? *The Tempest* or something for the spooky season—"

"Not that one." I glanced at the bookshelf. "Something light-hearted. How about Wodehouse?"

"Done. I'll find one of his books."

I recalled the author's works. "Not *Heavy Weather.* I have it already, and it's a poor choice for a flight."

"Excellent point," he said. "I thought about you during this trip. The flight was from Chicago to New York to London. And across the

Channel are Paris and Milan. I can practically see those cities from my hotel. That's the fashion perfecta, the runway cities, right? How'd the rehearsal go—"

"We'll talk about it later. I'm late for a meeting with Hank Leigel. Can we chat when you get back?"

"Sure, but look in the sky at about seventeen-hundred hours. I'll be vectoring to Minneapolis and pass over Cinnamon. I'll do a wing wave. Or would you like me to skywrite something?"

"How about 'Shop Local for Boo Bash?'"

"Those 'Bs' might be tricky, but I'll try."

"If you can't, I'll send Cousin Lou up on a broom."

"If anyone could do it, Lou could."

"Fly safe," I said.

We hung up. In the years I'd know Rand, I never discussed bad news when he was flying a trip. Anything negative happening in my life could wait until he and his passengers were safely on the ground.

It was hard to process the death of Ichabod Hall. If I shared that with Rand, he could cancel his schedule and show up at my doorstep.

I didn't need that right now.

If Rand traveled to Cinnamon, it would complicate everything.

10

HANK LEIGEL'S LEGAL OFFICE

I walked to Hank Leigel's real estate office under *unfriendly* skies (gray, moody-looking), weaving through shoppers, thinking about Captain Rand Cunningham.

We broke up last year but kept in contact. More than when we dated. He and I got along better, ironically.

Rand seemed happier and inquired more about my life and work. I felt less frustrated while speaking to him.

The past summer had been a plot twist. Rand wanted to get back together. I said no, diverted as they say in aviator-speak, because I'd met Cole Lawrence.

Was it true Rand was seeing Pauline—?

"Boo! *Boo!*"

"You scared me!" I grabbed my scarf and swooned.

"Boo!"

A "haunting" of ghosts floated on the sidewalk, the breeze twirling their sheets around their knees.

The group flowed out from Hank's office, *boo-ing* at passersby, showing off their goodie bags of stickers and glow bracelets.

For Boo Bash, shop owners gave out treats not just on October thirty-first but the whole week prior. Costumes were encouraged in Cinnamon, no matter the season.

A mom smiled at me. "Excuse us, we're just flying through. Happy Halloween."

"The same to you." I noticed the parent ghosts were empty-handed. "Wait, didn't you get your properties? Hank was handing out real estate to adults this week."

They laughed. "We'll have to stop back," a dad said. "I'd love to move to Cinnamon."

"I recommend it," I said. "Please go haunt the Bell, Book & Anvil. We have three floors of artists who need a scare."

"*Boo!*" the tiny ghouls yelled.

I entered Hank's place, which had been redecorated by Halloween elves with a JD degree. On a side table was a plastic hatchet with a large sticker saying, "Exhibit A."

Next to it was a ceramic witch's cottage with a roofer sliding down its shingles. An attorney stood on the lawn holding a contract, an ambulance in the driveway.

Pictures of scary real estate hung on the brick walls, infamous properties listed for sale. For low-ball prices, home shoppers could purchase the House of Usher, the Amityville Horror two-story, or the Pfister Hotel, a Milwaukee landmark allegedly so haunted major league baseball players refused to stay overnight even though it was the official team hotel.

A framed quote penned in Ye Olde World text was on the desk.

I read it: "First, let's kill all the lawyer *jokes*. Spoken by Shake-speare's attorney, I assume?"

"If The Bard could hire one after writing that," Hank said. "I imagine it was difficult to retain counsel."

He stepped around his massive desk, the old floor creaking. Hank was sixty, gray-haired, stocky. He dated a friend of mine, Susan Victory, and loved the heck out of the woman. She was a silversmith, one of the first vendors in my mall.

She was out of town this week on a health retreat. Susan had been to rehab earlier in the year, but healed marvelously.

"It's good to see you," Hank said, taking my jacket and scarf. "You okay?"

I sighed. "You heard about Ichabod?"

"Yes, Wooly Gallagher told me." He pointed to a leather chair. "Have a seat. What can I get you? I have Halloween drinks on tap. Would you prefer a Claw & Order or a Misty Meanor? Both taste like ginger tea."

On the side table, a crockpot simmered, its contents blooming, filling the office with comforting scents. It was like autumn originated right there, within the wooden floor, brick walls, and comfy furnishings.

"A Claw, please," I said. "I'm feeling disordered. Maybe it'll help."

"Two hot teas coming up." He hung up my things, then nodded at the spooky real estate listings. "May I interest you in a nightmare property? Something with bleeding ceilings or a spirit in the attic?"

I played along. "Do you have a haunted cottage by a lake?"

"No, but how about *The Addams' Family*? I've got a creaky colonial with a leaky roof and graveyard in back."

"No moat?"

"Sorry, not this listing."

"I was hoping for a moat."

Hand pondered. "I've got a remote island. Just listed by a fellow named Prospero—"

"From *The Tempest*?" I scanned the room's shelves, fearful of falling books. "No, Hank, positively *not*."

Hank served tea. I served up questions about my bookstore next door.

The Bell, Book & Melville shared a wall with Hank's digs. As the unofficial village historian, he knew its backstory.

I tasted the tea. Ginger and cinnamon with a honey finish. *Mmm.* Like Wisconsin's fall season in a mug. "Did an event occur there that wasn't, ah, advertised?" I asked.

"In the bookstore? Heavens, no," Hank said from behind his desk. "It was exorcized before I listed it—"

"*What?*"

He smiled. "I'm joking, Mel. It's the time of year. What's up with the question?"

"I'd like to know more about its history."

"It was a cobbler shop for years. Then the fellow passed, and it sat vacant. It fell apart, basically. Prior decades were hard on Midwest villages." He sipped from a black mug with "Statute Sorcerer" scrawled across it in blood-red letters.

"Then what?"

"A few businesses tried to make a go of it but none lasted. The roof leaked and it had a septic issue, as you know. You purchased it at a fair price, fixed it, and now Cinnamon has a great little indie bookstore."

I sipped tea. "The cobbler, did he marry, have a family?"

Hank shook his head. "No, Shaugnessy Shulman did not."

"He lived above the store?"

"Yes, 'Shue', that was his nickname, lived in the apartment you're updating, as most shopkeepers did at that time."

"So he could have passed ... " I had a hard time saying it due to the tragedy in the Promenade ballroom. "Shue could have ... ."

"Slipped on the proverbial deadly banana peel in his own home?" Hank sighed. "I'm afraid so. Ask not for whom the banana tolls, Mel. It tolls for thee."

In shockingly poor timing, the chime above the door dinged. Wooly Gallagher barged in, out of breath. "I'm glad you two are here," he said. "I've got news about Ichabod Hall's death."

"Goodness, Wool, it looks like you've seen a ghost," Hank said.

"Have a seat. I'll make you hot tea. Mel, would you lock the door and close the blinds? It looks like we'll need privacy."

I followed orders, closing the blinds and shuttering the office to make it seem like we'd disappeared.

WOOLY TOOK THE TEA FROM HANK, NEARLY SPILLING IT.

The editor's hands shook. He was so pale he looked white as the mini-ghosts I'd met on the sidewalk. Where had he been? Not in my bookstore. College students staffed it today. Crystal Broadway, the manager, was due back soon.

Hank returned to his seat behind the desk. "Wooly, I haven't seen you this rattled since that time in the cemetery—"

"Ichabod Hall's death is the strangest I've encountered," he interrupted. "People are saying he was killed by something supernatural. There are clues that don't make sense. Our village isn't safe."

As he spoke, thunder rumbled, vibrating the floor as though a freight train passed by.

Cinnamon didn't have tracks or a train.

"What can you tell us?" Hank asked.

"The toxicology tests are not complete. The man could have been strangled but that would require someone with exceptional strength." Wooly looked at me. "You found him. What did you see in that runway?"

I still had to speak with Detective Bruce DuWayne and didn't want to compromise that conversation. "For a potential crime scene, it didn't appear ... unusual."

Half true. Discovering a dead person was a shock but *anything* could appear on a fashion show runway. Coffins, for example. Thom Browne showed models lying in caskets in 2012. In 2000, Alexander McQueen's models flew on wires over a pathway of nails.

A man lying deceased wasn't odd, arguably.

Hank scowled. The genial real estate mogul was replaced by Richard III, criminal defense attorney. "Hold on, Mel. Before going into detail, let's discover what's being implied. Was there a press conference or an official statement, Wooly? Or did this intel come from gossip at the Tool & Rye?"

Wooly shook his head. "I can't reveal sources, but it was beyond gossip. People who *saw* things."

That meant Doc Graves or Pauline. Maybe Nathan Gould, Alicia Cliff—or even Wooly's wife, Cozette. The word "saw" could be a loose definition. Unlike attorneys, reporters used hearsay evidence from deep background sources.

Did the person have a reason to claim there was zero evidence? A perpetrator would misdirect on purpose—perhaps because they had something to do with it.

Wooly's odd story "captivated my ear," to quote *The Tempest*, the story haunting my life currently.

Still, I didn't ask a follow-up question. Nor did Hank, and Wooly didn't elaborate.

I'd never seen him so distressed, but perhaps the spooky time of year added to his misery.

We sat in a silent triangle, two people facing a desk and one seated behind, in an office of brick walls, an ancient plank floor, and macabre real estate listings.

We were like ghosts, three beings trained in the strategy of quiet observation. Well, two of us were formally educated. Then there was me, a former mannequin, an expert in posing and keeping her mouth shut.

I made use of those years of standing still, which was OJT in evaluating body language. I was never a supermodel, but I did have a superpower—I could read peoples' expressions and posture to discover who *spaketh* truth and who *dideth* not.

Wooly stared at the mug he held, a red one with a raven squawking the phrase "I CAW-GHT you!"

The editor knew more than he revealed—*why not tell two of his closest friends?*

My phone pinged on the desk. I'd placed it there after removing my jacket. I reached for it, figuring the text was from Detective DuWayne asking to talk. I glanced at the message.

Nope, wrong. It was Cole.

Finally.

I stood up. "Excuse me, I need to speak to someone."

II

THE HAUNTED APARTMENT

I grabbed my jacket and exited via the back door into the alley behind the two- and three-story buildings of Main Street. The structures were brick or limestone, built in the 1850s by Cornish and German immigrants.

The structures cast shadows on the narrow alley. It seemed like I walked a medieval street. The wind whipped in a Venturi effect, coldly slicing through my jacket like a dressmaker's shears. I shuddered. It felt like a season of discontent had descended upon sweet Cinnamon. No—a season of discom*bob*ulation was a better description.

Bob, bobbing for apples, fall, Halloween, and all.

I trudged to my bookshop, mentally weighted down as though my clothes had metal washers sewn into the hems like in fashion's old days.

Scenarios and suspects weighed on my mind. I felt like a criminal leaving a crime scene. *I'd* found Ichabod Hall dead on the runway. Had Wooly's discomfort been a sign? Was *I* a suspect?

It wouldn't be the first time.

Last year, a woman was killed in my mall, and yours truly was accused of the crime. I'd catwalked through that investigation like a supermodel, a class of fashionistas that Mel Tower, commercial girl, definitely was *not*—I'd been a worker bee in the industry, never a queen.

Rand and I broke up during that time, too.

What a disaster!

My heeled boots clacked on the steps leading to the back entry of The Bell, Book & Melville. I opened the door and waved at the college women staffing the shop. Crystal Broadway, the manager, returned in a day or two.

Enticing aromas floated toward me. The store smelled of books—vanilla, smoke, wood—plus coffee and baked treats. On a table near the front was a pot of drip brew, plus cups for customers, and the Tool & Rye folks sent over cinnamon roll bites for the week of Boo Bash.

At my right was a staircase leading up to Shue Shulman's pied-à-terre, the apartment being renovated. A chain barricaded the stairs, but it wasn't much of a deterrent, just plastic ghosts holding hands and a sign that said, "No Spirits Past this Point. We're Making the Upstairs Boo-tiful!"

I unlatched it and climbed upward, dual purposes on my mind. To paraphrase the adage, I'd kill two ghosts with one stone.

I sought a private spot to speak with Cole, and if a spirit resided in the place, it was time to tell it to scram.

I didn't have an eviction spell—I'd politely order the ghoul to catch the next frequent flyer departing Cinnamon. And if my order didn't work, I'd dispatch Louella Jingle, a witchy cowgirl who feared nothing except empty cupboards because that meant she couldn't conjure up treats to serve the masses.

There was a temporary keypad by the door. Sunny Days Restoration, the firm doing the reno, installed it. They were artists with drywall, paint, and tile. I tapped four numbers, "1513," Quarterback Bart Starr's jersey number, plus the number of Green Bay Packers' league championships.

Was the code too easy?

For a lifelong Wisconsinite, human or ghost, yes. Especially for ghosts because Packer fans are known for their team *spirit*.

The guys at Sunny Days suggested the code.

I should have it changed.

I entered, expecting to be bathed in light even on this cloudy day. The place had only four rooms, but its tall windows overlooked the street with its vintage-style lamps and bright storefronts. The effect made the place seem large—*except today*.

The windows were covered by opaque plastic and taped because the walls were to be painted. I flipped the switch to the sitting room's new chandelier. *Nothing*. The narrow passage I'd entered into remained dark. The sitting room was to my left. The kitchen, bed, and bath to my right.

CLANG!

What was that?

It sounded like metal—was someone in the kitchen?

I pressed my back against the wall, glancing at the sitting room. A worktable displayed cans of paint, brushes, and stir sticks. Also, a heat gun, Green Bay Packers bandanas, and a box of Chicago Bears towels, cleaning rags, probably.

I tip-toed to the table, my back to the wall. Pressing my phone camera to "on," I propped it against a can, grabbed the gun with its wide, short barrel, and crept down the hallway to stand at the kitchen's swinging door. It had been stripped of paint and refinished, redeemed to its original polished wood. Work done when I'd been occupied by the fashion show.

I knocked loudly. "Who's there?"

No answer.

"Come out with your hands up—police!" I braced my legs and clasped the gun in my fingers, pointing at the door. I'd been a police officer in a photoshoot once. I wore a uniform and modeled "All Day Slayers" footwear.

The photographer said I *laced* it.

The memory gave me confidence.

I deepened my voice. "Cinn Police. Come out. *Now.*"

I pushed the door. Quick like, to catch the ghoul off guard, bash his nose in case he floated near it—*did ghosts have noses?*

The door swung back, no satisfying *thud* as it bopped against a nose, face, or anything. Cold air blew toward me when the door whooshed shut.

"Police!" I yelled.

CLANG!

What the—?

The noise sounded familiar. There was a window over the sink, I recalled. It opened to the space between the buildings and had a curtain hung with metal clips ... could the window be open?

I kicked the door. It swung inward, then out. I snagged it with my foot and held by bracing my heel against it, using the door as a shield in case the ghoul came out.

I waited. *Nothing.*

In a fast move, I pushed the door, whirled around to step inside, and—*crash!*

Feet meet metal toolbox. *Ouch.*

The kitchen was empty. Of humans, anyway. The old cupboards were stripped of paint. Cleaned tools were on the counter by the window, which was cranked open a few inches. The clanking sound was the metal clips used to attach the curtain to the rod. When the wind whipped, they rattled loudly.

The white curtain fluttered. The lightweight fabric lifted and fell as though alive.

It reminded me of ... *a ghost.*

My toe hurt, and my head was still sore, too. Injuries were piling on.

I closed the window, but the kitchen still felt chilly, like a spirit from a distant realm had blown in. I thought about firing up the heat gun to warm the space, but my phone rang in the sitting room.

It was *The Lone Ranger* theme song—Sheriff Cole Lawrence.

I quick-stepped from the kitchen and grabbed my cell. "Hi—"

"Mel—break now," he said. "—wanted—talk."

I glanced at my phone. The WiFi wasn't working, and the service in Cinnamon was always sketchy. Too many hills. "I can't hear—"

"Can't talk—long. How—fashion show?" he asked.

"I need to talk to you. Ichabod Hall had an accident and—"

"—at the quarry. I'll call later, Mel. Can't—hear."

He hung up.

I stared at my phone. My vibe with Cole during the last few weeks was odd, as I'd mentioned. I disliked playing cat and mouse, but Cole had a way of avoiding things like I used to do.

Opposites didn't always attract. Sometimes, they were frustratingly alike.

Also, Cole was *awful* at goodbyes. He'd hang up quickly without mentioning when we'd speak again. He didn't do it on purpose, I was sure. It was self-protection, a disengagement that guarded his ego.

I understood. I used to do that, too—*but of all the times I needed to speak with Cole Lawrence, this was it.*

I HEARD A MAN'S VOICE AND SHOES ON THE STAIRCASE. NOT THE HEAVY clunks of a plasterer carrying drywall or paint. Or Steven Delavan, a best friend and god of delivering packages, toting a box. He was out of town with Crystal Broadway; the two were an item.

The footfalls were lightweight, the sound of someone schooled in dance. Or flying, perhaps. There was a knock on the door, *tap, tap.*

"Melanie, are you in residence?"

A man's voice—*Swan.*

"Come in," I replied.

He floated inside. Talk about ethereal. In the years I'd known Swan, I was never sure if the fellow opened doors or shimmered through them. Upon his entrance, the apartment immediately warmed and brightened.

"Your staff in the bookshop said you were here," he said, kissing both my cheeks. "I hope you don't mind a visit."

He wore a cashmere overcoat, and his cologne drifted to my nose. He smelled of orange, cinnamon, and pine, autumn in a bottle.

"Do you have a moment?" he asked. "There were rumors about Ichabod's death. I wish to inquire because you were the person ... to discover him in such an unfortunate state."

I nodded. "Dying *is* unfortunate."

"I'm very sorry you experienced such a shock, Melanie."

He spoke quietly as though fearing we'd be overheard. No, that was incorrect. Swan always spoke softly. It was why he was well-respected. His elegant demeanor and calm reserve said volumes.

He sighed. It sounded like the lament of a Nobleman perched on a throne. "Ichabod was at odds, sadly. Forces conspired against him. He was like a castaway among the fashion set."

"A castaway? What do you mean?"

"Yes, it was as though he resided away from the others in a remote locale. An island, almost."

I gulped and stepped away from the table of tools. When islands were mentioned lately, my person was in harm's way.

I touched my sore noggin.

"Have I said something to offend you?" Swan asked.

"No, but why are you telling me this?"

"There were associates ... plotting against Ichabod." He paused as though searching for an explanation. "Innocent players are being maligned. In your charming little burg, fair is foul and foul is fair."

"But that's the fashion business. Didn't Ichabod use that theme on the runway a few years ago?"

Swan chuckled, his perfect teeth flashing. "I've always enjoyed your humor, Melanie. But the game is afoot, I fear."

Afoot? I thought about my toe throbbing in my boot.

How did he know I'd bashed it against the toolbox? And why was he dropping cryptic clues as though he were a genie—or Prospero?

It seemed like I was receiving an assignment, a role in a tragicomedy involving a deceased designer and unknown antagonists.

Between Swan and Wooly, I felt like I was being cast under a spell to solve a murder.

Cousin Lou wanted to involve me, too, but she'd never use magic. She'd persuade me to investigate with a batch of truffle brownies.

Swan continued, "To protect yourself, you must put yourself at risk."

An irony for circumstances surrounding murders, I'd discovered.

Since being in the proximity of two victims within the past year, I'd learned that things *never* were as they seemed, and staying *out* of trouble meant risking *my* neck.

I shook my head. "Fortune sometimes brings in ships that are not steered."

In other words, the question of who killed Ichabod Hall may solve itself without my expertise, limited as it was.

I was an amateur when it came to murder cases, even though I had skills finding fakers. All those years of standing still trained me to read body language—but two men would *not* be pleased I was nosing around: Detective Bruce DuWayne, and a handsome sheriff.

Cole wouldn't enjoy hearing that I was Scooby Doo-ing it. For my own safety, he'd say, "I'd rather you Scooby *Didn't*, Mel."

Swan said, "Decades ago, you were sent on a journey to New York." His voice was smooth as silk. "It was a quest to find yourself."

"It was a quest for a paycheck. My parents were gone. I loved them dearly, but they left me just enough for a bus ticket. I had to work to survive."

"And you rose to the occasion."

"Because I'm tall." I straightened my shoulders. "The modeling industry had a height requirement. It was like the army, but its boot camp required walking in heels while balancing a book on my head."

Swan was unfettered. "Now, instead of you traveling away on a journey, it has come to here. To paraphrase the adage, if the spyglass fits, Mel, you must wear it."

Grumpily, I said, "In other words, ask not for whom the bell bottoms toll, they toll for thee."

He smiled. "John Donne. He also said no one is an island. Rather, she is a piece of the continent, a part of the main. Each death diminishes her, for she is involved in humankind."

Again, with the island theme, but point taken.

He glided toward the door. "Take care of yourself, my dear. Stay vigilant and beware of the Ides of October. Misfortune doesn't become a lady such as yourself."

Then Swan disappeared, floating through the door and down the steps as though he wore invisible wings.

I dashed to my car due to an emergency text from Inga.

She wrote: Mel, the dating show was rescheduled for tonight! Meet me at my cottage to help with an outfit?

I replied: Of course!

And so, like a genie soaring over the Kettle Moraine countryside, I ended up in Inga's sitting room drinking tea with her Pomeranian dog, Mocha, in my lap.

The dog and I watched while Inga modeled clothes from her previous career as a librarian—brown, gray, and black pantsuits.

After the third number, I asked what was wrong. "Inga, you've got a fun, artistic style. You're like Wisconsin's Betsey Johnson. Why are you pulling career wear from years ago?"

She studied her reflection in a mirror. The ends of her gray hair were dyed purple, and she wore mismatched earrings, one an artist's palette, the other a paintbrush.

After retiring, as a second-career, Inga became an award-winning calligrapher—but regarding the outfit she wore, her hair and earrings were where Inga's artsy personality ended.

She frowned. "I don't know. You always wear dark colors, Mel."

"That's because models were mannequins. The designer projected their vision onto us. We were a blank canvas."

"Ironic, isn't it?" She poured tea from the pot on the table into my mug. "In a creative industry, you weren't allowed to be creative."

True. Among designers, stylists, and hair and makeup artists, I was the least creative person in the fashion biz.

Inga sat down next to me. "I'm sorry, dear. I didn't mean to insult you. I'm so nervous."

"If it's too much pressure and you're uncomfortable, don't do it," I said. "It's not worth making yourself upset."

"Good heavens, Mel. We're not women who back down when something is scary or uncomfortable."

She put a hand over mine. I was wrong about her personality ending at her earrings. Her nails were painted orange with little black triangles that made pumpkin faces.

"I don't mean to be difficult," she said. "I'm working through something. I miss connecting with a partner. It's making me ... "

Her voice trailed off, and I finished her thought: "Wear career couture from the eighties?"

"But they're power suits—we all wore them!"

I squeezed her shoulder. The padding felt thick and stiff. She could deliver a decent hit to a blocking sled. "You and your new fella could try out for the high school football team," I said. "That's a unique thing to do on a first date."

"We'll tell them we're a pair of 'senior' walk-ons—think they'd notice?"

She giggled until she snorted, the emotion I wanted to see. "Golden-agers are doing all kinds of cool stuff now, Inga. You'd have a blast."

I giggled, too.

Just like magic, my spirits felt lifted.

WE SETTLED ON A BLACK JACKET AND SLACKS, BLACK PUMPS, AND A BLACK handbag.

No, those were my suggestions.

To Inga's credit, she didn't blackball me on the spot and throw me out into the "wrathful, nipping cold," as Shakespeare would describe the blustery weather.

The sky had turned the color of tombstones and trees twisted, lashing to and fro, their branches bent, their leaves soggy and brown.

We'd moved to her bedroom. Mocha occupied the bed while I sat on an overstuffed chintz-covered chair watching Inga as she rehung suits and dresses.

For the quiz show, she'd picked a smashing purple dress with a bag shaped like a pumpkin, a Betsey Johnson. She held up the orange purse. "What do you think? I got her a few years ago. It's the 'Oh My Gourd' bag."

"It's perfect. You know what they say: Go Big or Gourd Home."

She scanned her outfit in the full-length mirror. "I'll give 'em *pumpkin* to talk about tonight, eh?"

"Speaking of talking, have you ever heard of something ... weird happening in my bookshop?"

I tried to sound nonchalant. Asking about weirdness—ghosts, spirits, hauntings—could seem *extra*-chalant in any context, but especially during the week of Boo Bash.

No sense in alarming Inga before her dating show debut.

She paused, holding a hanger in mid-air. "Why?"

"No reason. Just wondering if there's been a rumor of a ghost."

"No, but years ago, it was a *boo-tique*, you know. Anything could be possible."

"Very funny."

"You know Wisconsinites, we love coupons and bargain *haunting*."

She smiled, and the cozy bedroom room lit up as though lightning struck. Inga looked great, and her personality and positive energy would attract tonight's fellow, whoever was replacing Ichabod, like a magnet.

I didn't press the issue about the history of my building. No sense in affecting her confidence. Given Inga's smile and sassy personality, the other contestants should watch out!

I STOOD BY THE ARCHED FRONT DOOR, A MAHOGANY SLAB OF CENTURY-OLD wood. I felt like Gretel from the fairy tale and wondered what lurked outside. Wind battered the door, and a peek through its glass sidelights showed a monsoon had arrived in southeast Wisconsin.

Inga pulled a tent and waders from the closet and tried to cloak me in them. "Wear these to get to your car."

I refused. "Are you worried I'll melt? I'm tall. No one would notice an inch or two off the top. I'll be okay in my jacket."

She set the rain gear on the floor. "Sorry, I don't mean to be overprotective. I want everything to be okay, that's all."

"You're not having second thoughts, I hope." I hugged her. "You look stunning, *boo-tiful*. You'll be the Queen Cheesehead among lesser cheeses, the ones with all the preservatives."

She paused. "Am I doing the right thing?"

"Sure."

"I'm putting my dating life out for people of Cinnamon to judge and criticize—in the Whoopee Den, no less." She frowned, and it was like seeing the Halloween Fairy break her wand.

"It'll be okay. Most people in the crowd will already know you, and they *love* you. And the only scandal I've heard about in the Den is when a prankster switched out a Bingo card for one with all FREE spaces."

"That prankster was named Louella Jingle." Inga flipped on the porch light even though it was only four o'clock. "The image on all those spaces was a pair of spurs."

I couldn't confirm or deny her accusation. In The Case of the Great Bingo Card Caper, I knew nothing. "Try not to worry. It'll be a new experience for an evening."

Inga sighed. "I don't know about dating at my age. I have plenty of friends. Why bother?"

"Think of it as meeting someone new. Not dating, per se."

"But I *do* want to share time with someone. It's odd—I'm confused, happy, and scared at the same time. It's like being a teenager again."

"If there's anyone who can handle an experience like this, it's you." I smiled. "But if you want to date privately, we all know single fellows. I'm sure we could *dig up* a nice guy for you."

She laughed. "Enough—get out, Mel, before you cast me in a starring role in Romeo and *Ghouliet*."

Her phone pinged on the side table with a message. She picked it up, looked at the voicemail ID, and then showed it to me: Detective Bruce DuWayne.

She met the man a year ago when a woman died in my mall, I recalled.

She stared at the phone. "He probably wants to know what I've heard about Ichabod. I'll call him back later."

"You've kept in touch with Bruce?"

She shook her head. "Not often. He's been in the mall a few times to shop for gifts, and we've chatted. That's it."

Thunder rumbled, and the floor shook as though a train rumbled through. Or maybe a pile of boulders had broken loose from a mound in the Kettle Moraine and crashed downhill.

The thought of rumbles and crashes gave me goosebumps. The skin on my neck tingled as though sprites danced on my skin.

I couldn't ignore the sensation.

What was going on in Cinnamon?

12

THE WHOOPEE DEN

I was supposed to be congratulating Ichabod on a successful rehearsal and re-bagging garments.

Instead, I'd been drafted as a backstage assistant for The Golden Cheesehead, a combination senior dating game and quiz show.

The event had been rescheduled given what had happened to Ichabod.

I stood near the prop table, yawning. I preferred to be home, reading a book by the fire while Max snoozed beside me. It's amazing how the older I get, the earlier it got late, if that made sense.

I'd have cancelled this thing, if anyone asked, which they hadn't. Despite the death of a fashion designer, the show must go on, more than one person said while setting up tables, chairs, and a balloon arch of hearts on the stage.

The competition's premise was simple: Three ladies, including Inga—a walking torch song—asked questions of a senior bachelor. The audience provided laughter and encouragement, and then voted on the best match.

The winners received An Afternoon on the Town in Cinnamon. Lunch at the Tool & Rye, gift certificates to stroll and shop at my mall, a vision test at the eyeglass place, and a consultation for cush-ioned insoles at the shoe store.

No, I'm kidding about the last two. My sarcastic side emerges when I'm tired. Or stressed. *And I was both.*

Instead of medical appointments, the lovebirds had a chocolate shop tour and a wine tasting with hors d'oeuvres to end their date. Also, they had front row seats at the Reader's Theater event on Sunday.

Hank Leigel was emcee. He weaved toward me through the congested backstage area. He wore a tuxedo and cloak over his shoulders that ruffled in silky waves behind him as he walked.

"Did you hear, Mel?" he asked. "You're our 'Vanna' for the evening. Thanks for volunteering."

I must have heard wrong. "No, I'm the backstage assistant—"

"How do I look?" Hank twirled to show off the cloak and tuxedo. He had a ruffled shirt and gold rings on every finger. With his pompadour hair, he looked like Walter Busterkeys, a.k.a. Liberace.

"You look great," I said.

He frowned. "I was going for mystical, a bit menacing. Keep up with the Halloween theme."

I nodded. "That too."

He didn't appear ghoulish. More like a grandpa hired to play card tricks, but Hank was an attorney. White lies didn't count.

He studied my outfit. Black, of course. "We're going to need to refit you."

"I beg your pardon?"

"Our original 'Vanna' canceled because her grandkids are visit-ing, and she couldn't accommodate the reschedule." He snapped his fingers. "Wardrobe!"

"Wardrobe?"

Gowns hanging from a silver-colored rack rolled into view. It was like the rack moved under its own power. I recognized the clothes from the fashion show. Hank looked through them, clicking hangers. "We have permission from the House of Hall to use these. Here, try this black number printed with red tridents and guitars. Fiend meets rockstar."

"*No*, Hank."

He pulled another one and held it up. "Orange sequins with a green fedora?"

"I'd look like a tall, shiny pumpkin."

"Gourd Glam is the trend for fall—"

"I'll pick one myself, thanks," I said.

I stood by the three-way mirror in the dressing room. Cousin Lou stared at me, evaluating the gown I'd selected. It was the most pedestrian garment of the collection, a black dress with orange chevrons at the shoulders.

"It's got a Charlie Brown vibe," she said. "It's the squiggle line across your chest. Ya could be Lucy goin' to work at her corporate job. Or a funeral."

"Good grief."

She smiled. "You sure you don't want sequins—"

"No."

"Your dress comes with a matchin' hat." She reached for a hat hanging off the rolling clothing rack. "The squiggles go the other way. You wanna add it?"

"*No.*"

Lou clucked her tongue as though encouraging a horse to trot. "Hey, cowgirl, why so glum? I'm the one under suspicion that I fed Ichabod somethin' sketchy." She pointed to the apron she wore, the fringe on her blouse swinging as she moved her arm. In black letters, the apron said, "Be Nice, or I'll Poison Your Food." Lou lowered her voice. "Not to talk shop, but did ya chat with Cole—"

"Yes, he and I spoke."

Lou's eyes widened. "*Uh oh*. You two kids havin' trouble? He got his gun belt in a knot cuz you're solvin' another murder?"

"I'd rather not talk about it *here*."

"You wanna take a load off and compete in the show? I can corral ya as a guest last-minute to fill in for Trudy. The battery in her hearing aid went kaput, so she can't participate."

"I'm sorry for Trudy, but no."

"She's mad as a hornet cuz she can't be on stage, no idea what happened. I guess that means you and Cole didn't break up if, ah, you don't wanna compete for a new fella."

I'd never compete for a relationship, but I didn't answer. The noise out front grew louder. The audience had arrived, and they were taking their seats.

Lou rubbed her hands together. "You know what to do, right? Give Hank his note cards. Escort the Man Candy to his seat and make sure he doesn't see the gals. For the boxin' round, you prance around like a show pony holdin' up a sign."

"There's no boxing, and I'm not prancing."

She laughed. "Yeah, I know. I suggested Feats of Strength, but nobody went for it. Still a good idea. I said it to make ya smile, Mel."

I smiled.

"Geez, put some sparkle behind it. You're a model. *Fake it.*"

"Who's the Man Candy?"

"It was supposed to be Ichabod, but he got breaded, unfortunately. Everything got changed up: there's no First Wedge, nothin' like that. They swapped out a stud from a Big Outfit."

"Who is he?"

"Todd Morgan. A suit, corporate guy. Likes my tea and knows the English code word for cookies: biscuits. Nate Gould nominated him."

I hadn't heard Nate mention the man. I thought of Inga and the other women on the panel, bless them for participating because I could never. "What happened to Trudy? Why, exactly, can't she do this?"

Lou looked away.

I knew it.

"She's got hearin' aid problems. She, ah, can't."

"You didn't."

She stomped a foot. "You know Trudy! She's sooo competitive. She'd get on stage, and tonight would turn into Datin' Game meets a bar fight. I couldn't help it if her battery was on the counter in the kitchen, and it ended up in the disposal. It slipped."

Trudy did the same thing to Lou's favorite pair of cheater glasses once. Fair's fair.

"Who's the third contestant?" I asked.

"Some senior-age hottie from Illinois. Last-minute entry. The committee let her in. We're tryin' to be more inclusive to Flatlanders. Edith Mackie's her name."

"Edith Mackie?"

"You know her?"

I paused. "No."

"Crowd's pourin' in—don't be nervous." She studied my heels. "You're not worried you'll trip in those things? Flub a cue or tip over on stage?"

"Not until now."

"If ya do mess up, remember what rodeo clowns say, 'If ya fall, make it look smooth and classy—*like Rodeo Drive.*'" She stood on tiptoe to peck me on the cheek. "Ya look great, like Charlie Brown's mom. I gotta go wrangle the snack bar, and make sure Trudy doesn't sabotage my food."

Audiences took sides and added sound effects. Rotten fruit and tomatoes were never thrown, but cheater eyeglasses, stuffed animals, and pool floaties—for the shipwreck scene in *The Tempest*—had been tossed in the past.

The crowd cheered damsels and booed bad guys. It was like attending a UW-Badger football game in a smaller venue.

The crowd in the Whoopee Den for The Golden Cheesehead were the same energized folks. The Den was the Promenade's comedy club, and it was like being at a venue in a big city. The lights were dim but still caught the sparkly threads in the stage curtains. The audience sat at round tables with flickering candles, watching the show.

Hank stood in the middle of the set. The "contestants" sat in large, open-fronted pumpkins (think Hollywood Squares, but the boxes were orange and with prop "stems" at the top).

Stage left, the three women were in their gourds, unable to see one another. Todd Morgan, the last-minute addition, sat in his own pumpkin box, stage right.

Hank's host costume set a silly tone for the proceedings. He opened with a pun: "Welcome to The Golden Cheesehead, a senior dating competition where *demons* are a girl's best friend."

He laughed, and the audience did, too. They didn't need a warm-up to get into the act.

I stood in the wings, watching Inga and the other ladies, Sally Clam and Edith Mackie.

Hank continued, "I will ask questions of our lovely contestants. You, the audience, will vote on the best match. However, there's an added supernatural element to the matchmaking tonight. We won't just vote. There's more to this prospective relationship."

On cue, the audience responded, *"And what's that, Hank?"*

He grinned. "Our new couple must have matching horror-scopes."

To describe it, the show began as a *CAT*-astrophe but then soared upward like a raven taking flight.

Hank introduced the ladies. Then Todd Morgan, a dapper fellow in a double-breasted jacket and an orange cravat tied at his neck.

It reminded me of the garb Ichabod Hall always wore. Morgan's look may have been an homage to the fallen designer, and he pulled off the vibe admirably.

His bio claimed he was from Chicagoland, but he spoke with a British affectation.

He was a good sport and charmed the audience with his opening remarks: "Friends, Wisconsinites, Kettle Morainians, lend me your ears. I arrived yesterday from a land to the south. Mine is not to praise Illinois, but to—"

"We'll give ya a chance," a fellow in the audience interrupted.

Morgan smiled. "Thank you, sir. I shall endeavor to not disappoint." He raised the glass of bubbles he held. "Rather than bore you with a speech about me, I toast to the women of Cinnamon. Here's to finding love in the land of cheese, sunsets, and pine trees ... and of beautiful, golden ladies."

The audience cheered.

Hank gave the rules: For the first round, each contestant could ask three questions. The ladies had cards to hold up after hearing an answer. She could show a smiley pumpkin for something she liked or a ghoul for something she didn't.

"We'll begin with Sally," Hank said. "A vibrant gal who tonight wears cat ears, cat-eye glasses, and a dog-print cardigan."

The dog joke brought whistles from the audience. Sally, laughed, but then she showed her claws and nearly coughed up a hair ball at Hank's remark. Sally operated a local feline rescue. A potential fellow had to be a cat lover—*no* dogs allowed.

Into her microphone, Sally purred, "Are you the cat's meow, Mr. Morgan?"

"I would be, my dear, if my allergist allowed it. I'm terribly allergic. My eyes swell when I'm near a cat, and I can hardly breathe." Morgan dabbed his eyes and loosened his cravat as though recalling a recent attack.

The crowd groaned, "*Awwww.*"

"Even hairless cats?" Sally asked.

"A cat by any other name would be as deadly. If the question is to cat or not to cat, it is *not.*"

Sally flashed the ghoul card.

A woman in the audience offered encouragement: "It's okay. I have an uncle who loves cats and has several rescues."

She grinned but folded. Her chair was on rollers, and she rumbled over into Edith Mackie's pumpkin. Edith wore a black dress and pearls, a lovely outfit. She had short gray hair and wore tinted glasses that shielded her eyes.

She was hesitant, soft-spoken, and looked intimidated—who could blame her in this environment?

The arrival of Sally encouraged Edith. Brought her out of her pumpkin, so to speak. Sally whispered in her new friend's ear, and Edith asked questions.

Todd Morgan answered all three inquiries satisfactorily: what were his favorite supper club, cheese, and Northwoods lake? He received all smiles in response. The two women chatted first, then held up the sign together.

The team effort was admirable but ultimately didn't matter.

Inga stole the show like an enchantress with special powers.

And when I said *stole*, I meant it.

13
THE WHOOPEE DEN, LATER

Hank explained that the second round was the cheesiest pick-up line. "Let's face it, folks, by the time we've reached our age, we've heard *all* of them."

"Yeah, especially from attorneys," a man shouted from the audience. "Why'd the lawyer—"

"Overruled!" Hank interrupted, squinting in the stage lights. "This is for contestants only. I sentence thee to an evening of hard labor in the kitchen, assisting with clean up after coffee and dessert."

Haw, haw. Har, har.

A crew member brought me a stool, and I perched on it while watching the silliness from the wings. The banter between Inga and Todd was worth the price of admission.

Even Sally and Edith Mackie quit after a few minutes, laughing and declining to participate.

Inga spoke into her mic, her voice low, the purple dress enhancing her skin tone. There was something magical about the color, truly. She looked grand, like witch royalty.

"I looked into my crystal ball, and it showed us having a wonderful future together," she said.

"My goodness, dear woman, you're casting a spell on me," Todd replied.

A few ladies fanned themselves. The lines kept coming, with Inga setting the pace of the repartee. Todd had to keep up with her. He either was a great actor or impressed by her wit and energy.

"Would you like to meet for *I-scream* later?" she asked.

"I certainly would, m'lady," he replied. "In the back of the room, they are setting out the after-show repast. I am partial to turtle sundaes."

"Why did the senior chick cross the road?" Inga inquired.

"I have no idea."

"To enjoy the early bird special."

He smiled. "A bird? No, my dear. Surely you are a swan."

I would not have imagined the night working so well for Inga, Hank, and the crowd.

Given what had happened to Ichabod in the ballroom, it was the best outcome for everyone involved—except for Ichabod, of course.

"Todd, I've taken up photography," Inga said. "I can *picture* us together."

"Dear lady, you're sending my blood pressure up!"

"Would you like to see what's in my medicine cabinet?"

He gasped. "Do you have allergy prescriptions, as well?"

"When annual enrollment time comes around, let's apply together for Medicare Part *I* and *T*," Inga teased.

Hank stepped in before things became too risqué, like before they began sharing vision and dental coverage. "Ladies and gentlemen, this has been a delightful evening for the Golden Cheesehead Dating Game. Our winners are obvious. Without further ado, I sentence Inga Honeythorne and Todd Morgan to a week of fun on the town in Cinnamon."

"You two are Cinn-sational!" a woman said. She sounded like Cozette Gallagher.

Inga and Todd emerged from their pumpkins, finally seeing one another. He appeared shocked, placing a hand on his heart.

He stepped back and gave Inga center stage, encouraging her to twirl to show off her glorious dress.

After rounds of applause, Cousin Lou emerged from the back. "Food's on! Take your bows, and c'mon back, Inga and Todd. You guys and the crew get first bites of mini eclairs and cream puffs."

All eyes were upon the happy couple.

Except for mine.

I observed "Edith Mackie." While the curtain call was organized, as cast and crew assembled to take bows, she maneuvered her way to the end of the line of people.

Like a black cat moving on silent paws, she tip-toed past Hank, the happy couple, and Sally Clam. She snuck past the crew to stand opposite of where I was, the wing on the other side of the stage.

She could hardly be seen.

After bows and applause, rather than follow everybody into the audience toward the refreshments, she about-faced in her expensive shoes.

She wore stunning Christian Dior kitten heels.

I'd noticed them when she settled into her pumpkin to begin the show—*click, click, click.* They'd made such a delicate, light sound.

Then, "Edith Mackie" disappeared from the stage into the wings —*POOF.*

It was like watching Samantha from the TV show *Bewitched.* She seemed to wiggle her nose and vanish.

The food smelled delicious. Aromas of coffee and chocolate lured me toward the tables laden with Halloween-themed goodies.

I ignored the temptation, difficult as it was, and followed the well-dressed mystery woman into the darkness behind the stage.

"EDITH" TRAVELED THE BACK PASSAGES OF THE PROMENADE LIKE A stowaway familiar with navigating a maze. Her kitten heels may as well have been tennis shoes. She sprinted like a fox, cornered like a rabbit.

She'd slipped out a door on the opposite side of the stage. I followed, but she had a head start.

I saw a form in front of me but couldn't shorten the distance.

The Promenade had a network of hallways, stairways, and freight elevators. That way, staff could move fast and transport linens, foodstuffs, and paper products without bothering residents. I noticed the stairs could be accessed via unlocked doors, but elevators needed a key.

Had Ichabod's killer used the network of hallways?

Thinking of the designer made me determined to discover the identity of "Edith." She was traveling up to higher floors. I heard a door creak open and then footfalls rattling on metal stairs.

The Whoopee Den was on the Lido Deck. The guest suites, meeting rooms, and Moon Cafe were on the upper floors.

My phone buzzed with a text. Surprising, given that I was in a tough spot to receive a signal. I looked at the message while quick-stepping toward a door. *Cousin Lou.*

She wrote:

> Where r u? Trudy's gonna spike my punch.
> Need you to keep eye on her!

I tapped back:

> Be there soon.

> Wehn?

> ASAP

> Cool looking 4 U

I wasn't wearing my readers. Neither was Lou, given her misspellings. I said:

Back soon as poss.

I climbed higher, figuring I was near the Moon Cafe. I couldn't hear footsteps any longer. I pushed out an exit, expecting to step into the hallway outside the cafe.

Nope!

Icy air blasted my cheeks.

I'd exited to an outdoor deck high in the air—*wow, it was cold!*

I stepped to the edge railing.

Below me, orange lanterns hung from trees, blowing to and fro. They were the pumpkin decorations around the grounds of the Promenade. They swayed, the movement making it seem like I *was* on a ship, floating along in a dark ocean.

I was on the observation deck!

On my right was a long glass wall with two slider doors into the Moon Cafe, which was dark except for its glowing exit sign—*had Cozette Gallagher closed early because of the festivities in the Den?*

I moved back to the door I'd come out of, following the glass with my hands to cold white brick—*did the exit lock behind me? Could I get back to the stairs?*

Temps were in the forties—*but that wind! Brrr!*

I tested the door.

Locked, darn it!

I checked my phone. The WiFi indication was an exclamation point. No signal. My teeth chattered.

Now what?

I *HOPPED* AROUND DOING JUMPING JACKS TO WARM MY TOES. THE DECK surface was hard tile, and I wore heels. Ouch.

I took a *leap* of faith and yelled, "Woman overboard—help!"

My cries were swallowed by wind clipping at about fourteen

knots by my measurement of swaying tree branches and pumpkin lanterns.

The Moon Cafe was on the unpopulated side of the "ship," and it faced stars, the nature path, and the meadow. There wasn't a soul around on this cold night.

DHOOT! DHOOT!

An owl's call pierced the darkness, and I felt weird, like fingers danced up my spine and over my skin.

My body was telling me something. It was like being back in New York City working as a mannequin—*my body always warned me when things were off.*

Times were different then. It was before cell phones and social media, before discrepancies or illegal behaviors could be recorded and used as defense. Or evidence, even.

When I sensed danger, or a person who behaved more like a predator than a designer, photographer, or stylist, I'd sense the same odd energy and the skin on my neck would tingle.

I stepped to the glass slider doors and yanked—*locked.* The latch rattled, though. It was flimsy. By pulling back and forth, I could crack open the doors. I looked down. No dowel in the track to stop me, either.

The handles felt like ice in my hands. *Brrr. C-cold.*

The wind swirled in the cave-like deck, chilling my bare legs. The borrowed dress I wore only came to my knees. I leaned over the door handle. If I could pull hard enough ... back and forth ... I could ... break the lock.

I gritted my teeth. If I pulled hard ... the lock would ... come loose.

It snapped—*CRACK!*

The door popped open!

"Whoa!" I teetered, gripping the handle, struggling to not fall.

Another *CRACK!* My heel broke!

I tipped backward. *I did not want to fall on the tile!* I grabbed the edge of the glass door, barely keeping myself afloat.

The cafe's lights flickered on—so bright they were blinding. I put an arm up to block the glare. I blinked at the contrast from dark night to bright cafe.

Who just walked into the place?

"It's like I was shipwrecked and rescued by a k-kindly w-witch," I said, shivering at a cafe table, gripping a mug of tea.

Cozette Gallagher removed the witch's hat she wore and set it on the checkout counter. "Like the Island of Caliban from *The Tempest*?"

She said it, not me.

Heavens to *Hamlet*, Boo Bash was turning into a nightmare.

Cozette had jumped to action upon finding me. She'd hauled my carcass inside, wrapped me in a blanket, and brewed tea.

I offered to pay for the broken doors. She refused, saying they'd been damaged before my visit and a work order for repair had already been turned in.

Besides the witch's hat, she wore an apron saying, "Be Nice, or I'll Spice Your Food."

She'd been assisting at the refreshment tables in the Whoopee Den, but zipped upstairs because she needed an ingredient. A spice, a sweet. A foodstuff of some kind. Essence of Beer Batter Wort. Elixir of Turtle Sundae.

I couldn't remember.

My head ached from the falling book at Fern Bubble's place. Now, my toes were frozen.

I'd chased a woman through passages, gotten stuck on an observation deck—a*nd a designer was dead!*

Even before finding Ichabod thirty-six hours ago, I'd felt confused. While working in fashion again, I traveled a twisty path in my mind, a runway of horrors.

Memories of angry people and conflicts made concentration

difficult. Like a long, glamorous, *haute couture* veil clouded my thoughts.

I searched for answers—*but what questions did I have?*

What did Ichabod Hall and the fashion biz trigger in my memory bank?

It reminded me of how hard I'd worked, speaking of banks. How I'd scrimped to survive in an expensive city and a subjective, image-obsessed industry. Then, add Eden Hoff to the mix. That was like draping spider webs over the veil!

I was "too commercial," she'd said. Too curvy. Too *catalog*.

Catalog was a fashion code for common. Not elite or exotic.

At first, I attended every casting available and booked shows and editorial shoots. As I aged, rejections mounted like sky-high heels, so I stopped. I told my agent to send me for catalogs, fit modeling, and body parts.

I'd made peace with my career, I thought.

Sure, I quashed feelings during my time as a mannequin. I had to because rejection and isolation were unpleasant parts of a "glamorous" job.

The irony never escaped me while working in the industry. Oscar Wilde said it best: "No object is so beautiful that, under certain conditions, it will not look ugly."

Ironic that an industry built on beauty and style was *not* in many ways.

My cell phone rested on the table. It was operating again, magically, and showed five bars. "You have powers that make phones work, Cozette," I said.

"It's not me. It's the WiFi booster. When I flip on the lights, it goes on to boost the signal. Cell service is always sketchy in this place." She winked. "I think the residents like it that way. Reminds them of the old days before technology."

"Or that they really are at sea, alone and lost in an ocean. Floundering and overwhelmed by the scope of their lives and mistakes they've made." I looked out the glass windows at the darkness.

"What's wrong, Mel?"

"Nothing that a silver crucifix and head of garlic won't fix."

My phone buzzed. I looked at it. *Cole Lawrence.*

Cozette patted my hand. "Answer it, dear. I have to pop into the kitchen for a minute. I'll give you some privacy."

On the fourth ring, I picked up. "Hello?"

"Mel, it's me."

"Hi."

"Did you get my message? I told Lou I was looking for you."

I recalled her text with the misspellings, "Cool looking 4 U." *She'd meant Cole.* "Yes, I did. Sorry, I was busy."

"Not getting into trouble, I hope."

I looked at the broken slider door. "Not much."

"I wanted to say I'm sorry."

"For what?"

He paused. I heard chatter in the background. Others were talking, and their voices echoed.

I envisioned an exhibit space with hard floors and concrete-block walls, a conference hall-turned-cop-camp with a safe house with trap doors, a manmade lagoon where they practiced rescues, and mannequins on tables to teach lifesaving measures.

"For not getting back to you right away," he said.

"It's fine."

"No, it isn't. I miss you."

"Something's happened," I said.

"I know. Lou filled me in. She wants me too—"

"Do *not* do anything affecting your job."

"Let Bruce DuWayne handle it. He's a good detective. Just stay safe."

"But—"

"As soon as this conference is finished, I'll drive down."

"No, you have a county to run up north. It's hunting season. There are licenses to issue. Trophy bucks to harvest."

"Mel, I'm coming to see you."

"But the loony tourists—you need to help them pack and fly south for the winter."

"The loony tourists?"

"Loons, I mean. The birds."

"My deputies can handle things. We need to see each other, Mel."

Cole hung up before I could deter him.

He was *not* great with goodbyes.

Sadly, I wasn't either.

14

THE MOON CAFE, LATER

Before Cozette returned from the kitchen, I studied the sliding doors that opened to the deck.

If I could wander hidden service hallways and break into a room, so could Ichabod Hall's killer. If I were a certain nurse-pickleball player, I wouldn't need to break in. I'd have keys or entry codes to everything on the "ship."

After several minutes, Cozette re-entered the cafe carrying a specimen jar of bloody eyeballs and a velvet pouch of magic fairy dust. She wanted to recite a spell of protection for the danger that haunted my future.

Kidding.

She came toward me carrying cherries and edible glitter for the dessert condiment bar. I realized I hadn't eaten, and a turtle sundae with bourbon cherries and gold sprinkles sounded exactly like what a Wisconsinite would prescribe.

She set the food on the table, then pressed her cheek against my forehead. "You're warmer. That's good."

"It was the tea." I tapped my head. "My mom used to check my temp that way."

"I know. I loved your mom."

Cozette and Wooly Gallagher knew my parents. They'd all grown up together in Cinnamon.

"Do you think she'd be ... proud of me?" I asked.

She smiled. "Your mom was a tough *kringla*, her favorite Swedish cookie. That's where you got it, Mel."

Kringla were excellent but formed into twist shapes. "Yeah, I'm knotted up right now."

She smiled. "I meant toughness, Mel."

"That, too. Since moving home and starting the craft mall, I've felt like the famous statue in Copenhagen. The Little Mermaid rock that's slowly transforming into a human."

"She's a fish gaining a human soul, dear."

I paused. "You get my point, though, right?"

"Yes, your mother would be proud of you." She pointed upward. "I inform her about your success. From the day you left for New York City twenty-eight years ago, I've kept her updated."

I looked around the cafe. "It's the WiFi booster, right? It links up to heaven?"

She laughed. "My prayer line doesn't need a booster. It's always open. And *The Cinnamon Roll* gets delivered up there, too, so your mom and dad saw your photos."

Wooly Gallagher kept an archive of images from my modeling days at the paper. My big hair, shoulder pads, and plaid skirts were recorded for posterity.

Heaven, too, apparently.

I drained my mug, then asked, "What do you know about Doc Graves and Pauline?"

"We must have ESP. I need to show you something," Cozette replied.

Cozette's dark eyes shined. "I just love mysteries. Death notwithstanding, of course. Poor Ichabod." She pulled her cell phone from a pocket in the apron. "I have pictures for you."

She swiped open her phone and showed a few. I saw a fashion portfolio and pictures of a collection of "flat lays," clothes laid flat and then photographed. The collection was athletic wear. Tops, skirts, and slacks. Most garments were black, with a few orange pieces added, a knit top, a scarf.

In addition to clothes, the collection included accessories like tennis shoes, pickleball paddles, and pearls. Lots of pearls. There were necklaces, bracelets, and earrings. And pearl trim on shoelaces, tassels, and sleeve edges.

The images were blurry. Like they'd been snapped surreptitiously over someone's shoulder. The background looked like the cafe.

One of the pictures showed the brand name. Two capital letters, black interlocking *B*s. I'd never heard of the company. "Ball Bash?" I asked.

Cozette nodded. "It's Pauline's fashion line. The first day Ichabod was in here, she showed up with a portfolio of pictures. He'd ordered a Wiscocoa, and I was about to serve it. Pauline grabbed the tray, marched over, and demanded he look at her designs."

The collection wasn't bad. Pretty great, in fact. American pickleball meets European chic.

Fashion brands were built by the bold.

I recalled the story about Michael Kors, who designed outfits as a teen and was discovered dressing a store window with his designs. The next thing he knew, he was delivering his first collection to Bergdorf Goodman in the trunk of his car.

I looked at the images again. "These could sell. The target market is buyers who want to elevate their game—"

"And sweat like wrestlers trying to make weight," Cozette finished. "Who wants to wear black knit in the sun on a blazing hot outdoor court?"

I saw her point. "It's a pickle, but fashion isn't practical sometimes."

"She put Ichabod in a pickle. He declined, and she got angry. Told him about her perfume and tried to sell him on that." Cozette crossed her arms. "That's where the money is in fashion. Perfume and accessories."

"How do you know that?" I asked.

"The newspaper office subscribes to every news reporting organization known to humankind, even the fashion biz. It's an excellent education."

I glanced at the phone. "Ichabod never mentioned this to me. It would have been too late to add other garments, and it would distract from the relaunch his brand."

"He made it clear he wouldn't share the spotlight." She lowered her voice even though we were alone. "The problem was Pauline was so pushy. Ichabod was having none of it. They had *words*."

Cozette described the argument between Pauline and Ichabod Hall. "It was short. He told her no. She said she'd speak with Nathan Gould and Alicia Cliff, the *real* people in charge. She packed up and stormed out."

Lightning flashed, and then thunder rattled the salt and pepper shakers on our table.

"Was anyone else here to witness the argument?" I asked.

"No, it was afternoon. I hadn't officially opened. At that time, residents go on a shore excursion to shop or volunteer somewhere in town. Or they nap. The Moon Cafe is for the night owls. Except for Pauline. She's not an owl, she's a night*hawk*."

"What's she like?"

"I adore working here, but no place is perfect. There are ... different social groups."

"Cliques, you mean?"

"Yes, but it's been worse since Pauline arrived. She's pushes her supplements—and she's *sooo* competitive in pickleball." She waved a hand toward the meadow outside, the walking trails viewed from the deck. "She wants to build a massive indoor court in the green space!"

"*No way.*"

"She's even persuaded them to test for a septic system. Can you believe they'd dig up that meadow?" Cozette's face hardened. "Not on my watch, Mel. They'll take away that beautiful view and lovely space for the animals and birds over my dead body!"

WE SPLIT UP. COZETTE DONNED CLIMBER GEAR AND RAPPELLED DOWN THE side of the building. I took the elevator.

JK.

We both took the sensible route, the elevator.

However, Cozette was so fired up after our conversation that she could have roped down.

She toted the goodies for the dessert table for the Golden Cheesehead, and she loaded my arms with books for the Little Free Library in the Promenade's atrium entrance.

"On your way out, tuck the books on a shelf," she said. "Residents love sharing things to read."

Before accepting the volumes, I scanned for a certain work by Shakespeare that was haunting my life. If *The Tempest* was among the books, *I'd* rappel down and flee to Cinnamon, never to set foot in the Promenade again.

I was safe. The books were delightful horse stories written by C.W. Anderson and murder mysteries written by local authors.

I dropped her off at the Whoopee Den, stole into the backstage area to grab my bag, and then rode down to the atrium. The car stopped once, and several giggly residents stepped on.

They'd been at a costume party.

One couple was Mr. and Mrs. Incredible. Their companions were Charlie Brown and Snoopy. Snoopy studied my dress and then spoke to his companion. "Charlie, we finally found your mom. She's carryin' books. It looks like she's a librarian!"

Hee, haw. Har, har.

Charlie and I stood next to one another for pictures. "No one is gonna believe this!" he said.

Snoopy invited me to the after-party in the Dockside lounge, a watering hole off the atrium. "Sarsaparilla's on tap," he said. "Great mocktails, too. As Top Dog, I'm buyin'."

I thanked him but declined.

I'd had enough fun for one day. But I recalled the other people I'd seen in costume—or disguise—since Ichabod died, and it gave me an idea.

15

THE ATRIUM

I placed the books into the little library and walked toward the front entrance, my shoes tapping the tile floor of the atrium—*clack, slap, clack, slap*.

The broken heel affected my catwalk.

Laughter floated out from the Dockside lounge just off the elevators.

I stopped to scan the atrium, taking in its height, glass ceiling, and potted plants. During the day, the space welcomed visitors and residents with sunlight, greenery, and live music.

There was a grand piano in a corner where members of the music club, the Yamahahas, practiced songs and entertained residents.

For Boo Bash, the decorating committee went seriously macabre. They'd downshifted from a bon voyage vibe to a ghost ship.

The dragon trees and snake plants were decorated accordingly. Ghosts of all sizes hung from wires, their white gowns fluttering.

Lightning flashed in the skylights, and rain tapped the glass.

It felt like I was underwater. The curved glass distorted the sky, and it was like watching a storm from the underside of a wave.

There was a guard's office at the front entrance. I had to speak with Tony—I heard a woman's voice behind me:

"Melanie? Is that you?"

I whirled to see a ghost—but not just any ghost. This spirit wore a gown from Ichabod Hall's collection!

I'd recognize the dress anywhere: Velvet, with a heavy sash that conflicted with Hall's casual aesthetic. Instead of showing how easy and elegant his pieces were, the dress looked like a white armor.

It was an editorial dress, one meant for publicity—*who wore it?*

The ghost wore a mask. One of those plastic things. Not hard to find because they were everywhere on cafe tables and the marble concierge desk. The selfie photo op at the entrance, too—as I mentioned, the decorating committee went all out.

"Who are you?" I asked.

She nodded toward the elevators. "I'm attending the costume party in the lounge."

Her voice was distinctive. The "ghost" possessed a measured elocution.

"Not what I asked," I said. "*Who are you?*"

She removed the mask.

Before me was a spirit from my past—and she wore a garment representing heaviness and bad juju. It was like seeing a nightmare come to life.

Standing in front of me was none other than Eden Hoff.

"WHAT DO YOU WANT?" I ASKED.

"I need your assistance, Melanie. It will benefit both of us."

She tapped the gown's bodice as though reminding herself to breathe. Her nails were manicured to sharp points, and their blood-red color matched her lips. Her eyes were dark, almost black, and reminded me of the inside of a coffin.

"Ichabod is gone—and you are a suspect," I said.

"You discovered him, Melanie. That means *you* also are under suspicion."

She smoothed her hair, a razor-edged bob.

I marveled that Eden Hoff could leave New York City, but the city would never leave her. Even under duress, while hiding in a senior community in the middle of nowhere, she was still a diva.

I rebuffed her attempt at guilt. "You're the one wearing a disguise. What do you have to hide?"

"*Nothing.*"

"Okay. Well, nice seeing you—"

"Wait, Melanie. I have information for you."

"No, you need help, you said."

"I, er, *we* need assistance. I have information that will assist *us.*"

"Have you spoken with the authorities?"

"The new owners of the House of Hall, you mean? They instigated this terrible circumstance and perpetrated danger on *us!*"

"The police, Eden. *Law enforcement.*"

"On, those people. I have not."

I pulled out my cell phone. "I will give you Detective Bruce DuWayne's phone number—"

"Is he the older gentleman? The fellow wearing business casual meets grandpa chic?"

"You need to speak with him—"

"We have not been formally introduced. Perhaps you will speak to him on my behalf."

A request to have an underling complete a task was typical for someone with Eden Hoff's career background. One may wonder why she approached me instead of hiring an attorney at this difficult time.

Because lawyers were expensive, and she already had piles of legal bills. When Eden lost her job at the magazine, she'd fought the firing, lost, and been ordered to pay her attorney fees and the magazine's.

There'd been rumors she sold clothing and jewelry to stay afloat.

I'd never wish that on anyone, even Eden Hoff.

"I'll give you the detective's phone number," I said. "We have attorneys in town, if you need one. Reasonably priced, and they don't charge for the first hour."

That was a fib.

The attorneys I knew would charge her double because they'd sense disaster when she walked in, especially if she wore that outfit.

I'd put in a good word.

"Melanie, you're an amateur sleuth of sorts." She smiled, and it looked painful. Like she'd stepped on a nail. "We should work together. It would be satisfying to solve this case. Like old times."

"We aren't allowed to be *old* in the modeling business."

No, no, no, I did *not* say that—*I wanted to, though.*

"I'm being set up for the murder of Ichabod Hall," she said. "I didn't do it. I-I promise."

"Do you have an alibi?"

"I wasn't anywhere near the ballroom, if that's what you're asking."

It wasn't. It was a half answer that would prick the ears of a detective like a seamstress stabbing her thumb with a needle.

I studied Eden's face. In her coffin-like eyes, I saw fear. There was even a furrow of worry between her frozen eyebrows.

Eden Hoff killed a lot of careers. She tried to kill mine because I didn't fit her ideal of a model. Did she kill Ichabod?

I had my doubts.

Eden told me she'd lurked about the Promenade, wearing whatever costume she could cobble together while listening in on conversations.

Also, she'd been "Edith Mackie," the mystery contestant on the Golden Cheesehead.

I held up a palm to stop her from speaking. "I won't be an accessory or charged with obstruction."

"But you did a photoshoot in handcuffs once—"

"*No*, Eden."

"I didn't do it, Melanie. Nathan Gould is setting me up to take the fall!"

"Why?"

"I-I don't know."

She began to weep. It seemed like I was in a graveyard watching a statue cry. Tears dripped onto the dress. The scene reminded me of *Midsummer Night's Dream* and Puck with the magic potion he poured into unsuspecting characters' eyes.

Was I being cast under her spell?

"You'll help me ... please?" she asked.

"I can't promise anything except that I'll seek the truth."

Music drifted from the Dockside lounge. It was karaoke night, and they'd begun singing *Ghostbusters*.

"If I need to reach you, where will you be for the next few days?" I asked.

She clenched her teeth. "I cannot say."

"Your choice. Contact the detective."

"If I need the detective, I shall find him."

She replaced the mask and marched toward the lounge.

I made for the exit.

Eden would be fine with disguises and sneaky behavior. During her career as an editor in New York City, she was used to it.

I stopped by the guard's office. Tony Giugliano, the Promenade security fellow, had left for the evening, but an older gentleman watched the camera monitors.

He was dressed in a flannel shirt and slacks. A volunteer, most likely.

There weren't many monitors. They were black and white, small. Made sense. From what I recalled, the residents wanted privacy, and disliked their intrusion.

"Hello, sir," I said. "What's the score? Big game this evening?"

I kept it light. Tried to not be obvious about snooping.

The man stared over his half-glasses. "You're the umpteenth person to ask—I can't say what we have, or what's been given to the detective."

Fair enough.

"Good night, sir," I said.

My evening wouldn't be complete without a scare in the parking lot.

I almost had a heart attack. If I were to have one, though, the Promenade was the best place to do it. Defibrillators everywhere, a doctor on sight, and residents trained in CPR.

I walked to my Saab, one of the few cars in the outside lot. There was a fellow escorting visitors to their vehicles in a golf cart, the "Golden Dinghy," but he assisted the smart people who'd parked underground.

Those without a death wish, in other words.

It was after ten, and the air felt blustery.

I unlocked my car's hatchback to grab a jacket. The wind whipped, and I had to push hard on the hatch to close it.

"Mel!"

"Wha—?"

"Melanie!"

Good Lord. Someone in a dark cloak and scarf over her face called my name!

"Who are you?" I shouted. "Stop right there!"

My hands were full with the coat and keys. I had no weapons. Safety was a sprint away to the portico—*and a killer still lurked at the Promenade!*

"Stop!" I repeated.

"Melanie, it's me."

"*Who's me?*"

"Inga!"

Was she crazy? She was supposed to be in the Whoopee Den. Why was Inga Honeythorne haunting the parking lot of the Promenade?

I stuffed Inga in the Saab, then drove us under the lighted portico. The car warmed up while we talked.

The convo was short. She'd been so thrilled at meeting Todd Morgan that she needed fresh air to clear her mind.

She'd bundled up for a stroll, or *friluftsliv*, the Swedish concept of walking in nature to appreciate the moment.

She wanted me to accompany her.

"No, and do not walk in the meadow," I said. "Go back inside."

Scandinavians are built different, even septuagenarian ones. They're unaffected by frostbite, wind, and circumstances that would make other people hunker by a fireplace.

"Just a quick walk, Mel, to clear my head," she asked.

"No wandering in the dark. There's still a killer on the loose. *Be safe*, Inga."

"I'm just so excited," she said. "Todd is a perfect gentleman. Tomorrow, we're going on the haunted hike in the meadow. I can't wait to spend time with him."

16
THURSDAY MORNING

Dawn broke not with rosy fingers but with orange ones that stretched across the horizon like rusty ropes. Dark clouds lingered, too.

If a sunrise gave off a Halloween vibe, this one was it.

I stood by the patio doors of my living room. Max was still at Fern's. I planned to walk to the office early to catch up on paperwork, and I wanted to monitor the apartment above the bookshop.

My cell phone rang. I looked and saw a pair of spurs.

Cousin Lou.

I picked up. "Hello—"

"Mel, they got another body out at the Promenade," she said. "I'm comin' to get ya. We're goin' to Fern's ranch to strategize. I got coffee and breakfast packed up."

My throat clenched as though strangled by an invisible hand. "W-who was it?"

"Dunno. Someone poor soul wearin' a black coat."

I thought of Inga. She'd been wearing a dark jacket.

Please, no!

"Get here as fast as you can," I said.

At Fern's, Lou laid out a breakfast of egg sandwiches, fruit, and coffee before Fern got off the phone.

Fern stood by the sink, speaking with Bruce DuWayne. It was after eight, and sunlight streamed in. The dark clouds had drifted off.

Outside, horses in a paddock munched hay.

The sight of them made me less anxious.

Fern frowned, eyes downcast. "Thanks, Bruce. I'll let them know."

Let us know what?

Lou shoved a cup of coffee into her hand. "Wait before ya say anything," she ordered. "Have a sip of Cinnamon Punch, my special brew. The cinnamon grabs ya, then the caffeine punches right in the vein. Helps a cowgirl think clear when she needs to."

Lou turned to me and filled my mug. "Drink up, Mel. You gotta be the smartest of all of us. You got *two* murders to solve now."

Macabre as it sounds, Bruce texted a picture of the corpse.

Lou went ballistic. "I shoulda known! Trudy and the Spices are gettin' revenge. They read too many crime novels. Trudy and her Werewolves is more like it."

The "body" was an old scarecrow someone found in a barn. It had been dumped on a trail in the Promenade's meadow as decor for the haunted hike.

It was dressed as Louella Jingle, unfortunately. Spiky straw hair, cowboy hat, boots, plaid shirt, and long duster jacket.

Lou pounded a fist on the butcher block table. "I donated those clothes to the church rummage. Trudy snatched 'em and dressed that gal just like me on purpose." She looked between us. "Who put her and her hyenas in charge of decoratin' the meadow?"

Lou, probably.

A month before Boo Bash week commenced, the committee met at the Tool & Rye to assign tasks to the volunteers. My guess was Lou suggested the coldest job—decorating a meadow out in the elements—go to Trudy, et al.

I wasn't going to remind my cousin. And Fern wasn't talking. She still had worry line across her brow.

"Is everything okay?" I asked.

Fern stared out the window, her eyes puffy. "That was quite a fright. I have PR work to catch up on and still need to muck stalls."

Lou continued her rant. "I'm mad as a tiger with a toothache. I'm gonna scrub down this kitchen—heck, I'll scrub the whole house. You gals go tend the horses."

We skedaddled to the barn. Max came with us. He knew to scram when Aunt Lou had her hackles up.

Fern handed me a pitchfork, but I hesitated. "What's wrong?" I asked.

"It's Bruce." She sighed. "I feel guilty about talking to him. It seems selfish to be thinking about *me*."

"What is it?"

A horse nudged me in the shoulder. We stood in the middle of the barn, and the animals hung their heads over the stall doors, watching us.

Fern patted a soft muzzle. "Bruce and I were seeing each other *a little*. It's not ... good. I'm too old to date."

"Not true."

She looked around. "I have my horses and my business. That's enough. I'll stay happily single."

"You can tell him. It's okay, Fern."

"It's an awkward time ... I don't want to lead him on."

A horse snorted, sounding like the blast of a ship's horn. Tulip, the giant mare I sponsor, was summoning her maid—*me*—to tend to housekeeping.

Before entering her stall, I said, "Fern, be honest with him. You'll be relieved, and he can focus on the investigation."

"I hope you're right. I don't want him to resign from the case. I feel so guilty."

I tossed a pitchfork of manure into a wheelbarrow, thinking about Eden Hoff.

Yes, a joke. True, also.

When one worked as a mannequin, a human island, one perfected the skills of observation, silent humor, and irony. Since escaping people like Hoff and moving home to Cinnamon, I was *not* an island, I'd discovered.

I had a family. Max, Cousin Lou and her husband Jason, and their rescue animals. I had friends. Two businesses, also. The mall and the bookstore.

While living in New York City, I'd been a castaway. I'd worked hard. Squirreled away my pennies because living there was dangerous and expensive.

I'd lived in the same cheap apartment for years because my job and income were perilous. In fashion, one day you were in; the next you were selling designer clothes "paid" to you as compensation.

Working in fashion again had caused my sour mood and reinforced that I did not *wish to be an island.*

Seeing racks of clothes, softbox studio lights, and a snake-like runway had given me flashbacks. Haunting memories of losing my parents and struggling in a volatile industry. The trauma had caused me to pull back from commitment and relationships.

It had taken me a few years, but now I sought family and genuine friendships. Romance, too. A relationship with a man who didn't fly away for a living or use his job as an excuse.

I shuddered, tipping soiled straw from the pitchfork to the stall floor. Perhaps that was why *The Tempest* haunted me? Prospero had been banished to an island and—

"Mel, watch out!"

Fern rolled a cart of straw bales—they began to tip!

I was blocked in—Max was nearby!

"They're falling! I can't stop them!" Fern yelled.

I dropped the fork, then grabbed the metal bars of the stall front, stretching my body away from danger. "Run, Max!" I screamed.

The dog scrambled down the aisle, his nails scratching concrete —*scrape, scrape, scrape!*

Bales crashed, tipping the wheelbarrow, barely missing my legs.

Tulip spooked and jumped to the back of her stall—straw and manure flew everywhere!

"Mel, Max, Tulip—that was my fault," Fern cried. "I'm so sorry!"

She hustled to me, yanking bales. "I could have killed you!"

"I'm okay—it's okay," I said.

"No, it isn't. I feel t-terrible." She started crying.

"Breathe, Fern."

"But—"

"It's okay." I hugged her and tried to lighten the mood. "Dying on a concrete 'runway' in a barn wouldn't be the worst way to go. Better than a catwalk."

Fern winced. *Oops, to macabre.*

"Sorry, that was inappropriate," I said.

She pulled out a kerchief. It was orange and reminded me of the one Ichabod Hall always used. Or used to use.

She dabbed her eyes. "I'm so sorry—I'm not myself."

"You don't have to explain," I said. "Please take time for *you*. It's okay to step back."

"That's best ... I think."

Fern disappeared into the tack room while I swept the mess in the aisle, pondering what to do.

She was a trusted resource. She and Wooly Gallagher, editor of the newspaper, were the people I relied on for objective advice.

I had yet to tell Fern about Eden Hall's appearance in the Promenade's atrium, or Swan magically showing up to the bookshop apartment.

Fern was busy with her horse rescue, business, and podcast. Let's face it: the PR game was like doing social work for companies. And now she had relationship troubles.

It was not the time to burden her with amateur sleuthing—but if she distanced herself from Bruce DuWayne, my link to inside intel was broken.

I pushed the wheelbarrow to the big sliding door and yanked it open. The compost pile's rich scent hit my nose. I dumped the cart, wondering about who could assist me in the death investigation of Ichabod Hall.

I was on an island again. An amateur sleuth needed a sidekick.

I pushed the wheelbarrow back inside, then slid the door shut. The old dairy barn was warm and snug. Its alfalfa and leather aromas were an earthy perfume that felt comforting despite my frustration.

After the barn was shipshape, the stalled horses needed to be turned out to join their friends in the pasture.

I clipped a lead to Tulip's halter and walked her out, the wind swaying the trees. Tulip jogged sideways, her hooves crunching leaves, vibrating the ground with every footfall.

Tulip was *big*.

Holding the giant horse was like holding back an Airbus that wanted to throttle up.

"Easy, girl," I said. "Mind the toes."

I wore boots borrowed from Fern's tack room. Broken in, and the color of sun-soaked earth, a gorgeous golden leather patina. *Authentic.* If the boots were presented on a fashion show runway by a designer, they'd cost a fortune and someone would pay it.

They weren't much protection from an eighteen-hundred-pound horse that wanted to fly like Pegasus.

Fern opened the gate.

I led Tulip through, then turned her head toward me and relaxed my shoulders and slowed my breathing, a signal for her to stand quietly before I removed the halter.

I patted her. "Good girl."

She spun, then ran off like she'd been launched from an aircraft carrier.

Speaking of flying, when I returned to the house, events spun out of control like a turboprop without its propeller.

The farmhouse kitchen had been scrubbed to OR standards.

Lou even changed the light fixture's bulb to a brighter wattage. The room smelled like bleach. The gold fixtures at the sink shined as though polished for display in an emperor's tomb.

She handed me my phone. "Ya left it on the table, so I answered it."

"Oh—"

"You and Captain Rand are double-datin' with Inga and her new fella, the Golden cowpoke."

"No—"

She nodded. "Yeah, Inga wanted ya there, so she set it up. She called Rand in Minneapolis. Told him everything. He's on his way."

"He didn't have a trip?'

"Guess not. Said he'd help her out. You guys are gonna do the haunted hike, then have dinner. I confirmed for ya."

Maybe Rand was coming to see Pauline, too.

Not. My. Business.

"Cole's coming to town," I said.

I looked at Fern, hoping for backup. She ignored our conversation and flipped through a To-Do list on the counter.

Lou continued, "So what? The sheriff likes Rand. Everybody does. And you and Cole aren't hitched." She tapped a finger on her left hand. "'Bout as close to gettin' a ring as the Chicago Bears are to winnin' one." She shrugged. "It'll be fine. If the sheriff fusses, tell him you're helpin' Inga. Cowgals need each other."

17

THE HAUNTED MEADOW, LATER

My hour had almost come,
When to pickleball witches with spells and paddles,
I must surrender myself.

Not my quote. Shakespeare wrote it. I just paraphrased.

The four of us arrived for the haunted meadow tour at dusk. The paths of the acreage near the Promenade glowed with flickering lanterns. Plastic pumpkins dangling from tree branches. Ghouls lurked behind every rock.

Grandmas warned their grandkids about the danger ahead. The kids ignored them and jumped about, giddy with excitement.

The walkers—or were we victims?—dressed for the temps in flannel jackets, scarves, and hats.

It was a shotgun start.

Groups mingled at different takeoff points staffed by ghosts. I suspected the spry phantom under the shamrock-patterned sheet was Wooly Gallagher, but he stayed in character and wouldn't say *boo*.

At the recorded screech of a crow calling *CAW! CAW!* we were released.

Lanterns marked winding paths. Signs told us to avoid a spot of dirt mounds—a place where perc tests were being conducted for those awful indoor courts, apparently.

Inga, Rand, and new friend Todd appeared to be in great spirits, no pun intended. After about fifteen minutes of being spooked by skeletons hiding behind trees, pirates rattling sabers, and a hodag with an ear-shattering scream, a scarecrow caught my gaze.

I stopped to see if the mannequin wore cowgirl clothes similar to the one discovered earlier, the one I'd feared was Inga, but dressed like Lou.

Bad idea—I got lost!

I made a wrong turn at the intersection of Gloomthorn Crossing and Abandoned Ruins Boulevard.

The path would lead to civilization eventually, I figured, so kept walking.

The parking lot wasn't *that* far away.

I trudged toward voices but found myself on the far side of the meadow, the light and safety of the resort behind a hill.

I saw flames—a campfire—and stumbled out of the trees to see three women standing near burning logs. An iron cauldron hung over the fire. It bubbled with a liquid that spilled over the pot's edges and hissed.

Eye-of-newt soup, perhaps?

I waved. "Which way back to the popcorn and Wiscocoa—"

"What fresh hell arrives to our coven?" one woman shrieked. She threw her head back and cackled.

The voice sounded familiar. *Pauline Pickle*? She wore a raggedy black gown. They all did. They stood with intense expressions and braced shoulders, looking like warriors—*double, toil, and trouble, the trio took their cosplay seriously!*

With their poses and fierce faces, they could have been eighties-era runway models.

It seemed they'd stepped from the pages of a Shakespeare play, Macbeth. They were the story's three witches, but angrier.

They'd added a pickleball twist to their roles by accessorizing with orange visors and paddles. They began waving their racquets and chanting as though casting a spell.

"What evil yonder this way comes?" the Pauline Witch caterwauled.

"It's Mel Tower. I'm not evil. Just lost."

"What is the password?"

I paused. "Keep calm and pickleball on?"

"Argh, we shall curse on her!" a second witch screeched.

I noticed wiffle balls on the dirt by the fire—had they been burning them?

I scratched my temple. "Could you curse me with something helpful? A map? I'd like to get back to my group."

"Let's get her!" The first witch screamed.

I turned and sprinted—they gave up the chase quickly. Their dresses slowed them down, and the uneven path of the meadow wasn't like a smooth pickleball court.

After a minute, I found a group of giggly septuagenarians and warned them about the coven. They asked how to find them.

I did not have getting hunted by witches on my evening's bingo card, but life was strange. After a career in fashion, one of the goofiest professions on the planet, one realizes anything is possible.

What's fair is foul, what's foul is fair, after all.

In the kitchen of the Moon Cafe, Lou pulled a scorecard from her pocket.

"I did not have you gettin' chased by witches on my bingo card." She marked a square on the card with a pen. She wore jeans, an orange T-shirt, and an apron, a black one patterned with images of different cheeses. The text on the apron said, "Pick Your Poison."

I looked down at my shoes, Bally pumps I'd had for years. After the hike, I'd changed into a dress and heels. Black, of course, like my mood. "There's a bingo element to Boo Bash?"

"Nothin' official. It's a competition between anonymous cowgals. Need-to-know basis only."

"What's the over-under on who bingo-ed Ichabod Hall?"

She ignored my question. "How's it goin' with Rand?"

I looked at the door. "How are things between Inga and Todd, you mean? He's charming. Inga is smitten. They're already talking about their next date."

She frowned. "I mean you and Rand-O."

"Fine. Why?"

"Did he … ask anything? Hand over a velvet box with somethin' sparkly in it?"

"*Absolutely not—*"

"I'm kiddin'. Don't get a burr in your bustle." She stared at me over her cheater glasses, sassy orange ones outlined with rhinestones. Betsey Johnson meets Halloween. "You're so testy lately. I'm the one under suspicion. *I'm* the one that should be actin' like a hunk of cod 'bout to get beer-battered."

"Why did you ask about Rand and a ring? Or someone else?"

"I was *kiddin'.*" She frowned. "Those witches you ambushed—what were they doin'?"

"Not sure. It could have been a photoshoot, and they stuck around to 'haunt' the meadow."

"Yeah."

"What?'

"You heard about Rand and Pauline?" she asked.

"It's none of my business, Lou."

"Fine, but watch yourself around her." She handed me napkins pressed into flat pumpkins. "Here, take 'em. It's the reason why you came in here."

True, but our table had plenty. Our server had given us fresh ones with dessert.

I'd made up an excuse to speak to Lou, but it was a mistake, clearly.

I stared at the napkins. Cotton with an excellent "hand," or feel, to the fabric. They reminded me of what Upper East Side women purchased at Bergdorf's. These had a Wisconsin twist and were patterned with cow skeletons.

I recalled the scarves Ichabod always wore.

"What's the matter?" Lou asked. "You look like ya saw a ghost."

"N-no. Just haunted napkins."

"Nice, eh? Expensive, but I used Kohl's cash. 'Serviettes,' they call 'em, but a napkin by any other name works as good."

She stepped to the workstation, its counter a slab of glossy black marble that reminded me of the runway in the ballroom.

Gold-dusted chocolates were stacked on trays.

She handed me a tray. "Take these and skedaddle back to your table. Don't make plans for tomorrow, even if Rand proposes."

"He. Is. Not—"

She laughed. "*Relax.* We're having a girls' dinner to dish about dating in our golden years. Inga, Fern, you, and me. You guys will ask questions. I'll give advice."

Lou hadn't dated anyone since age eighteen because she married Jason, her high school sweetie, after graduation.

Taking her advice would be like asking butter for ideas about cutting calories or spurs for tips about going slow.

I didn't mention it. With Lou, it was best to pick one's battles.

I swooshed out the kitchen door with napkins and a tray of chocolates stacked to my eyebrows. Diners seated at the few tables in the small room stared.

I hadn't gambled on Lou joking about engagements—what got into her?

Further, everyone was acting oddly: Fern Bubble was "off her feed" to use cowgirl vernacular. Cozette Gallagher suddenly was a sleuth. Eden Hoff wanted me to prove her innocence. And Pauline Pickle may be out for me.

It felt everyone in Cinnamon was under a spell.

What would happen next?

I HAD AN EMBARRASSING DISAGREEMENT WITH TODD MORGAN, THAT'S WHAT happened next.

The moment felt surreal.

Hours earlier, I'd been fleeing witches in a haunted meadow. Then, after a salad and swordfish in the dining room, I was practically spearing an honored guest.

I'm a quiet bird. If odds were offered of me squawking like a pelican in the Moon Cafe or of a real pelican doing it, folks who know me would bet the actual bird.

I almost flipped the bird at Todd. He took a wrong turn at the intersection of Big Yellow Taxi Avenue and Joni Mitchell Street.

He commented off-hand about a pickleball court being constructed in the meadow. "Paving over paradise wouldn't hurt," he said, chuckling. "It's just a vacant lot." He gestured toward the windows.

"A vacant lot?" I fumed. "A field where Brown Swiss grazed to give nourishment and this state its heritage?"

VIPs in the room stared. Well, if Cinnamon had them. The only VIPs in our state lived in Green Bay and wore green and gold on Sundays. But Alicia Cliff and Ethan Gould glanced in our direction.

The mayor's wife looked at me, then whispered to her husband. Doc Graves and Pauline were seated at a table by the fireplace.

She and I had avoided each other during cocktails (brandy old-fashioned with cinnamon), the appetizer course (mushroom-gouda puffs or salad), and the entree (prime rib or fish).

I'm old enough to accept responsibility for my emotions, but seeing Pauline made my blood boil.

She glared in my direction—I recalled the bubbling pot in the meadow.

Rand placed a hand over mine. "Would you like coffee, Mel?"

"Milk. Served *cold.*"

"We're having ice cream drinks for dessert," he said. "Remember that place in New York where we'd go for grasshoppers?"

"No."

Morgan seemed oblivious to my anger. "I'm an equal-opportunity bovine-enthusiast. Holsteins, Jerseys. Brown Swiss, too." He snapped his fingers. "Ichabod Hall was designing a cow print dress collection for spring. What were they called?"

"*Muumuus,*" I said. "He made his name creating them." How did Todd Morgan, the new private equity owner of Ichabod's design house, not know that?

"Is that what they are? Ironic, eh?" He smiled. "I focus on ROI, not clothes."

"How about those ice cream drinks?" Rand asked.

"I'll take mine to go," I said.

Rand and I were in his rental vehicle, a *Ram* truck. He patted the dash. "Don't get ideas, Mel. You're mad as a bull."

"Todd Morgan should not be in the fashion business."

"I play *moo-sic* to cool you off?"

We'd left the Promenade and parked on a hill. At night, the building's exterior lighting created the outline of a cruise ship, a sight made even more stunning by a storm retreating in the distance.

Cousin Lou had packed us ice cream bars to-go. Homemade by her, of course.

Rand unwrapped the bite-sized treats. "We've got Effie's

hazelnut biscuits with vanilla bean or cocoa biscuits with peanut butter ice cream. Which would you like?"

"The one you don't want."

"I'll take the peanut butter." He gave the other bars to me. "Why don't pilots like vanilla?"

"I don't care."

"It's *Boeing*."

Since our breakup, Rand had become funnier.

I tried not to overthink why he'd changed by *not* having me in his life.

I tasted the sandwich, savoring the hazelnut and creamy vanilla flavors. "I have mixed feelings about the fashion business, but there are talented designers who create beautiful things. Ichabod was one of them."

"I'm glad to hear that. You should be proud of your career."

"Fashion has a purpose," I said. "It makes people feel special. Wearing beautiful things brings out confidence."

"That's true. Our company's new uniforms were a big hit."

Viking Ship Airlines, Rand's company, had used an up-and-coming designer to reimagine its uniforms, and they'd been a smash.

The fashion press loved them, as did flight crews, who had choices of tailored jackets, slacks, and dresses in hues of blues or greens, the colors of the Northern Lights.

Their planes matched, too. Snow-white airliners with stunning blue-green swirls painted on their tails.

Rand added, "After the redesign, ticket sales went up, and company morale improved."

"Fashion has a raison d'être."

"*Oui, oui.*"

"It's more than ROI," I said.

"Roger, that."

"Could a person get killed over it?"

He stopped mid-bite. "*Mon Dieu*, I hope not."

"I'm serious. Todd Morgan would pave a meadow—"

"Don't stress, Mel. He was just making conversation."

"What's an empty meadow when it could be bulldozed for a return on investment?" I felt myself getting warm.

"That's not what he said, and Inga seems to like him. She's a good judge of character." He glanced at the take-out container. "'It is not the man who has little who is poor; it is the one who always desires more.' Would you like the last one?"

"No, go ahead."

Right or wrong, the thought of Todd Morgan taking over Ichabod's business was like waving a red flag. I finished my treat, but it had lost its flavor.

"Why couldn't Todd have something to do with Ichabod's death?" I asked. "He knew Ichabod's schedule and had motive if the brand wasn't making money."

"Think, Mel: The relaunch was just starting. They needed the face of the brand to regain its audience. Losing Ichabod was a setback."

Rand was correct, probably.

It was difficult to admit because the Aries in my pedigree interfered red flags and rams. Some people think I'm stubborn, but I refuse to believe them.

Rand drove me home. Tomorrow would be busy. I had a mall to run, a fashion show to reschedule, and a murder to solve.

Mon Dieu, indeed.

18

FRIDAY MORNING

When I entered the Bell, Book & Melville bookstore, Crystal Broadway, its manager, was standing at the checkout counter unwrapping a sign.

The young woman held it up. "I found it on our trip and bought it for inspiration. What do you think?"

It was a quote by Georgia O'Keefe. I read it silently, and a spark jolted my nerve endings. Max felt the energy.

The dog stood near my legs but jumped quickly to the side.

Animals know.

The phrase on the sign hit me at the intersection of Ichabod Hall's death and my encounters with *The Tempest*. I read it the quote loud: "To create one's own world takes courage."

"Great, huh? It'll keep me motivated while I'm in school. It reminds me to stay true to my vision."

"Your 'own world' means ... "

"I'm on an island, yeah." She nodded, her blond curls bouncing. "It reminds me to, like, honor my ideas while being grounded in worldly elements. Georgia did that. She painted ordinary flowers in ways no one else did. I want to do that with sportswear."

I winced.

Not because of Crystal's explanation. I feared being knocked in the noggin again with a flying book.

Crystal studied the sign. "Isolation hurts but, like, solitude is sweet—what's wrong?"

My gaze darted to the shelves. "Has anything odd happened in the store lately?"

She shrugged. "Steven and I were on vacation, so I can't say."

"Anything weird before you left?"

"Sure, it's an old building." She placed the sign on the counter. "And it's a bookstore. Weird stuff should happen, or it's no fun."

"What about up in the apartment?"

"I hear voices up there sometimes. It's probably ghosts." Her eyes lit up.

"*What?*"

"Sorry, did you, like, see one?"

"*No.*"

Crystal adored books and had an eye for design. She'd set up the bookshop, combining the space's exposed brick walls and wood floors with expertly merchandised shelves and curated artwork. She managed my store while taking classes at Mount Mary University in Milwaukee.

"Have you gone upstairs?" I asked. "I should have told you not to."

"It's the first thing I did this morning. Love it up there."

"The installers are coming today ... to finish."

She scanned a schedule on a clipboard by the cash register. "Yeah, it looks like they'll be done soon. Then we can start decorating. What do you want to do with the space, exactly?"

"I'm not sure yet."

She studied me. "I heard things went crazy at the Promenade while we were gone. Everybody at the Tool & Rye is buzzing about it —oh, Rand is there. I'm super sorry about Ichabod Hall. Are *you* okay?"

"I'm managing." The bell jingled, signaling a shopper entered behind me. Max *woofed* gently. "Please be careful. No one is sure what happened. Stay vigilant."

She nodded. "I've got pepper spray. And the store has good security."

I'd paid for self-defense classes when Crystal began working for me. The shop had a hidden alarm embedded under the counter. I hadn't installed cameras because the line-of-sight inside the shop was excellent; it was a small place.

There were cameras on the exterior of the building, though. I'd checked them and only seen tourists, shoppers, and workmen coming and going—*but ghosts don't show up in photographs.*

"Mel, did you hear me?" Crystal asked.

"No—what?"

"Sheriff Cole. He's, like, behind you." She waved. "Hiya, Sheriff?"

Max tippy-tapped on the wooden floor, then *woofed* again. I felt an arm around my shoulder.

"Hello, Mel," Cole said. "I got here early. I needed to see you."

"H-hi," I replied.

COLE KISSED ME, THEN GAVE MAX A TREAT FROM THE JAR ON THE COUNTER.

The sheriff and Crystal chatted while I remained quiet, observing them, a habit learned during my career.

Cole looked great in jeans, boots, and a denim shirt. His engaging smile and arresting blue-green eyes made one want to be arrested.

Me, anyway.

His face was perpetually tanned from living in the Wisconsin Northwoods, a land of sunshine in the summer and snowshine in the winter, nine long months. He stood over six feet. His muscled body thrived on walleye, maple syrup, and pine-scented air. Turtle sundaes, too. Cole and I shared those every time we were together.

His hair was salt-and-pepper—had it become more gray since we'd met about a year ago? Did I see worry lines around his eyes?

I adored him. The emotional distance between us *hurt*. But I had to set boundaries to establish what I needed in our relationship.

He talked to Crystal about the conference in Green Bay. "It was a learning experience. They showed lots of camo and black this year."

"Did they accessorize with badges and leather belts?" she asked.

Cole shook his head. "Pumpkin donuts with orange sprinkles."

She smiled, then pointed toward the window facing south, toward the bakery-hardware store down the street. "Will you guys pick up the shop's order at the Tool & Rye? We have chocolate chip cookies for customers today."

"Certainly," Cole answered. "Do you have time, Mel?"

Before I could answer, Crystal spoke. "Go on, you two. Max can stay with me"—she stopped as though realizing something—"unless you don't ... want to, Mel."

The look in her eyes revealed she suspected Rand was still at the Tool & Rye.

He'd stayed overnight at Inga's place in the country in her mother-in-law cottage.

Cole took my hand. "I could use coffee and a cinnamon roll."

I looked at Crystal, who grimaced as though saying she was sorry.

It would be fine. Cole and Rand got along—sometimes better than I did with either of them!

I didn't want to stress my relationship with Cole more than it was, though. He had an intense job, and we were long-distance. I didn't want him to overthink, and suspect Rand and I saw too much of each other, which we did *not*.

"Mel, shall we go?" he asked. "I'd like to talk."

I nodded. "Me, too."

We entered the Tool & Rye, Cinnamon's gathering place for chats, celebrations, informal town meetings, and general problem-solving. Forget TV and social media; face-to-face conversations are prized in our little burg.

Aromas of cinnamon, yeast, and coffee tickled my nose. A fire blazed in the pot-bellied stove, and I smelled the smoky richness of burning embers. It was like entering a ski chalet on a mountain. All it needed were skis propped against the knotty pine wall and snowflakes falling outside the windows overlooking Main Street.

The display case showed off homemade breads. A sign listed specialty coffees, which changed with the seasons. Tables were scattered near the fireplace and front windows.

Customers with home or yard projects could step through a connected entrance into the hardware store to purchase hammers, screwdrivers, nails, or plants. At Christmastime, this was *the* place for freshly cut trees.

The floors creaked with age, and the T&R was always decorated for holidays. The theme for Halloween this year was ghosts, lucky me.

White goblins floated from the ceiling and in corners, their draped sheets wafting gently as though the ghouls were alive. The song "Somebody's Watching Me" by Rockwell pipped quietly from hidden speakers.

When we'd entered, everybody looked at Cole. People always stared. With his height, long stride, and bright eyes, he was Charisma in denim. It was like seeing John Wayne, the movie star, reincarnated.

He turned to me. "Will you get a table? I'll get us the usual, two Wiscocoas."

"No, I'd like campfire tea. Extra hot."

He stopped, his boots thumping the floor. "Oh?"

"I need energy and mental focus."

The T&R's campfire teas were from the hidden menu, known to only locals. It was code for a caffeinated black tea, and *hot* meant to add orange peel, ginger, and a B vitamin. It was a Red Light order and transcended season and time of day.

I needed it. I'd scanned the patrons on the Tool & Rye, and suspects in the murder of Ichabod Hall were in the place: Alicia Cliff spoke to Nathan Gould.

Pauline had been leaving when we arrived.

Eden Hoff sat in a corner in disguise. I couldn't claim to be a former model if I didn't recognize her luscious Donna Karan suit in white wool. She wore a gray wig so perfect that it could only come from a shop in New York, one that had fitted me when a different hairstyle was required for photoshoots.

Where was Lt. Bruce DuWayne, and what was happening with the investigation?

With Fern Bubble out-of-sorts, my connection to inside intel was broken.

I felt Cole's gaze upon me while I scanned the room pondering suspects, Ichabod's death, and murder. *Awkward.* Cole knew what I thought, for sure.

At least Rand wasn't here—nope, I lied.

He walked in via the hardware store carrying Halloween decorations. Orange twinkle lights, a skeleton, and ghosts, darn it—*I couldn't get away from them!*

Rand set the decorations on a table, then extended a hand to Cole. "Nice to see you, sheriff. Happy Halloween."

"Same to you. What brings you here?" Cole looked at me.

"Boo Bash and a Halloween emergency," Rand said. "A friend ran low on decorations and needed assistance. It was a near miss, one might say."

"He's here for Inga," I explained. "She wanted him to be a chaperone for her blind date. Long story."

"Inga was the winner in the Golden Cheesehead dating game," Rand said. "Mel is the other 'player' in our foursome. We had dinner last evening. Next, it's Readers' Theater. It's all for Inga."

"Yes, for Inga," I agreed.

Cole smiled. "Let me guess: It's for Inga."

Rand picked up the Halloween goodies. "Wish I could chat, but I've have a delivery to make. It's like having a plane to catch, except via ground transport. Nice to see you again, Cole."

"Same," he said. "Buckle up. Keep your tray table upright and in a locked position."

Rand laughed.

The two men were *so* much alike.

It was embarrassing, really. I had a type: Tall, handsome, and funny. Hard working. Lactose tolerant. Wisconsin was the Dairy State. Summer date nights often included frozen custard sundaes or root beer floats.

He also must be kind to seniors, dogs, and yours truly—*why did I push away men who seemed perfect?*

A year ago, I broke up with Rand because I'd wanted more. Now, I distanced myself from Sheriff Cole for the same reason.

Maybe the problem was *me.*

"Maybe the problem is you, Mel. People keep dyin' around ya," Lou said.

My cousin stood at our table. She'd entered and spied us in the corner. She wore jeans, an orange vest, and ghost earrings that swung back and forth as she moved.

Cole came to my defense. "They do that around me, too, Louella, unfortunately."

"Not the same. You're a sheriff. Price of the gig. You know about Ichabod, poor fella—did ya know I'm a suspect?"

"You, Louella?"

She nodded, and the earring ghosts swirled. "I set out snacks and he sampled the cheese curds. We all know *I* didn't do it, but a n'er-do-well coulda sabotaged it to set me up. To be the fly in the beer batter, so to speak."

Cole looked at me. "And Mel is on the trail, eh?"

"Yes, she's huntin' down the killer like a hodag chasin' an Illinois tourist."

The couple at the next table looked over. They wore orange and blue jackets, Chicago Bears' colors.

"No offense, folks," Lou told them. "That's only if Minnesotans aren't prowlin' the woods. Hodags eat them first."

Cole sipped his cocoa, pausing as though taking in what Lou revealed: *Mel was on the trail.*

It was the moment I dreaded, the one I knew was coming.

When men like Cole go silent, things were serious.

After about a year, Cole asked, "Would it be best to let the authorities handle the investigation?"

"Sure, if we could *find* our authority," Lou said. "Bruce DuWayne has gone missin'." She scanned the cafe. "Haven't seen him for a while."

"He needs privacy—" I protested.

"Naw, he's semi-regular. He'd stop before Ichabod passed away, even. The Tool & Rye is a destination in southeast Wisconsin. Like your craft mall."

"Cole, it's not unusual for a detective to be absent a day or two, is it?" I asked.

"It depends on the detective and how he prefers to work."

"Bruce liked to work on coffee and fresh bakery from the Tool & Rye," Lou said.

Cole spoke firmly: "Whatever his situation, I suggest letting the lieutenant work without interference."

"Mel's not interferin'," Lou countered. "She's like my private investigator-legal eagle rolled into one. A mashup of Scooby-Doo and a Charlie's Angel."

"No—" I began.

"Cole, could you get a hold of Bruce? It's not like him to pass up today's special, pumpkin bars with maple icing."

"I'd like to try those." He pulled out his wallet and handed over cash. "Would you mind?"

"Sure thing," Lou said. "Don't solve the murder before I get back."

She hustled to the counter, her boots thumping the wood floor, *thump, thump*.

There was a long line. It would take a while before she returned.

Cole turned to me. "Tell me what you know, Mel."

I sipped tea before speaking. Finally, I said, "What are investigations, after all, but journeys of self-discovery?"

Pithy. Sounded smart. Best I could do on short notice.

Cole frowned. "My investigations are journeys to handcuffs, usually."

"Why do popular Wisconsin places stash handcuffs under the counter?"

"No idea."

"Because they're for *two-wrists*."

Oops, the couple next to us heard me. They got up and left.

Cole sighed. "Mel, you have a right to ask questions about a tragic event you were involved in."

Leave it to him to take the high road while I made jokes.

"Finding a man you liked and respected dead must have been a shock," Cole said.

"I haven't processed it yet, to be honest." I looked out the window. Clouds with white tops and gray edges billowed above Main Street. the vision looked surreal, like the marshmallow man scene from *Ghostbusters*.

"I get it," Cole said. "It's hard to accept, and you can't move past it until the perpetrator is caught."

"Bruce DuWayne will find him. Or her."

"Do you believe that?"

I nodded. "I believe the killer will be found, whoever it is."

Cole reached for my hand. He. Had. To. Pull. It. "Loosen ... up ... Mel. Murder investigations shouldn't come between us."

"I don't want them to."

This was the conversation I feared.

I'd been involved in three murders in the past twelve months, a conflict of interest when it came to dating a law enforcement officer. It was like dating a hedge fund manager and being religious. Like dating a pilot and working at the FAA, for *Boeing's* sake.

Cole caressed my hand. "You're drifting away. I'm not sure why, but I don't want to lose you."

"Me, either."

"Rand was part of your life for a long time, but old boyfriends or murder investigations shouldn't affect us. *I love you, Mel.*"

Just then, Lou marched over with pumpkin bars, enough to feed everybody in the place.

Her eyes darted between us. "What's the matter? You guys look like ya saw a ghost."

Lou left the platter, then hustled off.

For once, she didn't interfere.

"Don't say it back," Cole said. "This isn't the time or place. I wanted you to know. It should have been said in our favorite spot."

"On a hike in the Northwoods?" I asked.

He smiled. "Close, but no."

"Your horse barn?"

"No, that's Max's favorite spot."

"My backyard?"

"Still Max's favorite."

He leaned toward me. I smelled his cologne, pine tree in a bottle. I saw his skin, smooth and tan, exfoliated by cold air blowing off a Wisconsin lake—how could I *not* fall for the man?

Softly, he said, "It should have been said in *The Root Beer Float* on a summer night, with stars overhead, a blanket over our laps, and a loon calling in the distance."

The *Float* was his boat, a vintage Cris Craft, a floating treasure with bench seats, red cushions, and fuzzy dice hanging from the dash.

"Don't say it back," Cole repeated. "We'll talk later. I have to get back up north. Paperwork for a trial. Nasty weather's on the way— thundersnow, they call it."

"Thundersnow?"

"Humidity, a cold front, plus convection. Snow and a thunder- storm. It can get bad quick." He glanced toward the counter. "Lou's coming back."

"Hate to break up your convo, but I saw Bruce DuWayne" Lou nodded toward the window. "He's walkin' down the street. You wanna chat with him, Cole?"

He looked at me. "I won't leave unless it's okay with you."

"I'm fine. Go talk to him."

"I'll call you."

He kissed me on the cheek, then left. It was like a Giant Sequoia exited the room, taking Big Forest energy with it.

Lou watched him go. "Now, that's a *man*."

19

FRIDAY, LATER

Lou sent me packing with a delivery for the Moon Cafe. No, in case anybody wondered, she did not work for the Tool & Rye, the Cafe, or the Promenade.

She and her husband owned an excavating business. She volunteered like it was her job, so seeing her everywhere in town wasn't unusual.

We stood by my car. The wind gusted, but temps felt mild.

Lou slammed the trunk. "Take these pumpkin bars to Cozette. I'll talk to Fern Bubble."

"What for?"

"In case I get incicted. She's my legal counsel."

"*Indicted*, you mean?"

"Same thing."

"Fern's not an attorney," I said.

"I know. I'll try my case in the press before court. Gotta have a PR person on staff like you do for the mall and bookstore."

"You're not going to court, Lou."

"You and I get that. Not sure if Bruce DuWayne does. I wish he'd stopped in the cafe. Place was full of suspects—did ya notice who left?"

I nodded. "Pauline."

"She probably went to the Promenade to hide evidence. Get your tail out there and arrest her."

"I can't do that."

"Make a citizen's arrest! Don't forget to read her rights: You got the right to play pickleball, but not in the meadow, no court shall be formed there. You got a right to play on other courts, but no servin' outside the lines." She laughed.

"Where will you be later?"

"Waitin' for Cole to come back, and then pump him for information."

"Please don't."

"Okay, I won't."

"*I mean it, Lou.*" I looked down the alley. "Did you really see Bruce DuWayne?"

"Sure, yeah." She shrugged.

"You didn't just say that to get rid of Cole, and then ask me what we were talking about?"

"No, but what were you two lovebirds talkin' about?"

I sighed. "Horses. Boats."

"It was more than that." She waved toward the backdoor of the Tool & Rye. "What's the point of a small-town coffee shop if you can't gossip?"

"What Cole and I discuss is none of your business."

She studied my face. "The light's comin' back to your eyes."

I ignored the comment, opening the car door. "Go easy on Fern if you see her.""

"What's up with Fern? She need cinnamon rolls?"

"No."

"How 'bout pumpkin bars—"

"Give her space."

"Gotcha. I'll just chat with Cole, then."

"He won't be back to the cafe. He's headed up north."

Lou frowned. "We need him on our side with Bruce being AWOL."

"Are you sure the detective is missing?"

"My spies haven't seen him."

I waited a sec to see if she mentioned the well-dressed spy in the cafe, Eden Hoff—*those two shouldn't tangle.*

She stared down the alley, not mentioning the woman in the gray wig, and I didn't bring her up.

"Get to the Promenade," Lou ordered. "Find Bruce—and find out who did it. We got our girls' chat out there tonight, too."

I paused. "It's at Inga's, I thought."

"Nope, moved it."

"Why?"

"D-don't know, exactly." She looked skyward.

I sighed. "You're not trying to set us up as decoys? Tempting the killer to appear during our talk?"

"*Nooo.*"

"Good, because the Promenade has residents and visitors every-where. The killer won't return to the scene of the crime."

"Right, they *never* do that."

I climbed into my car, my mind spinning. Was Bruce DuWayne really missing? Would the other women and I be decoys tonight?

Cole said he loved me.

Movement at the end of the alley caught my gaze. A figure—a woman?—wearing white. I caught just a glimpse. She, it, moved quickly in the direction of my bookstore.

Was it Eden Hoff—or had I seen a ghost?

I LEFT WITHOUT INVESTIGATING.

I detoured past Fern's ranch on my way to the Promenade.

Clouds wafted over the countryside, billowing like steam from a train.

I cruised over hills and around curves as though driving through smoke. I passed sheared-off cornfields, the stalks broken and brown, the crops cut and stored for the winter in barns dotting the landscape.

Turkeys gleaned what was left. They strutted across the fields, pecking the terrain. In the haze, they looked like a short, bronze-colored army with razor beaks and clawed feet.

Fern's place was same-as-usual.

The horses ate hay in their paddocks, their heads down. In the gloom, they looked like four-legged ghosts. Except for Tulip. With her giant Draft horse size, she looked like a medieval warhorse grazing among modern, light-boned animals.

I slowed to squint at the office attached to the barn, checking if Fern was in residence. The curtains were closed, but the lights blazed.

She was working on her to-do list, probably. Between her PR clients and the rescue, it was a long one.

The office was the barn's milk house that Fern converted into a workspace. From my angle on the road, I saw the office first and the barn behind. The office was painted white. The barn, deep red.

The office looked alone, like an island. The image reflected the vibe from Fern: That she was isolated, perhaps frustrated.

Oh, I wanted to talk with her about Cole! Poor timing though, especially if she was stressed.

Bruce DuWayne's sedan wasn't parked on the gravel by the office door. Was he really missing?

My cell rang, a muffled *Ring! Ring!* because it was in my purse.

It was the old-school jingle of a rotary-dial telephone. I didn't answer. Service in the country was sketchy, and the call likely would drop.

The Promenade was about a twenty-minute drive. Thirty if I took a trip past Inga Honeythorne's cottage.

Her place was isolated, too. *Another island.* Ironically, the theme for Ichabod Hall's fashion line was vacation dresses and loungewear. Where does one go on vacation?

Islands.

I drove toward Inga's place, sensing a clue.

At Inga's cottage, I pulled into the drive.

A black-clad figure emerged from behind a shrub. It carried an orange blob—*a head?*—and it dragged glowing wire. Weapons were scattered near the monster's feet: a trident, a sickle.

The sky had grown dark even though it was midday—*what was I seeing?*

Was Inga okay?

Her car was gone.

I cranked the wheel, then slammed the brakes in front of her guest house, white-knuckling my vehicle to a stop in the drive. *SCREECH!*

The ghoul saw me. The blob he carried had a grotesque smile and freaky eyes. It oozed orange blood from its mouth—*hideous!*

I was trapped.

Stopping was a terrible decision!

The house blocked my way, and I couldn't back up—*oh, no!*

Okay, no. The "monster" was Rand in a raincoat.

He'd carved pumpkins and left their guts on the ground. He placed them around dwarf pine trees. Macabre decor and strings of twinkle lights were strewn on the lawn.

Forgive me, but I joke when I'm stressed. The fashion people in New York loved it.

Yeah, no.

My silly side drove editors like Eden Hoff nuts, but to paraphrase Shakespeare, "If humor is the spice of life, joke on."

Rand opened my car door. "Mel, great to see you so quick. You look gourd-geous. What's up?"

"Is Inga here?"

He scratched his temple with a glove, a pair of those prank ones with fuzzy hands and neon-green nails. Looked like they belonged to a werewolf. "She's working at the mall. She's, ah, your manager. Opens and closes the place? Takes the slings and arrows for you?"

"*Riiight.*"

"Is anything wrong?"

"No."

"Do you have time to help decorate?" He pointed to the roof. "I need someone to get up there and string lights. I can't because I'm afraid of heights."

A pilot afraid of heights.

Hee, haw. Har, har.

I turned off the car. "Sure, I'll help."

WE STRUNG THE LIGHTS AROUND SHRUBS AND DECORATED THE ENTRYWAY TO the guest house, a tiny place consisting of three rooms, one closet, and a fireplace.

A mouse hole, basically.

Rand loved the place. "Anything bigger than a plane cockpit is a mansion to me," he said, hanging a ghost from a light fixture.

The cottage was white, its front door painted glossy orange, and its fixtures matte black. Spectacular and perfect for the season but a risky combo for a house.

I stood by the door admiring the place, thinking about Inga, who possessed an artist's heart.

She'd always been bold and creative. She'd have been a hit with the New York City fashion elite if she'd chosen to become a designer.

Inga had taken up calligraphy and penned notecards that sold out at the mall quick as she made them. The isolation of post-modern life was her inspiration.

While putting cards in the display racks, she always said, "Humans crave one-to-one contact. 'Mass' market is out. 'Close' market is in." Then she'd add a worrisome phrase: "When the world goes mad, civility to one another is all humanity will have left."

Her warning resonated with me. *Isolation.*

Islands, in other words.

Rand and I finished decorating. He removed his werewolf gloves and looked at his watch. "It's time for the beverage service. Can you stay for coffee, tea, or soda? I have pretzels, too. Duty-free."

"Hot tea, please."

We sat in the living room, a cozy den with space for a loveseat and a bookshelf.

Rand stoked the flames in the fireplace. The heat felt comforting and warm—like him.

He handed me a cuppa and settled beside me. The couch's worn cushions slanted inward. We tilted toward each other, and my tea nearly spilled from its mug.

"I love this room," He said. "It contains the real necessities in life."

I nodded toward the hearth. "Except for a dog. Max would fit perfectly right there."

"Right. Where is my favorite collie?"

"At the bookstore. It's his turn to read to the kids for story hour."

"If any dog could read, it would be Max."

There was a coatrack near the door. Aside from the kitchen pantry, it was the only "closet." Was a certain black windbreaker hanging on a hook? It was covered by another jacket, so I couldn't tell for sure.

"When did you get here?" I asked.

He nodded toward his phone, which was facedown on the tiny coffee table. "Inga called me, and I was 'wheels down' shortly after." He spoke in a satisfied voice as though proud of his quick action.

He rarely responded quickly when we'd been dating, especially after a trip, but I'd never called for help, either—was he here for Inga? Or more?

"How do you feel about islands?" I asked.

"Excuse me?" He sipped tea.

"Islands. What's your theory?"

"I don't mind them." He shrugged, and my arm swayed; that's how close we were. "Oops, sorry. I work on an island if you think about it. An airliner is an island in the sky."

An excellent point. "What do you think about them?"

He smiled. "I enjoy them. They're just *beachy*."

"No, seriously—"

"What's an island's favorite meal?"

"No idea."

"A *sand*wich."

He was missing my point. I pressed on. "Do you have a favorite? You've been all over the world."

I expected him to say a tropical paradise. An island in the sun with blue water, sunshine, and white beaches. A picturesque locale that negated the loneliness and desperation I alluded to.

"Motorized or non-motorized?" he asked.

"What do you mean? This is the twenty-first century. Or are you a time traveler? Does your plane go back to horse and buggy days?"

"We never went to Mackinac Island, did we?"

"No."

"It's stunning. Historic. Named for turtles, in fact." He sighed, then surprised me with his answers: "If motorized, I'd say Minocqua, Wisconsin. Non-motorized would be Mackinac. The Grand Hotel, the Hotel Iroquois, Arch Rock—and the only way to get around is horses and bikes." He set his mug on the coffee table, its top no bigger than a tray table in economy class. "We are going somewhere, Mel. It feels like we're in an airplane."

"Yeah."

I gulped.

It did, but the view in front of us was flames.

Rand and I sat shoulder-to-shoulder, but I felt so, so frightened.

Rand walked me to my car. He looked at the ghosts swinging from the fixtures and the pumpkins on the steps. "This looks un-boo-lieveable. Well done, Mel."

"It was just the two of us, a skeleton decorating crew, but t-thanks." I shuddered. Stepping out from the cottage made me shiver.

He smiled. "I hope Inga thinks it's *spooktacular*."

"I'm sure she w-will."

"Are you okay?"

"Yeah. Just cold."

"Need a vacation to a warm place? I know direct routes. No extra fees or delays, I promise." He held up a hand. "Pilot's honor."

"I'll think about it."

"Mel, wait a sec. Why did you ... stop out here?" He studied my face.

"I wanted to talk to Inga," I said.

"Oh, *right*. Shall I give her a message?"

"No, thanks."

"See you soon, then. Are we still on as chaperones? You won't *ghost* me?"

"Nope."

He opened the car door. "Drive safe, Mel. Watch out for turbulence. There's still a ne'er do well on the loose."

20

THE PROMENADE, LATER

The metal cart I pushed rumbled loudly, the sound of its wheels echoed against the concrete block walls of the dark passage.

Delivering baked goods to the Moon Cafe gave me an excuse to study the behind-the-scene network of the facility.

I heard footsteps. Not just any footfalls—the sharp *CLACK* of stilettos. Quick, forceful, and louder than the metal cart, even.

Who was she?

An outsider, not a resident.

The senior fashionistas of the Promenade wore low-heeled shoes. Sneakers of all kinds: cushion-sole, slip-on, performance. Platforms with rhinestones.

Or, ballet flats, kitten heels, or sassy French heels. Boots—rubber Wellies, hikers, or tall, English-riding style—for those who walked the meadow in the cold season.

A door opened, then banged shut, *CLANG!*

I pushed faster, searching for the escape hatch. I wound through the hallway and hurled around corners like a cat after a mouse, the cart rattling, the boxes of treats nearly tipping off.

There—a door!

I reached for it, but it opened and light flooded the passageway. I blinked, my eyes adjusting to the glare.

"Hey—stop!" a voice said. "You almost hit me."

Pauline Pickle.

I looked down at her shoes. *Orange sneakers.* "Were you just in the hallway?"

"I'm headed downstairs. Would you move that cart so I can get past?" She carried a tote bag with her company's logo on it. She shifted it from one hand to the other.

The heels could be in it; she could have changed in a flash. I'd seen models switch out shoes quick as lightning. "May I ask what's in the—"

"Out of my way, please. I'm late for a meeting."

A meeting to speak with Bruce DuWayne about your whereabouts when Ichabod died? A meeting to discuss bulldozing the meadow for an indoor pickleball court?

She pushed the cart aside and swished by on feet silent as a chee-tah's. I barely heard her move as she walked past and disappeared.

Before I could tap on the door to the Moon Cafe, it burst open. "Mel, I've been waiting—got intel for us."

Cozette Gallagher pulled the cart into the cafe, dragging me with it. She slammed the door, its "Closed for Private Party" sign slapping the wood.

"Help me put these treats away. Then you and I are going for a walk," she ordered.

"Great, I could use one. That track around the Lido Deck is calling me—"

"No way." She nodded toward the windows. "We're heading to the meadow."

"But the weather—"

"I have gear. Don't worry about it."

"*Okkaay.*"

Cozette looked around as though invisible beings—*ghosts?*—were watching us. "I don't want anyone to overhear."

COZETTE FITTED US IN LANDS' END ALL-WEATHER JACKETS AND WELLIES. She kept a supply in the storage closet for "mind-clearing strolls" in the meadow. "We shall walk. It's our chance to be girls again: half-savage, hardy and free," she said.

The quote from *Wuthering Heights* fit the environment.

Fog pooled in the meadow's low spots. The scene resembled cauldrons separated by gently rolling hills and trees. The shrubs were shrouded in mist. The illusion reminded me of the witches I'd encountered on the haunted hike.

I shuddered despite my warm clothes, a raincoat, scarf, and boots. "The next mystery I solve will be in somewhere warm," I said.

Cozette walked next to me, her boots tromping on the mulched path. "Excuse me?"

I glanced back at the resort, a beacon in the gloom, a white ship bedecked with orange lights. "Any chance the Promenade is sailing south? Can I book a ticket this winter?"

She patted my hand with a mitten. It was soft wool with a cat face stitched on it. It looked familiar because we sold them in the craft mall.

"We're staying put to solve this mystery. As far as I'm concerned, our prime suspects are Nathan Gould and Pauline Pickle."

The same list as mine. "How'd Pauline do it?"

"You think it's her, too?" She tugged her scarf away from her neck as though needing air. The cozy muffler matched her mittens—we sold it, as well.

"What's her motive?" I asked.

"Anger, for sure. She was furious that Ichabod wouldn't include her sample garments last-minute."

"She didn't ask me about it, and I was assisting with the line-up."

"She waited for him, then ambushed him." Cozette said. "Choked the poor man. Then she took off. Seeing her speed-walk through the building was normal. No one would suspect her of *anything*."

We turned and walked toward the ship, er, building—it was easy to confuse the two! "Have you spoken with Bruce DuWayne?" I asked. "We want to forward with the show, but I need to confirm it with him."

"No, not at all." Cozette sighed. "It's a funny thing. He was here all the time, then he vanished."

Cozette stopped me near an open space. "This is where they want to put the courts."

I looked around, appreciating why it was considered a perfect location. The space was flat, with a view of the grounds. The pool and the outdoor dining area were nearby, too, though closed for winter.

There was a better, less invasive place for indoor pickleball.

Now that I'd walked the meadow a few times, an idea came to mind.

I pointed to the parking deck near the building. It wasn't a huge structure, just enough for visitors' cars for special occasions. The top of the deck was flat and empty of vehicles. "Why can't they put courts up there?"

Cozette shook her head. "That's for parking."

"It's overflow. Otherwise, no one uses it. It's the least favorite place to park. It's too hot in the summer and too cold in the winter. I've been here many times and noticed it."

"People do prefer the underground level. Or the lower decks."

There also were the weirdos like me who parked in the farthest place in the exterior lot near the entrance—no-woman's land—lot to protect her ancient car against door dings, plus get extra daily steps.

"There's already an elevator up to the top," I said. "Add a roof, and it could work."

Cozette stared at the structure as though considering my idea, then began walking again. "I'll call for an emergency meeting and take it to the board."

I rubbed her shoulders from behind as though she was a prize-fighter. "You can do it, Champ. I'm sure your suggestion with be a *smash*."

THE HALLOWEEN DECORATING COMMITTEE AGAIN SHOWED ITS FANTASTIC sense of humor.

Around the pool were life-sized skeletons and ghosts reclining in lawn furniture. A sign announced that it was a "Ghouls by the Pool" party, and attendance was by "Invisible Invitation Only."

At the pool bar, a hut with a thatched roof, ghosts were seated on chairs while skeleton bartenders served drinks. A disco ball whirled above them, its mirror lights flashing brightly against the gray sky.

Cozette pulled me under the canopy of the bar. At my left was a ghost drinking what appeared to be a fake brandy old-fashioned. Plastic ice, a cinnamon stick, an orange slice, and cherries swirled in a plastic glass.

"Mel, I need to tell you something, and I hope it doesn't hurt you." Cozette's voice cracked.

"Sure, what is it?"

"You know Wooly and I always loved Rand. And we adore Sheriff Cole. Whichever fellow makes you happy is the one we hope you marry."

"I may not be the marrying type, but thanks." A gust skittered leaves across the concrete, and I coughed.

I wanted to confide in Cozette about what he'd said earlier—I love you —but the wind choked the words from my throat.

"I have information about Rand," she said. "I do *not* know if it's true."

A shudder traveled from my neck to my toes. "*Okay.*"

"There's a rumor ... he's seeing a gal."

"I've heard. It's fine. Rand has male and female friendships like I do."

"Yes, but ... it's Pauline." She patted my glove. "The story is she was a flight attendant, and they knew each other a long time ago."

That would explain his cheerful mood recently if he had a rekindled love interest.

"It's not my business," I said. "I have no control over it."

"I know, dear." Cozette's eyes teared up like she was about to cry.

After a moment, I realized something awful. "She's our number one suspect in the death of Ichabod Hall—we suspect Pauline Pickle of murder!"

"Isn't it terrible?"

I turned to the skeleton bartender. "I need a drink."

A SECURITY GUARD APPROACHED, TONY G. HE WORE A DARK DUSTER AND looked like a ghost moving through fog. "The detective has released the ballroom. You guys can get on with the fashion event."

Cozette nodded. "Good, Ichabod would want that."

"Tony, when did you speak with the detective?" I asked.

"Him? Earlier today."

"So Bruce DuWayne is here somewhere?"

"He was, but then left to work off-site." The cap the young man wore shielded his face, but a few snowflakes landed on the shiny visor, reminding me of a polka dot print dress in the show, a snazzy black and white muumuu.

"You actually saw the detective?" I asked.

"Yeah, no, we talked on the phone. Then he sent a text." He pulled his phone from a front pocket, scrolled, and showed the screen.

I read it. *Seemed legit.*

"Thanks for informing us," Cozette said. "That's good news."

He looked around. "You ladies comin' inside? Don't get stranded out here like castaways. Nasty weather on its way."

"That's our cue; it's time to seek shelter." Cozette linked her arm through mine. "C'mon, Mel, let's get back to civilization."

21

THE ATRIUM

Not having those trusted friends to rely on during a murder investigation made me feel isolated.

"I'll contact Lou about food prep for the show," Cozette said. "I'll also get word to the staff here."

I nodded. "I'll work with Nathan Gould and Alicia Cliff. It'll be hard without Ichabod, but we'll find a way to honor him."

"That's the spirit." She hugged me, whispering, "Do *not* worry about Rand. Don't dwell over it."

The atrium buzzed with activity. It was a mini-Times Square. Seniors gathered in groups—some around the coffee bar. Others near the grand piano, singing scales, warming up until Yamahaha practice began.

A cluster of women wearing black pickleball outfits stood at the concierge desk. The outfits looked *sharp*. A luscious combo of sportswear mixed with understated elegance. Pearl trim and buttons accented the casual slacks and zippered jackets. Visors were glossy black, reminding me of the shiny runway in the ballroom.

Outside, a bus idled under the portico, its marquee above the windshield showing a camera and row of black hearts.

The players' transportation somewhere, obviously.

Pauline Pickle appeared in a hallway across the atrium, directly across from where I stood. She stepped with long strides. I studied her walk, reconciling her movement with the footfalls of the person I'd heard in the passage earlier.

Pauline moved purposefully, unlike the mystery woman. The unknown gal had *clacked* on the hard floor. Pauline placed her feet softly, carefully. She could have been a runway model.

Models lead with their hips. They maintain a neutral facial expression, keep their chins low, and limit the sway of their arms. Walks vary, and some models become known for a signature stride.

Still, most followed specific guidance from designers or runway coaches.

Pauline wore a black tracksuit with white piping. Its zipper flashing with rhinestones—*eye-catching*.

She swooped to the concierge desk. "My models and I are leaving for the photo studio. Be back in a few hours." She snapped her fingers. "Come on, ladies, let's do this—it's gonna be epic."

She stepped toward us, unable to avoid Cozette and me because we blocked the exit.

"The collection looks great, Pauline," I said.

She raised an eyebrow. "Thanks—excuse us, we're playing through."

We moved, then watched them board the bus and putt-putt away, the vehicle looking like silver-white ghost.

"Do you think she hurt Ichabod over *not* showing those outfits?" Cozette asked. "Did she get so mad that she killed him?"

"I don't know, but I'll find out," I said.

MY PHONE RANG, AND COZETTE SKEDADDLED AS THOUGH THE JINGLE WAS A warning siren. "Answer it. I'll see you for our girls' chat in the cafe."

I answered but wished I hadn't.

Nathan Gould gave me an earful. "Mel, I called earlier. The show's on, and you're in it."

"Yes, I'll be a dresser, no problem. The order shouldn't change, but what if we add a few pieces. I know it's last minute, but hear me out—"

"You're in the show, I mean. You're gonna open it. Alicia Cliff and I agreed."

"Excuse me?" I'd moved into the entry lobby, away from the crowded atrium. My words echoed off the walls. The distress in my voice bounced back to me. Talk about an island—*it was like I spoke to myself!*

"Your friend Fern won't do it," Gould said. "She isn't well. That means you're *it*."

"I can find another model."

"The New York gals went home. Alicia contracted with a couple local agencies. Those women are on their way."

"They got paid, I hope."

"They did, I promise."

"Have one of the locals walk—"

"Ichabod wanted you. Do it for him. He thought you could tell his story. You were someone who understood his vision."

"He said that?"

"Yep. Don't be afraid, Mel. Be our 'it' girl. *You're gonna open the show.*"

I DROVE FROM THE PROMENADE BACK TO TOWN. I PARKED IN MY DRIVEWAY, then hiked several blocks to the bookstore. Something drew me to the place.

Crystal Broadway stood by the counter. When I entered, she closed her sketchpad and hugged me. "Fern was in here and told me about the show. I've always wanted to, like, see you on the runway—*go for it, sista.*"

The young woman's enthusiasm was endearing. She made me believe I was on a bigger island. One with a link to the mainland.

"Your positivity … is something the fashion industry needs," I said. "You have a gift, Crystal."

"You're gonna open? Be the first look?"

I nodded. "Fern's out, I'm in."

"Gotcha—does Cole know? He'll want to see you."

"I texted him. He's busy with paperwork. I doubt he can make it on short notice." I glanced around the store. The place's aroma of books, wood, and fireplace comforted me.

"This is a big deal," Crystal said. "'You're gettin' back on the horse,' as your cousin would say."

"It's just one quick walk back and forth, that's all."

"Don't do that, Mel. If you don't mind me, like, saying that."

"What do you mean?"

"I told Fern the same thing when she came to get Max—you don't mind she took him to the farm?"

"Not at all. She needs a little canine therapy."

Crystal smiled. Since she'd started working in the store and begun taking classes, she'd blossomed. "Believe in who you are and what you can do. No matter your age or past. And make sure the people you love know that."

Behind me, the door jingled.

Right after she spoke those wise words, Eden Hoff strolled in.

Eden Hoff still wore the disguise.

Crystal whispered, "she's been in here before. I like her."

She clacked across the wood floor, the sound of her heels clipped, like her elocution, *click, click, click.*

There were a few browsers in the shop, and they glanced up. Even in disguise, Eden had a commanding presence. Her coat was white wool with silver threads; it sparkled under the lights in the store.

"Good afternoon, Crystal," she said. "How are those sketches coming?"

"Really good, ma'am, thanks for asking," the young woman replied. "Do you know Mel Tower? She, like, owns the place."

Eden extended a gloved hand. She wore Ferragamos. Soft as butter and stunning. "How do you do?"

I nodded. "How do you do."

"Melanie, you are the person I was looking for, in fact," Eden said. "A woman at the craft mall said I may find you here. Do you have a moment?"

Crystal's eyes widened. "Do you guys know each other?"

The lights flickered—caused by the bookstore ghost, no doubt.

"We have similar styles, you might say," I answered.

EDEN AND I MOVED TO THE APARTMENT UPSTAIRS. SHE SUGGESTED IT, AND I agreed. She'd be good for the place, an exorcist. Even ghosts paused in the presence of fashion editors.

The work crew had finished. The walls were freshly painted, the light fixtures by the fireplace glowed with golden light, and the maple floor gleamed.

She walked to the window—again, the *click.* "Melanie, I wish to apologize. I was rude the last time we spoke."

Eden Hoff was sorry? Perhaps the banishment from New York City changed her. She'd been on her own island, come to think of it.

"Losing Ichabod has been stressful," I said. "Apology accepted."

"I have information about his *murder*. Goodness, I can hardly say the word. I've presided over fashion editorials implying death but never encountered it—"

"Have you spoken to Bruce DuWayne? I can't talk to you otherwise."

She nodded, the strands of the gray wig swaying. "I left a message."

"When?"

"Earlier today. When he replies, I will make myself available." She smoothed the wig. "I shall turn myself in, so to speak—I did *not* kill anyone, Melanie."

"Who did?"

"There are two people I observed while undercover: Nathan Gould and Alicia Cliff."

I tested her. "Nathan had no motive. Losing Ichabod complicated everything and made his job harder. He needed him *alive*."

Something jangled in the kitchen. The curtains again, probably.

Eden didn't react to the noise.

Nothing frightened her, though. Well, seeing a commercial girl in a high-fashion editorial would, but that was beside the point.

"What would Alicia gain?" I asked.

Eden rolled her eyes. "What everyone wants—control of an empire. In this case, the House of Hall." She waved a glove. "In fashion, lack of control is the root of all evil. That, and being boring."

"The business is managed by a man obsessed with ROI. It's not like Alicia would have an open checkbook or decision-making power."

"Things have changed in the fashion industry, but not that much," Eden said. "It wouldn't stop her from manipulating further. Have you ever read the play *The Tempest*?"

I gulped. "I've … heard of it."

"To paraphrase The Bard: hell is empty, and all the devils are in Cinnamon—and one of them killed Ichabod Hall."

I felt a chill—*was a window open in the kitchen again?*

I moved away from its swinging door. "Have you heard I'm walking in the show?" I practiced my walk, stepping across the room, giving it my best.

Eden evaluated my stride, narrowing her eyes. I felt another chill. *Not* due to an open window. It was like I time-traveled back to my first audition for a runway show.

"Go again," Eden said. "Lift your knees a bit. Eyes forward."

I walked. No *clacks.* Just a silent footfall like a cat, my feet tracking a single line—hips pulling my body forward, shoulders back and down.

"That's excellent," Eden said. "I was terribly wrong to underestimate you for all those years, Melanie. Please forgive me." She brushed my hair behind my back. "You will share the catwalk with a dangerous woman tomorrow evening—*do not turn your back on Alicia Cliff!*"

WHEN I LEFT, EDEN WAS SPEAKING WITH CRYSTAL, EVALUATING THE YOUNG woman's designs in her sketchbook. Seeing my old nemesis standing in my bookstore, chatting with one of my staff, was *un-boo-lieveable,* but I shouldn't have been spooked.

Woolly Gallagher had warned residents in *The Cinnamon Roll* newspaper that Boo Bash would be a mystifying week.

I stepped into the alley, immediately sensing I'd erred. The wind gusted through the narrow lane between buildings, whistling like shrieks from invisible spirits. Halloween revelers flitted in the shadows.

It was dusk, and costumed teenagers, excused from after-school practices, were out searching for treats from businesses.

Please don't play a trick on me!

My house was only a three-block walk, but I wanted company

along the route. Max was at Aunt Fern's place. I called to see how he was doing.

"What's up?" Fern's greeting was clipped. She sounded irritated.

"This is Sherlock Bones calling to check on my favorite canine. How's his rawhide supply?"

She didn't laugh. "Fine, but things have gone to the *bark* side out here."

"Is he okay?"

"Yes, I'm the one who's *howlly*."

"What's wrong?"

"Bruce won't speak to me."

I stopped behind my craft mall, where the alley met the crossroad before my backyard. The back of my building had a giant spider crawling up the limestone. *Egads.*

"When did you—"

"I wanted to confirm things," Fern continued. "I called and texted. He refuses to answer."

A kid wearing a werewolf mask darted out, then dashed toward Main Street.

"*Yikes!*" I yelled.

"Where are you?"

"In the alley behind Main Street, walking home."

"Mel, there's a killer on the loose—that's a terrible idea."

"It was a werewolf, all bark, no bite."

She didn't laugh. "I'm okay with being alone, you know? I don't want to explain it to anyone. *I need a mental health break.*"

"I get it—you don't have to explain. Occupying your own island is nurturing sometimes. I've been there."

"I dumped the show on you, sorry."

"Ironically, it may be cathartic." I stepped onto my patio and pulled out a key. "We'll miss you tonight."

"Me, too, but while you're dishing about dating, I'll be taking a *boo-ble* bath to feel better."

"That's the spirit," I said. "Oh, and Max says he's *mutts* about you."

We hung up. I stepped into my house, locking the door behind me.

I missed being greeted by my dog, and my place needed TLC. It needed paint, the floors should be refinished, and its two bathrooms were tiny. At some point, it would need a new septic system.

It was paid for, though, and Max and I called it home. My friends and family dropped in without an invite.

For the first time, it felt like a kingdom to me.

I TAPPED OUT A TEXT TO BRUCE DuWAYNE:

Hello, Bruce. It's Mel Tower. If you'd like to talk, I can meet you in Hank Leigel's office. Please let me know.

Hank wasn't my legal counsel. He did real estate transactions and simple wills (only if customers had *few* skeletons in the closet).

It never hurts to have a legal mind in the room when one is speaking to law enforcement. By the way, how does a vampire lawyer start his letter? *Tomb* It May Concern ... .

My phone rang. The image was a spur behind the bars of a jail cell.

JK, just the spur. *Cousin Lou.*

"Mel, you need a ride to the Promenade tonight? I'm comin' to get ya."

I flipped on the kitchen light. "No, I can drive—"

"I stopped at the thrift store and picked up a cool mirror. Couple baskets for your place, too."

I looked around my living room. It had a second-hand sofa, a chair, a bed for Max, and his picture on the mantle. "That sounds extreme—"

"Nope, it isn't. Gonna granny-core your place whether ya like it or not."

"But—"

"We gotta talk about my defense, too. How'd the former fashion model prove her cousin was innocent?"

"No idea."

"She found out the evidence was *fabric-ated*. Good one, eh?"

I rubbed my forehead. "What time will you be here? How much time do I have to enjoy being alone?"

"I'll get ya in an hour. Wear jeans. I got us gals matchin' T-shirts that say 'No Time to Dye.' That's your gals' datin' motto and our new pickleball team's name."

I had a steady fellow and did not need a motto.

Also, between the mall, the bookstore, and Max, I had no time to take up a new sport.

Lou continued. "Kinda fun bein' an old fart, isn't it? Sixty is the new forty, they say. And eighty is the new sixty—"

I hung up, but she probably didn't realize it.

I needed peace and quiet before she arrived.

22

GIRLS' NIGHT

"It's granny-core, like I told ya," she protested.

"I prefer minimalist-core. Like Sweden."

She looked around the living room. "Like a jail cell, ya mean."

"I lived in New York City in a one-bedroom apartment. You get used to it."

"But you got artists right across the backyard that wanna give ya stuff." She pointed out the French doors toward the mall.

"They need to sell their work, not put them on my walls."

She held up a basket. It was sturdy wicker with a warm patina. It looked handmade. "Max told me he wants this for his toys."

"Okay, fine."

She approved of my outfit, a bright orange jumpsuit with fringe down the arms and bold black lettering.

No, *she* made that joke.

Her POV about possibly being arrested lightened the mood, certainly. I wore jeans and the "To Dye For" T-shirt over a black blouse, adding silver necklaces made by Susan, an artist friend.

We loaded into the quad-cab truck, its backseat filled with coolers of goodies for the buffet for the fashion show.

Riding in the loaded-up vehicle felt like we were piloting a supply dinghy out to its mother ship. We cruised down Main Street. Orange twinkle lights wrapped around fixtures and ghosts wafting from trees made it seem eerily peaceful, like a village out of a haunted fairytale.

Lightning flashed in the distance. Temps had warmed, and it was humid. Odd weather for October.

Thundersnow was coming—another prediction coming true about Boo Bash this year. Humidity plus convection, plus static charges in the clouds—Halloween sprites?—combined to cause lightning and thunder while snowflakes fell.

My phone pinged with a text, a reply from Lt. Bruce DuWayne:

> Ms. Tower, thank you for the notification of
> your availability. I'm in Madison for a meeting
> but will return soon. I'll be in touch.

Lou turned the behemoth truck down a country road, passing corn and hay fields, their crops harvested for the year.

Farmers got into the spirit by decorating giant round bales and positioning them near the windy road. I saw a giant pumpkin bale gobbling a scarecrow, a spider with pool-noodle legs, and a ghost bale painted white with black eyes.

Lou slowed the truck to observe decorations at a farmstead. "How about next year we set bales up in your backyard? You buy 'em, carry 'em in, and stack 'em. Your artists can paint the faces. We'll have a decoratin' night at your place. I'll serve hot cocoa with marshmallow ghosts."

"I'll think about it, Lou."

She looked over at me. "Ya didn't say *no* right away. This week has been good for ya, Mel."

"Darn tootin'"

"I talked to Swan. He told me you're first victim down the

catwalk."

"Not a great way to put it, Lou."

"Sorry, yeah."

"Did you speak to him on the Gold Deck by his suite?"

"It was at the gym. He was bench-pressin' locomotives but stopped to jaw when he saw me."

I knew the gym offered passes to outside guests. "Does he have info about what happened to Ichabod?"

"Not much, but he's got scoop about Nate Gould, Alicia Cliff—and Todd Morgan."

We turned onto a narrow road leading into the Kettle Moraine, a long route to the Promenade. The route detoured away from farmland and wound around Lake Cinnamon, or Lake Cinn, as it was known to locals.

The scenic road led us away from civilization; it was like traveling through an island forest. The truck's headlights were the only source of illumination. Stars and the moon were covered by clouds.

Lou took her foot off the gas. "Should I stop to tell ya what Swan said?"

"Not funny—keep driving."

"Is your door locked? Wouldn't want a pirate's hook arm to grab the handle and yank it open."

"I don't *have* to prove you're innocent. I can quit this gig right now."

"Okay, put it that way." She gunned it, and the tires spun on the gravel shoulder. "Accordin' to Swan, he thinks a bigwig did it."

"Which one: Nathan, Alicia, or Todd?"

"Keep listenin', and I'll tell ya."

Lou looked over, and the truck veered. "Why'd the bigwigs 'off' the fashion designer?"

"Eyes on the road, please. No idea."

"Cuz they couldn't *hem* the guy in."

I paused. "It was about profits, in other words?"

"Sure as shootin'."

"Swan thinks the murderers were Alicia, Nathan, *and* Todd? A coordinated scheme involving all of them?"

"Doesn't make *cents*, I know; I told him that. Hard to believe they'd kill the guy, keep it a secret between 'em, and then frame me. Not a great master plan. Too many cooks spoil a murder plot. One of 'em would spill the beans, and toss the other two from the fry pan into the fire."

She was correct. Swan wanted to cast light on the group for a reason. Like a photographer's key light, he shined it on them for us—me?—to investigate.

I had a theory about Swan and where he resided—and Eden Hoff resided—as the quest to find Ichabod Hall's killer continued, but I didn't share it.

Too many cooks spoil a murder investigation, as Lou said.

We pulled under the portico of The GP.

Lou grabbed a cart from the security guard's office. She jerked a thumb toward the office. "You catch up with Tony. I'll take the food to the kitchen by the Grand Saloon."

I stepped into the office. Tony Giugliano looked rested. Much better than the last time we talked.

"Hi, Mel, nice to see you," he said. "Have a seat."

I noticed a volunteer wasn't watching the cameras. Tony saw me glance into the little room adjacent to the office. "My volunteer was here. He just left to get a Wiscocoa and will be right back. He's stepped up since the incident in the ballroom."

I smiled. "Anything new since we talked?"

"Nothing."

I pulled out my phone and showed him a picture. "Is this woman coming and going this week?"

He nodded. "Yeah, she's a guest."

"That's what I thought." I put my phone away. "Thanks."

"Is she a problem? Should I stop her?"

"Only if she commits a fashion crime," I said.

In the Moon Cafe, I received a phone call. My cell worked fine on the upper levels of the place.

I saw who it was and slipped out the glass doors onto the deck to answer.

The air felt humid for an October evening. The meadow glowed orange with its Halloween decor swaying gently from the trees, and I saw the pool area, the thatched-roof bar, and the flat field behind it. The dirt mound for the septic test marred the scene. A metal building there would look like—*never mind.*

"Hi, Cole," I said.

"Home safe. I wanted to call and tell you."

"Thanks."

"I miss you."

"Me, too."

"I've never attended a fashion show before," he said. "What should I wear?"

"Excuse me?"

"Funny thing driving up here. The billboards announced that Mel Tower was walking in a show. Radio stations carried it, too. It was a Northwoods news bulletin."

I laughed. "Who told you?"

"Max. He called and spilled the dog biscuits."

"He's staying at Fern's tonight. They probably had too many dogtinis and were prank dialing.”

“What should I wear?” Cole repeated.

“You can’t come—what about work?”

“It will have to wait.”

“And the drive back—”

“Isn’t a problem when my sweetie takes on a challenge like this. I’ll plug in our playlist and the drive will be like drifting on a lake in the *Root Beer Float* where time doesn’t exist.”

Cole would turn around and come back? He knew being in the show reconciled my past with my future?

He’d never put it like that, of course.

He’d put it in law enforcement terms, military vernacular. A quote about being a warrior and conquering the mission.

I’d underestimated the man. Probably because I’d underestimated myself.

I didn’t try to talk him out of it, nor did I dismiss what the moment meant. “Wear denim,” I said. “Plaid, too. Be true to you. That’s what fashion should do: enhance a person’s features and boost confidence.”

“It sounds like you’re falling in love with it again,” he said.

“It was a means to an end, but I understand it better now.”

“Should I include a badge, too?”

I smiled. “Save that for later—with nothing else.”

He laughed. “I’ll see you sometime tomorrow. Break a leg, hon.”

Girls’ Night in the Moon Cafe got off to a scary start.

Pauline showed up, came out to the deck to admire the spooky landscape, and Cozette almost tossed her over the side.

I’d never seen Cozette angry, not even when readers fussed at her for something in her husband’s newspaper. Smiling, she always replied, "Wooly makes it look easy, but writing news objectively is darned hard."

I lingered on the deck, enjoying the view of lighted pumpkins swinging from the tree branches, which looked like skeleton arms.

Pauline appeared. I wondered who'd invited her. The evening was for Inga, Cozette, Lou, Fern, and me—*was Pauline invited because Fern declined?*

She fit our demographic and was dating in her older years. A certain pilot, if the rumor was true.

Pauline opened the slider and stepped onto the deck. "I need fresh air."

She wore one of her tracksuits. Black. Orange stripes down the legs. A bedazzled zipper that glittered in the dim light. Not a bad look. On trend, in fact.

"Beautiful spot," she said.

"Yes, it's peaceful."

"I'd love to own all of this one day."

"Excuse me?"

"C'mon, Mel, you're a businesswoman. You see the gold mine that this place is. A cruise ship on land is an amazing idea, a great franchise."

She put her hands on her hips and stretched side-to-side.

"This isn't a franchise. It works because it's community-based. The Clam family, the people who started it, live here."

She touched her toes. "For now."

I changed the subject. "Pauline, your line of womenswear is—"

"When I heard you ladies were up here, I wanted to drop off supplements." She twisted her head around, exorcist-like. "Twenty percent off, with one container complimentary. You should grab that one, Mel."

Cozette barged out to the deck. Faster than Lou, and my cousin barges *fast*. Working in the cafe had toned Cozette better than any supplement or gym. "This is a private event, Pauline. Please leave."

"I work here. *Chill*."

She pointed to the walkie-talkie on her hip. "I'll call security. This evening is invitation only."

Pauline nodded toward me. "Mel wanted to talk about my clothing line."

"Not here, not now," Cozette stepped closer.

"What are you going to do? Throw me overboard?"

"It's the fastest way down."

Crikey! I sensed a boatload of trouble. "Pauline, we can talk later about your clothes. How about tomorrow?"

"Come to my office on the Lido Deck." She stepped around Cozette. "I'll leave my supplements if anyone wants to feel more energetic. Ten percent off, too."

RESIDENTS WENT STARRY-EYED FOR THE MOON CAFE, AND I COULD SEE WHY; the place was out of this world.

The cafe came to life after dark. Its ceiling was decorated with hand-painted constellations that twinkled when its sconces were dimmed. Soothing music—Nep*tunes*?—played in the background.

The place was far out, like having a party in a planetarium.

Lou set out a spread of mini pizzas topped with moon-zerella cheese and alcohol-free cocktails. After that, homemade Milky Way bars, "star" bucks coffee, and gravi-tea were placed on the marble counter.

Lou and Cozette took turns giving the two singletons, Inga and Mel, advice about dating and men.

Lou blew on her tea. "You know what I say, cowgirls: if ya got it, *haunt* it."

"It's odd saying I have a boyfriend at my age," Inga said. "Like a time warp. It's been fifty years."

"You and Todd hit it off, eh? He's makin' you the center of his universe?"

She blushed, the color enhancing her full lips. "I wouldn't go that far. We come from two different worlds. He's from a land far, far away. I've lived in Cinnamon my whole life."

"You thinkin' he's out for just one thing?"

"Yes, and the Moon Cafe makes it more-so." Inga lowered her voice. "I feel *like a lady of the evening* in here."

Lou smiled. "Not what I meant—"

"Todd's dating Inga for her hands and beautiful calligraphy," Cozette interrupted. "She's the *write* one for him."

"In that case, I look much better on paper—and he's most likely an illegible bachelor!" Inga giggled.

"What's your instinct about Todd?" I asked. "Any vibes you can read?"

"It's only been a few days. I hardly know the man. He's calm ... but intense about certain things. Like his investments."

"That makes sense for a CEO," I said. "That's how they're trained to think. He was a good sport for stepping into the dating game last minute."

Inga nodded. "That's why I liked him right away. I knew we could get along at surface level. Turns out, we had great chemistry on that stage."

"Chemistry, shmemistry. If ya wanna know a fella's disposition, check out his whorls," Lou said.

The three of us froze—*a man's whorls?*

Cozette coughed. "Excuse m-me, Louella?"

"A guy's whorls tells all about his ... stuff." She raised her eyebrows.

"What sorcery is this?" I asked.

Lou stood up. "I'll get more hot water for tea—then I'll spill it."

"You sound spacey, Lou," I said. "Are you drinking a Cosmo and not tea?"

"I'm sober as the judge that'll lock up Ichabod's killer." She leaned in. "If ya wanna know about a guy, check out his whorls."

I looked around. "Are the whorls in the cafe with us now?"

"Stop makin' fun—I'm serious."

"I'm dying to know more," Cozette said. 'I've been married for forty years and never heard of this."

"If a guy's gonna spook, run off on ya, his whorls will tell the story." Lou touched her temple. "Check out his hairline. Easy if he's got a widow's peak. Hair swirls tell if he's gonna run off—*and which way!*" She drew concentric rings on the table. "If the swirls are super tight, he's high-strung. If they're looser, he's calm."

"I see," Cozette said.

"If the hair swirls to the left, backward, he'll return to an old girl-friend. If it goes right, he's gonna move on to a new gal." She scribbled wildly. "If he's got a double sworl, *watch out*. That's a storm. Life with him is gonna be a tempest. *Stay away*."

"Todd has a thick, full head of hair—and a widow's peak," Inga said.

Lou gasped. "Could be a runaway. Very unpredictable."

"My husband Wooly is balding," Cozette said. "That explains why we've stayed together, I guess. His hairline doesn't reveal anything."

A memory sparked—I recalled Fern saying something similar about horses. "Are you talking about the study that looked at the hair on a horse's forehead? The one that claimed to show temperament?"

Lou slammed a hand to the table. "That's it! A magazine reported it: *Farmer's Almanac* or *Gravel & Glam*. A science one. A good, solid study."

"I don't think the theory applies to men."

"*Pshaw*—why do ya think Fern gave up datin'? She got the scoop before everybody." Lou studied me. "What's Sheriff Cole's hairline tell about him?"

"His badge speaks for him. I don't worry about his hair."

"Yeah, he's gotta keep his cool." She poured hot water into my mug. "What about Captain Rand-O? What's his hairline say?"

I tapped my forehead. "It's covered by a pilot's cap. Don't know."

"Are you sure those two guys aren't the same person?" Lou nudged Cozette. "Mel's got a type: a silver fox in a uniform."

We all laughed—*true.*

"One could say I *gravitate* toward them." I glanced around the space cafe.

"Better safe than *starry,*" Lou agreed. Her gaze traveled to the containers of capsules near the cash register—Pauline's supplements. "You don't care if Rand-O could be seein' the Pickleball Queen?"

Inga coughed. "That's none of our b-business."

"Cowgirls—*it is!* Datin' when you're old like Mel means *baggage.* In Rand's case, it's an old girlfriend. But it could be an ex-wife, kids, or money trouble. What say you, Mel, about handlin' the traps a single, older cowboy's hidin' in his saddle bag?"

I sighed. "Our friend Fern is onto something. If a woman wants to date when she's older, get horses or animals instead."

"They should have an online site for gals who want to meet horses!" Lou exclaimed. "'Meet Your *Neigh*bor dot com'. I'll buy that domain, and you run it, Mel."

"No thanks."

"But for gals fed up with datin', it's perfect—"

I held up a hand. "The thing about baggage is, we *all* have it at our age. We've made bad decisions. We're marginally self-aware. We've got exes, kids, or financial issues." I glanced at Lou. "Or difficult family members."

"You don't suffer from that one. Take it off your list."

"It's not that we have baggage—it's what have we done with it."

Cozette and Inga nodded.

Lou said, "Yeah, like, have we fixed it, got the burr out from under the saddle pad. Like, gone for therapy at a shootin' range. Or robbed a bank to solve money problems."

"No, Lou."

"Just kiddin'. What you're sayin' makes sense, though. We all can't be as cute as Cozette, as intelligent as Inga, and as low-key as me."

Under the "No Time to Dye" T-shirt, my cousin wore a pink satin blouse. She also wore rhinestone-studded jeans, and crystal earrings shaped like ghosts. A typical understated outfit for a week night. On weekends, she glammed up.

"You're low-key, Lou?" I asked.

"Sure, in a bedazzled sorta way. Why be a wallflower when ya can be a butterfly?"

"Ichabod Hall used to say that." I smiled.

"I know. That's why him and I hit it off right away."

"Speaking of Ichabod, I have news," Cozette said, eyes glowing. "I'll lock the door and tell you."

After glancing in the hallway and locking the door, Cozette returned to our table, moving fast on cat-like feet. Working in the shop plus playing pickleball had leveled up her fitness.

The Golden Promenade had a reverse-aging time machine in Doc Graves' office, or the activity agreed with her.

"Pauline's supplements and clothes aren't selling." Cozette waved toward the containers on the counter. "She sunk a fortune into them and pushes them on all of us. People suspect she's done something drastic as a result."

Lou whistled. "People kill for one of two reasons—passion or fashion."

"No, passion or *greed*," I corrected.

Cozette continued, "Residents gave her a chance. They love her pickleball classes, but she's so pushy she alienated many of us. There's a sense of desperation about her now."

Inga sighed. "I've experienced the same thing in the craft mall. She's tried to sell with us but refuses to sign our most basic sellers' contract. I can't let her join without one."

That was news to me, and perhaps another reason why Pauline didn't like me.

"Mel, you tangled with ornery bucks in the Big Apple," Lou said. "Why're people like that?"

"Usually, it's fear. Greed sometimes, too."

"No, it was passion or greed, ya said—"

"That's when it comes to murder. Fear can be overwhelming when people try something new, like selling a product. Risk-taking isn't easy. Especially when you're introducing new ideas into the marketplace."

Inga nodded. "I see it with our artists. That's why we offer beginners' workshops. Vendors can ask questions and learn from one another. Pauline refused to take those, too."

"So she's committin' crimes of fashion, passion," —Lou made a fist and tapped the table, rattling plates— "and hard-headedness?"

"Would that make her desperate enough to kill Ichabod?" I asked. "That's a big leap, and I don't see the motivation."

"Heck yeah—if Pauline's checkbook is howlin' like a wounded coyote, it is!" Lou tapped harder. "She committed a crime of fashion, passion, hard-headedness—*and greed*."

"No, people commit murder for one of two reasons: passion or greed," I said. "They commit the crime unplanned, in a frenzy of emotion. Or greed motivates them. They pursue money or a golden trinket of some kind."

"A gold trinket like jewelry!" Lou exclaimed. "A crime of *fashion*, like I said." She drew a shape in the air. "We've come full circle. Made a lap around the rodeo ring, and here we are."

Inga set down her mug. "Do you really think Pauline could have done it?"

Lou nodded vigorously. "Yep, if ya ask me, that cowgirl is a real tempest in a teapot."

INGA AND I OFFERED TO HELP CLEAN UP BUT WERE REBUFFED.

"No offense, but that's too many cowgirls in one small kitchen," Lou said, holding a tray of dirty plates. "A *pane* in the *glass*. We break stuff bumpin' into each other. You two talk. I know you both got the hots for fellas in uniform." She winked.

Inga laughed. "Let's step out to the deck, Mel. I need fresh air."

On the patio, we looked over the railing, the balmy air refreshing. The unusual "thundersnow front" wasn't due until morning. I stood on my tippy toes and moved up and down, stretching my calves.

It felt good to stand after sitting so long.

The glowing pumpkins decorating the trees had timed out, but an owl called, *DHOOT! DHOOT!*

"It's like we're on a cruise." Inga inhaled deeply. "Except I smell leaves and moist earth, not the sea. The meadow is deep blue water, and it almost feels like we're moving." She pointed toward town. "Look, there's the lights of Cinnamon."

"It's so bright, almost like New York City," I said. "Minus millions of people and an Empire State Building."

"You don't miss it?"

"Not at all."

"You're glad to be back?"

"Very."

She sighed. "Me, too. I've traveled, but I love my town. It's home."

"What about Todd Morgan? Does he like it here?"

"Goodness, no. His private jet is coming, and he'll be leaving soon. The county airstrip is just long enough, he says."

"He should alert our public works employee to cut the grass before landing, or he'll have to use Crites Field in Waukesha."

She smiled. It was dark, but I saw the bulge of her cheek from the side. "Todd is a city mouse, and I'm country," she said. "It would never work ... but can I tell a secret, Mel?"

"Sure."

"I'm having a fling, and I'll ghost him. *Soon.*"

My jaw dropped. "*You*, Inga?"

She started giggling, then grabbed my elbow. "Can you believe it? The dating game at the Golden Promenade brought out the panther in me!"

INGA MEANT "COUGAR." "A COUGAR IS A WOMAN WHO DATES A YOUNGER guy," I explained.

"I'm learning new dating terms," she said. "Todd teased about it because he's a few months younger than I. What do you call a woman who dates a handsome older fellow?"

I smiled. "Mel Tower."

She giggled again. So hard she had to wipe her eyes. "I heard another one. I think it applies to you and me—we're buckle bunnies."

I shook my head. "No, that's if you're into cowboys. We're into uniforms—we're badge bunnies."

She hooted. Loud as the owls. I started in, too, and our carefree chuckles echoed across the empty meadow. It was late, and we were giddy.

Lou must have heard us laughing.

After a minute, she stepped out. "What's so funny? I got a call in the kitchen about two gals causing a ruckus on the deck. They wanna know what's goin' on and called police. The cops are coming to get ya."

23

SATURDAY MORNING

In the dark, my phone rang.

Max was dialing again. Border collies will run the world soon. They're smart, adaptable, and have great style. Who doesn't love black and white? The dogs wear tuxedos All. The. Time. They're the James Bond of dogs— ring!

I leaned up on an elbow to look at the clock. Six a.m.

Ring!

"H-hello?"

"Hi, Mel. Sorry to wake you." *Cole.*

"H-hi." I flopped back to the pillow. Dropped the phone. "Oops."

"Need a minute? I can call back."

"No ... it's fine."

He paused. "Late evening?"

I nodded—which he couldn't see. "Yeah."

"Hon, I'll let you sleep. Ring me back when—"

"No, I need to get up." I yawned. "Late night with the girls."

"Did Lou keep you out again?"

"Yes, she never stops chattering ... residents at the Promenade almost ... called the cops on her, in fact."

"Let me guess: she talked her way out of *jail* by bribing the officer with pumpkin *bars*." He chuckled. "She's tried that on me a few times."

"You're funny in the morning."

"Part of the job. It's the first commandment of law enforcement: Thou Shalt Use Humor First, then Handcuffs."

"In Wisconsin, I thought it would involve cheese."

"My jokes are plenty cheesy, so there's that."

Thunder rumbled. Cold air blew across the dark bedroom, fanning the curtain. I'd cracked a window last night before hitting the sack. "I have to shut the window" —I yawned again— "and make coffee. May I call you back?"

"Sure thing. I'll be here."

I got up and drew back the drape. Lightning flashed in the distance—thundersnow was on its way.

Why would Cole call so early?

Something definitely was wrong.

I CALLED BACK AFTER MAKING A CUP OF INSTANT.

Cole answered, saying, "Keep to your cabins, lest assist the storm!"

I froze, my mug stuck in midair. "Why are you quoting *The Tempest?* Is that why you called earlier?"

"No, hon. I'm reading a playbill from the local theater group. Just got it in the mail. They're performing the play. I'll buy tickets if you want to go—"

"Please tell me what's going on, Cole."

He paused. "I'm coming back down to see you tonight. I'm leaving shortly, as fast as I can. The weather looks iffy."

"I know." I glanced out the window over the sink. "I'm in the kitchen looking out at the backyard. Weirdest sky I've ever seen. Orange, purple, and charcoal gray at the same time."

"I have a four-wheel drive. I'll bring my chains and use them if I have to."

"Snow chains in October?"

"It never hurts to be prepared."

"What else?" I didn't have to see Cole to know there was more. I could read his body language over the phone.

"I've texted a few times with Bruce DuWayne, and he's advising caution tonight. He released the venue so the fashion show could continue. He thinks life should return to normal after a tragedy, and I agree."

"Has he learned anything? Are the toxicology reports—"

"Nothing I can reveal. Those things take a while."

"What do *you* think?"

"There are enough suspicious characters around him to want him gone." He sighed. "The company managing his brand had sketchy financials from the limited intel I could gather."

"I see."

"What's that quote you like about fashion? That phrase you say?"

"Personal style is a simple way to say complicated things?"

"No."

"Trends come and go; be yourself on purpose?"

"Sounds like you, but no."

"I shop; therefore, I am?"

He laughed. "No, definitely not that one. You're the opposite of that."

"Hell is empty, and all the devils work in fashion?"

"Yes, that's it."

That was a paraphrase from Shakespeare, not words from a designer. It didn't matter. *Point taken.*

"Be careful, Mel," Cole said. "I've been in law enforcement a long time. Greed or passion motivate people to do awful things—even someone you'd never expect."

I drove to Fern's ranch under an orange-red sky, bringing
a care package from the Tool & Rye.
Greed and passion were on my mind—I hoped Fern would
offer ideas while we dined.
Fern's wise counsel I sought—she was a woman who
couldn't be bought.

I'm a poet, I know it.

Turning into the drive, the Saab's headlights bounced off the barn. Its lights were off, and the horses were already outside, munching hay in their paddocks.

Tulip lifted her giant head as I walked across the gravel to the house. She was so large compared with the others that she seemed unreal, like a Renaissance horse, a knight's mount. She nickered as though alerting the other animals a visitor had arrived.

I knocked. "Fern? It's Mel. I brought breakfast."

After a moment, I heard footsteps. Then she opened the door. No makeup, damp hair, bathrobe. She'd just gotten out of the shower. "Is everything okay?" she asked.

"Yeah, sure." I held up the box of goodies. "Max called and said you needed breakfast." My dog stood behind her, wagging his tail.

"I'm exhausted, Mel. And the sun's not even up yet."

"I've got fruit, egg and bacon sandwiches, and coffee. Donuts, too. Frosted pumpkin that are *a-glazing*, they said at the Tool & Rye."

She stepped back. "C'mon on in."

Fern's eyes brimmed with tears. "I'm sorry I haven't helped you. I let you down at the worst time. I just feel ... so alone."

"Like you're on an island?"

"Yes … how did you know?"

"It's been a theme this week."

"I've *never* struggled like this." She blew her nose into a tissue.

We sat at the butcher block table in the kitchen. I'd washed a couple plates for us, but otherwise, dirty dishes overflowed in the sink. Empty bottles of wine were on the counter.

Fern had been indulging in a red blend called *The Tempest*, believe it or not.

Okay—no.

She'd been drinking *Prospero*. A reference close enough to be ironic and spooky, which I didn't care about anymore.

The time had come to be brave. To figure out who had turned Boo Bash into Boo Bad. *To burn the ships, so to speak. Well, that action would leave one stranded on the island that caused this mess, but—*

"Mel, did you hear me?" Fern asked. "I can't shake this mood right now."

"It's okay. It will get better, I promise."

"How do you know?"

"Because I've felt it, too. A week ago, even. I felt weird, different. But when I lived in New York City, it was *way* worse. In that huge city, I'd never felt more alone in my life."

"What do you do?"

"Be a burr—thou shall stick, as it's said."

"*A burr?*"

I nodded. "It's a favorite Shakespeare quote. When I was alone, booking nothing, I'd tell myself to be a burr, to stick to my goals. I'd visualize my future, even when no one hired me. I was too commercial, too tall, too short. Whatever the fashion trend Eden Hoff identified, I was the opposite."

"But you made a long career out of it."

"Because I was a burr—I stuck to the industry like those things that grab saddle pads and horse tails." I laughed. "It worked."

"So what do I do?"

I patted her arm. "You reach out. Your mind is messing with you right now. It tells you to sleep. Be alone. Stare at the wall" —I nodded to the wine bottles— "or drink. Do the opposite: call your friends. Take a walk. Get to your doctor."

"I haven't had the energy to contact her."

"Do it, and I'll drive you to the appointment. We'll have fun afterward. Try something new."

She paused. "How about pickleball?"

"Sure."

"You'd try it with me?"

"Yeah, and our team name could be Island Girls. We'll prove you can move forward in life one *atoll* at a time."

She smiled. *Finally*. "I'm not sure ... how about Cinnamon Spices?"

"Already taken by Trudy and her ganstas. You don't want to fight them over it, believe me."

"We'll think of something."

"We will. You're resilient and smart, Fern. You've built a great life in this community, and you have loyal friends who'll help with one phone call." I paused. "No, you don't even need to call. Tie a note to a dove like you're on an island. Send her out. Someone will come."

"I believe you."

"This feeling shall pass, my friend."

Max came over to check on us. He looked from Fern's face to mine, his dark eyes intense, nose twitching. He probably thought the job of an emotional support dog was hard enough for one woman, let alone two.

It was okay, though.

There was plenty of Max to go around.

Fern and I cleaned her kitchen. She washed the dishes; I dried.

Max sat at the table, reading a veterinary textbook named *Healing Hugs*. The canine already *paw-ssessed* practical knowledge in the subject matter but wanted an advanced *dog-ree*.

"Thanks for letting Max stay with me," Fern said. "He is a comfort."

"It's okay if he stays the weekend? I won't be home much between the fashion show tonight and Reader's Theater tomorrow."

"Of course. Maybe I'll even make that doctor's appointment and bring Max. Help me slay this depression dragon." She handed me a plate. "I'm sorry I dumped the show on you."

"It's fine, Fern. Walking in the show is good, actually. It redeems my past. Helps *me* slay a dragon."

I didn't want to pester with questions about Bruce DuWayne— or stress her further by talking about the investigation.

To my surprise, she brought it up: "I'm worried about Bruce. He'd normally call me during a time like this."

"You'd discuss cases?"

She shrugged. "Not because we were dating; we weren't, technically. During a difficult case, he'd ask for advice. Public relations people have insight."

"Do you have an idea where he is? Was he staying in town?"

"No, he was driving from Madison. It's only an hour."

We finished the dishes and tidied the kitchen. I didn't ask more questions. I didn't want to worry my friend—*but Bruce DuWayne was missing*.

I was sure of it.

DRIVING BACK TO CINNAMON, I GRABBED MY PHONE OFF THE PASSENGER seat. I needed to call Cole. It rang instead.

Captain Rand.

I answered. "Hi."

"Mel, I'm standing on your front porch. I stopped by with coffee and *plane* bagels. Where are you?"

"Breakfast with Fern at the ranch."

"This early? Must have been a top secret mission." Wind blew across the mic on his phone; it sounded like paper crackling. "Wow, the weather's changing. Time to start bidding on warm destinations."

"When are you going home?"

"I leave Sunday night. We're still chaperoning Inga and Todd for Reader's Theater, right?"

"Sure."

"I wanted to ask: Would it be inappropriate to bring a date for the fashion show? Lou told me you're walking in it. I'd like to ask Pauline to attend, if that's okay."

If Rand was with Pauline, she couldn't pull any shenanigans, jets *in case she had something to do with Ichabod's death and Bruce's disappearance.*

Not a terrible development.

I flipped on my blinker, taking the quick route to town. "I'm okay with it."

"You're sure? I want to be considerate. It's awkward, I'm aware."

"Rand, I'm seeing someone, too. It's okay."

"Just checking," he said. "You're amazing, *fly* the way. Running successful businesses, starring in a fashion show—"

"I'm just one of the models. Not a star."

"You are to me. Oh, and you solve murders. Top flight, I think."

"Thanks." I shifted to fifth gear, pulling my phone away from my ear temporarily. "Are you and Pauline on the fast track? Or, is this relationship more of a slow boat?"

"I don't know. For now, I'd describe it as an indirect route."

"Do me a favor and don't lose her during the show."

"Excuse me?"

"I'm kidding—but do you trust her?"

He paused. "That's an odd question, but sure. I trust her to be an excellent pickleball partner. She's a good person once you get to know her."

"Gotcha."

"How many fashion models does it take to put on a successful show in Cinnamon?"

"No idea."

"Just one. Her name is *Mel*, and I think she's pretty *swell*."

I smiled. "Thanks, Rand."

"Break a leg, hon."

We hung up.

Rand was an excellent judge of character. Pilots go around the world. The job was OJT psychological evaluations with citizens everywhere.

If he trusted Pauline, I could—*never mind*. I had to decide for myself.

Instead of going back to town, I turned toward the Golden Promenade.

24

THE GOLDEN PROMENADE

Tony G. wasn't in. The gentleman I'd spoken with previously observed the monitors.

"Hi," I said. "My name is Mel, and I'm looking for Tony. Is he here?"

He leaned back in his chair. "You're a model in the show tonight. I heard about you."

"Well, there's about ten models—"

"You're gonna open the show. Your cousin Louella Jingle told everybody. She posted it in the *HORN BLAST!* newsletter." He pointed to a piece of paper on the counter. "You're wearin' quite a dress."

"I am?"

"Yeah, looks like it's half pontoon boat, half ballgown. No offense." He handed me the paper. "See for yourself."

Sure enough.

There was a picture of dress that Ichabod had cancelled, but Alicia Cliff had wanted because she'd made it—a voluminous, orange tulle Statement Dress. Like a wedding gown for dump truck.

A Halloween editorial garment too fantastically fussy for Ichabod's laidback style, and almost impossible to walk in.

Alicia took over the looks for the show and changed the order-of-go!

I had to get backstage.

"Will you tell Tony I'm looking for him?" I asked.

"Yes, ma'am. When he finally gets back. He's here, but no one will ever find him. He's somewhere in the passages of the building, battenin' down the hatches for the storm. He's gettin' salt and shovels out to where we need 'em."

I nodded. "I'll check back."

"Sure thing. Break a leg tonight. My wife and her friends can't wait for the show."

"THAT'S *NEVER* HOW THEY RUN THE PARADE OF CHAMPIONS AT THE Midwest Horse Fair, I'm tellin' ya!"

My cousin's voice resonated into the hallway. I entered the dressing area to find her arguing with Alicia Cliff.

Lou wore a pink satin blouse and jeans. Alicia wore a scowl, a look so fierce I worried she'd kill someone.

Lou stood by a rack of garments, rearranging them. "Open the show with a big number—an Appaloosa. A golden Palomino. Bold color with chrome. Get the crowd into it." She pointed to the wacky orange tulle dress. "Start off with a fancy number like that, a wide body. Then, tone it down with somethin' demure. A dark color. Gray, maybe—"

Alicia interrupted her. "I will not compare my fashion show with a horse parade. I will select garments that tell *my* fashion story!" She clenched her fists.

"I'm tryin' to help ya, Felicia," Lou said.

"It's Alicia!"

"Wait—is this *your* story? Or poor, dead Ichabod's?" Lou nodded toward me. "Look, Mel's here. She'll solve this. Hiya, cuz."

"Hi—"

"Tell Keisha you're wearin' that dress big as a chuckwagon, or you won't do the show." She threw up her hands. "Mel's a diva. Ornery. Like a mean, old pony but tall."

I sensed a setup. This conversation was over the top, even for Lou.

"Why was the order changed?" I asked.

Alicia's face was bright red. "To improve it. This show needs to reach its market. We need 'likes' and social media shares. Your cousin intruded—"

"Mel's not walkin' unless she gets to wear the crazy ballgown," Lou interrupted. "Who made that monster? The House of the Great Pumpkin?"

"*Get out!*" Alicia shrieked. "*Leave—now!*"

The Moon Cafe was closed, but Lou used her walkie-talkie to radio Cozette, who appeared like a magic spirit, and opened the place so we could talk.

I looked at the clock. Noon, but it felt like midnight. The cafe's dark wallpaper, starry ceiling, and orb sconces made time even more of a suggestion.

Cozette flipped on the coffee maker. The cafe began smelling like pumpkin spice and vanilla. "I love solving mysteries," she said "How'd the scheme go, Lou?"

She mounted a stool. "Alicia did it. I messed with those dresses, and she started in about makin' money. Oh, she got mad! It was like lockin' a hodag in a zoo."

"Cozette, did you put the picture and article in the *Horn Blast!*?" I asked.

"Yes," she answered gleefully. "Just before the deadline last evening. Wooly helped me write it."

"We cooked up this scheme after you left last night," Lou explained. "Next up is Nate Gould and Todd Morgan. We gotta lure them in somehow. Get 'em to show emotion, reveal themselves. See if it was a group thing—"

Cozette frowned. "I don't think they had anything to do with it. Todd wasn't here; his plane hadn't landed. And I point-blank asked Nate. He looked shocked and explained how the brand needed Ichabod *alive*."

"I dunno. We gotta bust this thing like a bull seein' a red flag." Lou looked at me. "You'll be our rodeo clown in that monster dress, Mel. Attract the bad guy, jump into a barrel for protection, and then Cozette and I will come out—"

"I won't be doing that, Lou."

"Seems like a solution to me. How else are we gonna flush out the killer?"

I heard a tap on glass. Someone was knocking on the slider doors. I turned to see Tony G., the security guard, standing outside.

"Will you let me in?" He pointed to the handles. "I got locked out!"

Tony was installed on a stool with a mug of vanilla-pumpkin coffee and a blanket over his shoulders. "*Grazie*, ladies. I was salting the deck, and the passageway door slammed and locked behind me."

"*No problemo*," Lou said. "What's the scoop? You hear any scuttlebutt about Ichabod's killer?"

"Nothing new, but I read in the newsletter that Mel's wearing a knockout dress tonight. *Bellissimo!*"

"*Bull-isimo* is more like it," she said. "That thing could work as a signal flag for rodeo stock."

"Tony, have you spoken to Bruce DuWayne lately?" I asked.

He sipped, then nodded. "Yesterday. He was delayed in Madison, and said he wouldn't be coming out."

"You spoke to him? Or texted?"

"Spoke, texted," Lou interjected. "Same thing these days."

Tony shook his head. "I don't remember. I'd have to check my phone. It's back in the office."

"Lou or Cozette?" I glanced between them. "Have either of you spoken to Bruce?"

"Yeah," Lou answered. "How about you, Coze?"

She paused. "A day or so ago."

"You spoke to him?" I asked. "Or just texted—"

"Mel, if ya spoke, talked, texted, or FaceTimed, it's the same these days." Lou pulled out her cell phone. "These things do it all."

"No, I'm asking if you *spoke* to him—"

She looked around. "Yeah, we all *spoke* to him."

"Did you *see* Bruce—"

"I thought you were keepin' track of him. Or Fern Bubble was."

"No—"

"You guys lost him? How do you lose track of a detective in charge of a case?" She pointed to Cozette and Tony. "*We* didn't—we talked to the guy."

"Did you *talk* to him? Or text him?"

"It's the same thing!"

My cousin wore a long scarf around her neck. A quick yank, and I could strangle her with it.

I didn't, of course.

Too many witnesses.

I talked with Tony before he left. "I haven't been able to physically locate Bruce, but he'd want to be here tonight. Detectives observe suspects in their element. Will you contact him?"

Tony nodded. "Sure, I'll get him here."

Lou slammed a hand to the counter. "I just thought of somethin'! Have we seen Todd Morgan and Bruce DuWayne in the same room?" She looked between us. "Nope, we have not. That's why he vanished. Todd shows up, Bruce goes missin' *because they're the same person*."

Again, too many witnesses for me to act.

Before we broke huddle, Lou gave advice: "I gotta get to the kitchen and make snackies for after the show. Cook up a storm. Speaking of, we're expecting a smaller crowd cuz of the weather, Tony?"

He nodded. "It likely will be just the Promenade residents. Not many outsiders want to drive with the forecast."

"Got it," she said. "I'll only make half the double batches of everything, then. Keep it light on the buffet." She tapped her temple. "Cozette, you got the master plan stored away in that brain of yours?"

"Sure do. I *love* mysteries."

"What master plan?" I asked.

"The party tricks we cooked up for tonight. Flush the bad guy—or gal—out from underneath a rock. Or skirt, given that it's a fashion show."

"No, you shouldn't—"

"Speakin' of skirts, you're not nervous about walkin' in that nightmare dress?" she asked. "Not worried about trippin' on the runway in front of the crowd? Fallin' flat for everybody to see?"

"Not until you mentioned it, Lou."

"Good, wouldn't want to psyche ya out."

I paused. "We don't know that Alicia Cliff will use that dress to open the show."

"She will, by golly! The whole place is buzzin', can't wait to see it. It was splashed in color on the front page of the newsletter. You know how the fashion press is; they'll kill her if she doesn't show it. And the best part is, *you're gonna wear it, Mel.*"

TONY LEFT TO CONTINUE WITH STORM PREP. COZETTE STAYED IN THE CAFE, locking the door after Lou and I departed on the elevator.

I recalled the time we rode up to the Gold Deck after Ichabod was found—how had that been only days ago?

A *HORN BLAST!* newsletter was posted in the glass display case near the buttons. Lou waved toward it. "Great, huh? Cozette posted 'em everywhere. You're not afraid to wear that dress? I've heard of models goin' top over teakettle on the runway."

That scarf she wore was only arm's distance from me—

The elevator dinged, then stopped at the Lido Deck. Pauline Pickle stood in the lobby.

"Paula, just the cowgal we wanted to see." Lou held the doors. "Hop on."

"It's *Pauline.*"

"Sorry, Mel told me wrong. Come aboard. We wanna talk."

She stepped on. The sweat set she wore was outstanding. The stretchy black pants and jacket with pearl trim was eye-catching, comfortable yet stylish.

Pauline's Ball Bash clothing line could be an excellent seller for the right audience.

"Pauline, your outfits are killer," Lou said. "Present circumstances not withstandin'."

"Thank you."

"You ever consider puttin' 'em in the fashion show?" Lou smiled. "You could call it the 'Paulapalooza'."

"I just tried," she said. "Alicia Cliff would have none of it."

Lou's eyes widened. "She's still alive, isn't she? You left her standin'?"

"*Of course.*"

"Sorry, just making sure. We got a crab apple somewhere in the buildin'. A shark among the minnows. A fish hook in the party dip—"

"She gets it, Lou," I said.

"Pauline, if you're interested, Mel knows people in the rag trade. She can hook you up. She knows important stuff like ROI and IPOs."

"Not quite," I said, "but unique regional brands are the hottest thing in fashion."

"Yeah, Mel's got an office downstairs among the barnacles. *Alone.* It's like hangin' out in a cabin in the woods with nothin' around but hodags. Skedaddle down there if you wanna meet with her."

Pauline shook her head. "I will figure out my fashion business on my own, thank you."

She jabbed a button on the elevator panel. The car shuddered to a stop, and Pauline stepped out.

She wore tennis shoes. Trendy black slip-ons that camouflaged noise. Her walk amazed me; the woman moved silently as a cat.

After the doors closed, I scolded Lou: "That office was a temporary cubby hole. I'll clean out a few personal things, then turn in my key. If Pauline wants to talk, she can come to the craft mall."

"Sorry, Mel. Didn't mean to set ya up for an ambush in the basement and not tell ya. It was Cozette's idea to trap the bad guy." She lowered her voice. "When ya move out, do *not* go alone. Take Tony the security guard. Never know what could happen."

25

CINNAMON, LATER

Fair is foul, foul is fair.
Hover through fog and spooky air.

SHAKESPEARE AGAIN. MACBETH THIS TIME.

I paraphrased the line while driving through Cinnamon. Cruising Main Street was like driving through soup. Weather conditions preceding thundersnow were eerie.

Fog had descended. The shoppers on Main Street look like ghosts. Obscure forms moved through the mist, carrying bags that seemed to float by themselves. Smaller forms, mini-ghosts, swung pumpkins that twinkled. Treat containers with glow sticks, no doubt.

School was closed for fall break. The minis haunted Main Street businesses with their parents. A chill of little goblins—wasn't "chill" the perfect collective noun?—emerged from Hank Leigel's office. They flowed out the door to the sidewalk. I slowed as a precaution, pressing the clutch, the car's engine rumbling. The conditions made it difficult to see if a ghost wandered off like a lost duckling.

I turned left, then right, driving down the alley toward the bookstore parking space. I searched for the sign showing a ghost carrying a book, a funny Halloween placard drawn by Crystal. My store manager was so creative!

I parked, tooted the horn, and got out. I shut the car door hard. *SLAM!* The noise scared away demons, I hoped.

"Melanie, good afternoon."

"Oh—who's there!" I yelled.

"It's Swan. Sorry to frighten you."

He approached from behind the car. I hadn't seen him in the alley. It was like he flew over, landed behind the buildings, then folded in wings.

"I have news to share," he said. "I must leave Cinnamon."

"By car? Or magic carpet?" I asked.

"Covered wagon." He smiled, and his dark eyes twinkled like stars.

"Lou may be able to help with that."

"She could. Please give her my best. I won't see her before I depart."

"Headed back to Mt. Olympus, are you?"

"Gotham. I'm needed at White Owl Holdings. There's been a development." He frowned, and thunder rumbled, the *boom-booms* underscoring his statement.

No, just kidding—but it should have. What development? A change in leadership because a bigwig faced a murder charge?

"What's going on?" I asked.

"I cannot say."

"Sure you can. It's me, your buddy Mel." I punched his bicep. Felt like hitting granite. Or Lou's forehead. "Tell me. Fashion makes strange bedfellows, remember."

"Ah, a reference to *The Tempest*," he said. "But the phrase is '*misery* makes strange bedfellows,' is it not?"

"Not where you're headed. In Gotham, they say it differently."

"I shall miss your humor."

"You don't have to. Stick around. Big show tonight." I smiled.

"I'm in it, and there's karaoke afterward. But if you tried it, they'd call it opera."

"I must leave ... Melanie, you have done well."

"What does that mean?" I asked.

"Be not afraid, my friend," he said. "Though the isle is full of noises. Sounds, and sweet airs, that give delight ... and *not* hurt."

I swear Swan vanished after that. The man moved back, his wings unfolded, then he lifted to the sky, disappearing into the mist like a phantom. Swan was a friendly ghost who bequeathed wisdom and then disappeared.

What had he meant?

I sensed I'd find out.

I entered the Bell, Book & Melville via the backdoor. A bell jingled —*that was new.*

Crystal was descending the steps from the apartment. "Every time a bell rings, a ghost gets her crown. She already can fly, so no need for wings."

"I thought you'd say a book." I studied the bell, squinting up at it.

"I hope you don't mind. I found it in the apartment and installed it. It was used in the store at one time, I'm sure."

"It's great. An alarm, but cheerful. Very Wisconsin-like."

"Your friend was here."

I nodded. "We chatted in the alley."

'What do you think about it?" She reddened, and her bright cheeks reminded me of a kid at Christmas.

No, wrong holiday.

"About what? Whatever it is, it's swell according to your body language."

"I *would* love to move in upstairs," she said. "And, like, have a design studio."

"What—*no*."

"Oh ... you don't like it." She sighed. "I get it. I'm being forward. I'm just tired of living with mom, and I don't have a studio—"

"That's not it." I stared up the steps. "It's haunted, isn't it?"

"Sure!" she said. "That's why I *love* it."

AN ASSISTANT WATCHED THE SHOP SO CRYSTAL AND I COULD CHECK OUT THE apartment.

Before ascending the staircase, she visited the display case near the register. "I'll take up a black tourmaline to shield us from negative energy. Would you like a stone, too?"

"Do you have a heavy rock in that case? I'll use it to knock the ghost over the head—"

"No, Mel. We'll have none of that," she said.

Crystal was acting like she'd moved in. *Good.* Confidence was everything when starting out.

Upstairs, I stared out the front room window that overlooked Main Street. On nice days, light flooded in, bathing the space in a golden glow. "You're not worried about ghosts?" I asked. "Or thundersnow?"

The fog was dissipating, and thick, black clouds hovered over the buildings. They looked like giant, puffy warlocks. The wind blew down the street, and the trick-or-treaters' costumes tangled around their little legs.

Behind me, Crystal laughed. "If a ghost lives here, I'll *lift* his *spirits* with positive energy. When Edith Mackie said it was a good idea—"

"She was the person who suggested this?" *I assumed it had been Swan.*

The young woman nodded. ""She talked about how the fashion business needs original voices and ethically sourced fabrics. Repurposed fabrics, too." She smiled, though her eyes were fierce, determined. "I can do that."

"Yes, you can," I replied.

Wow, agreeing about the apartment for Crystal was the only time editor Eden Hoff and I had been on the same page—how long did the woman plan to stay? What if she was moving here? That was a catwalk too far!

How was she getting around the village? A broom, probably. Or a rental car. Something out-of-this-world. A Volkswagen Beetle *Juice*, no doubt.

"I'm proud of you, Crystal," I said. "If you're not afraid of a ghost, and you're willing to put in the time and effort to become a designer —or an artist, or whatever you choose—you can do it."

She smiled. "The bookstore and this apartment are like my sanctuary, *my* quiet place. They're my little island in the middle of everything."

INGA CAME UP THE STEPS CARRYING BOXES. I'D TEXTED HER EARLIER ABOUT needing some to empty my office at the Promenade.

Like a magician, Inga showed up with several. She set them on the floor. "Here are those boxes, Mel. Hello, Crystal."

The young woman grinned. "Hi, Inga. That color looks fire on you."

"It's nothing. A coat and scarf I've had for years."

"No, that scarf is new," I interjected. "It was knit by an artist in the mall—"

"Inga's got a *bae*," Crystal said.

She shook her head. "This time of year, he's better described as a *boo*."

"You're lookin' hot. Did you, like, get your lips done? This guy brought out the she-wolf in you."

"Wait—I thought the term was cougar."

Crystal clapped. "Your new man is younger? *Go for it, girl.*"

"Only by a few months. Todd Morgan is a nice fellow, but not for me. He'll be returning to New York shortly. Fun while it lasted, but I'm ghosting him."

"Naw, you won't—you'll mail a hand-penned card wishin' him well. Next, you'll put him on your birthday card list."

"Of course I will, but the term works for the season, does it not?" She smiled.

I tensed at the mention of Todd Morgan. He still was on the list of suspects in Ichabod's death. An outlier, but I wanted Inga to be cautious. "You're not seeing him again until Reader's Theater, right? Rand and I will be with you."

"Correct."

"You and *Rand*, Mel?" Crystal asked. "What's goin' on with that?"

"We're chaperones. Long story."

"Gotcha, yeah." She nudged Inga. "Will he be wearin' his uniform that night? I know how you two are about those."

Inga giggled. "We're badge bunnies—isn't that hilarious?"

"Everybody's got a type, for sure. Uniforms. Suits. Jeans. Cowboy hats."

I cleared my throat. "Or delivery uniforms."

Crystal's fellow, Steven, was Cinnamon's courier ace. The village could barely function without him cruising the streets in his yellow van. The place had lost some of its magic without him these past few days.

She laughed. "That makes me a delivery boy bunny, I guess. Can't hide it. Word's out—I got a type, too!"

Upstairs in my bedroom, I pulled a black bag from the closet. I hadn't touched the carry-all in years. It was an ancient Lands' End duffle with my initials embroidered on it.

It had been a gift from Inga years ago. "This is your model bag," she'd said. "Every model needs one. Do the research and figure out what goes in it. *You can do it, Mel.*"

That had been her way of pushing me from the nest. Telling me I had to swim—or I would sink in the Big Apple.

Manhattan was an island.

Ironic.

The idea plagued me this week.

I'd felt isolated when I'd worked in New York. This week, I'd discovered an island was of one's making, no matter where home was. And an island wasn't always a bad thing. One person's loneliness was another's solace.

The windows of my bedroom rattled. Frozen ice pelted the glass. Temps had dropped, yet lightning flashed.

Thundersnow had arrived.

No matter, the show must go on.

I filled the duffle with items a model needs. Not everything was provided at fashion shows. A professional model brought a hairbrush, hand wipes, and safety pins. Her own lip balm and mascara. Nude underwear and a strapless bra. A pair of heels, too.

There also was a thing called a comp card, a model's business card. A half-sheet of photos including a "digital," a black and white image of a model wearing a T-shirt and jeans. Measurements were listed, also.

If a model showed up at a casting and the measurements differed, things got crazy, believe me.

I'd seen many girls sent away in tears when the comp card and her actual size didn't match. The business could be brutal.

In the insular modeling world, the devil always was in the details.

26

THE GHOSTLY GALA

I parked near the porticoed entrance. Few cars were in the lot. The nasty weather kept townsfolk from driving out and attending the show.

This one would be for residents only.

I was okay with it.

The car's headlights pointed toward the meadow. The mound where the perc tests had been conducted stood out. An eyesore of a hill, sure—but a decent place for a photoshoot. Especially featuring that ginormous dress I had to wear.

A savvy editor would see that mound of dirt, the meadow with its glowing Halloween decor beyond, and the flashing, wild sky. She'd declare: "Lights, camera, action! We've got the perfect dress, the perfect season, and a great location for an editorial shoot. Let's get set up. This is outstanding!"

Eden Hoff would recognize it.

I gave the woman credit. A good editor captured moments. Fashion was about creating unforgettable images on film and influencing society. There'd been so many: The supermodels in white T-shirts by Peter Lindbergh. "Le Smoking" by Laurent, which introduced a man's jacket for womenswear. Dior's "New Look," a full skirt against a narrow waist, a design suggesting elegance and femininity for the post-war years.

Now, society set its own fashion rules. It was great to be an individualist while supporting locally made garments and regional designers.

Eden Hoff saw that, too, apparently.

Perhaps her attitude about fashion, models, and life was changing and softening—like mine.

I ENTERED THE GUARD'S OFFICE CARRYING MY MODEL BAG AND BOXES. "HI, Tony. Do you mind if I store these boxes here? I'll clean out my office tonight, but do the show first—"

"Mel, just the person I need to see. Let's walk down now. I'll carry your stuff." He took me by the elbow, ushering me toward a door.

"What's wrong?" I asked.

"Give me the boxes and the bag. You first."

"Wait—"

"No, let's go. Now."

"Tony—"

"Open the door to the passage. Now, Mel. It's urgent."

Before I could refuse, I was in the dark hallway—alone—with Tony.

It happened so fast.

"I'm *not* comfortable with this." I pressed my body against the wall, bracing my legs, locking my knees. The concrete block felt … like concrete.

He'd grabbed my bag and stuffed it in a box. The bag contained my cell phone and my only weapon, a shaker of fish fry seasoning, extra spicy.

It was a gag gift from Lou because I don't cook! The shaker had a pour spout pressured like a fire hose—it was all I had, okay?

He dropped the boxes and moved toward me. "We have to talk, Mel. Not in the office. I don't want anyone to overhear."

I shoved him back. "You stay on the port side of this passage. I'll stay here, starboard."

"I don't know what to do—I guard older folks. My usual mission is finding a lost wallet in the Whoopee Den."

"What's wrong, Tony?"

"It's Bruce DuWayne. He's missin', for sure. Guys are coming from Madison, but it'll be a while. The roads are slowin' everybody down."

"He's missing? Where?"

Tony's brow wrinkled. "If they knew that, he'd *not* be missing, Mel."

Good point.

"When was the last time he was seen?" I asked. "Glimpsed his physical person—not a text."

"Two days … maybe?"

"Do you think he's here?"

"No—I've watched constantly. Cameras are on in the atrium, the ballroom, and the Lido Deck. If someone got him, I'd know."

"So someone … dispatched Bruce … off property?" I hesitated to ask—*I didn't want to say murder.*

"Most likely," Tony said.

Where could the detective be? A barn somewhere? *Doubtful.* Our local farmers were diligent. With it being fall harvest, their barns were beehives of activity. A stranger wouldn't get past a busy farmer, their hands, or their watchdogs.

What about my mall? It had a storage space with closets and cubbies by the loading dock. But it was monitored by Inga and cameras—*again, doubtful.*

Main Street? No vacancies. Hank Leigel ensured it. The man bought, sold, and rented places like a realtor-magician. Same for the apartments above the businesses. All of them were occupied—*except mine.*

I refused to believe my apartment had nothing except the ghost of a shoemaker.

Crystal, Inga, and I had just been there—had we been alone? Maybe not!

"Give me my bag, Tony," I said. "When help arrives, have someone check the apartment over my bookstore. I'll give you the key and entry code."

"Sure thing." He dropped the boxes and handed it over. "The show can go on tonight. I'd prefer if it did. Everybody will be accounted for in the ballroom, safe in one place. The models came in earlier today. I won't let anyone else in, other than volunteers."

"Sheriff Cole Lawrence is on his way. No idea when he'll arrive," I said. "One person is coming you may not know: Rand Cunningham. He'll be with Pauline. If anything happens, count on him to help."

Tony pulled a pad from a pocket. I gave Rand's number and description: "He's tall, blue eyes, square jaw. Authoritative. Drives a Boeing Triple-Seven compact."

Tony stopped writing. "Huh?"

"Kidding, sorry. I joke when I'm stressed."

"Fear not, Mel. The catwalk of life never runs smooth. We'll find Bruce."

Tony knew Shakespeare? Who knew?

"Let's pray for the best," I said.

Tony gave directions to the ballroom's backstage via the passage, pointing to the metal staircase ahead. "Up one flight, take a right. Walk around to the door marked 'Globe Entrance.'"

"As in Shakespeare's Globe? Really?"

He winked. "I can joke, too. Look for 'Backstage.'" He nodded to the boxes. "I'll drop these by your office. Break a leg, Mel."

I turned, grabbed the doorknob, and fled the passage like a baby seal escaping a shark—who wanders a dark hallway when a killer is loose and a detective is missing?

Not Mel Tower. She was never a supermodel, but she had superpowers of self-preservation!

The ballroom was one floor above the atrium. Gracefully curved staircases rose to the second level; a glass half-wall provided a view to below.

I walked up the steps, staying close to the outside, my shoes barely audible on the marble stairs—*click, click, click.* I padded across the carpet to stand behind a Halloween decoration, a giant, inflatable cheese curd dressed as a ghost.

No, it was a palm tree with orange twinkle lights, sorry. The Golden Promenade was much too classy for giant inflatables.

The palm's trunk was too narrow to hide me. I stood there anyway. My dress was the same security blanket, cashmere gem I wore when finding Ichabod. It provided comfort—and semi-invisibility, I hoped.

A small crowd had gathered in the atrium. More attendees flowed in, looking cheerful, unaware of tension behind the scenes, of course.

If there was an argument for staging fashion shows to audiences beyond New York City, this was it.

Older ladies, silver swans, gathered in small groups, or "ballets." They admired one another's outfits. The star of one flock was a sassy senior in a sparkle tracksuit, her walker painted glossy black with a mini disco ball on its handlebar. She pressed a button on a keypad, and the ball rotated and glittered.

The swan's outfit was from Pauline's collection, no doubt—she should be walking in the show!

Gentlemen also gathered. A few wore suits, some with Halloween bowties. Others wore sport coats and pressed slacks. They looked handsome, smiling as though attending a real "senior" prom.

Their confidence was contagious. Their happiness affected me.

Fashion didn't make up for character. Or any virtue. But seeing the seniors' delight at attending a style event warmed my heart. I saw the industry from the point of view of those affected by what they wore.

It changed me. I felt like a fashion witch transforming into an angel.

No, not that—*Victoria's Secret already did it.*

I was a fashion ambassador, a voice for cheering on local designers—

"Pst, Mel. Over here!"

I looked around. Two women stood behind a twin-stemmed palm tree.

Lou waved an orange bandana.

Cozette stage-whispered my name: "Mel—we have news!"

WHAT DOES ONE CALL A GROUP OF AMATEUR SLEUTHS?

A "joke," that's what.

Yes, the little-known name for a cluster of amateur sleuths gathered in a hidden passageway in the Golden Promenade was "You Must Be Kidding."

Lou and Cozette dragged me to the catacombs. We exited via a camouflaged door, a life-sized painting of Bela Lugosi in *Count Dracula.*

We stood in a huddle in the catacombs.

Lou spoke first. "Alicia Cliff is missin'."

She glanced at Cozette, then me.

"What'd you do with her?" I asked.

Cozette said, "Nathan Gould and Todd Morgan aren't gone. They're here. Safe and sound."

"Yeah, they're fine," Lou confirmed. "Came into the kitchen. Sampled my deviled eggs for the afterparty. Loved 'em. Said they couldn't wait—"

"What did you do to Alicia?" I interrupted. "What scheme and whose idea?"

"Lou's—"

"Cozette's—"

I spoke through clenched teeth: "The show goes on in an hour. *Where is she?*"

"She'll be back," Cozette said. "Try not to worry."

"Yeah, she's not *that* mad; it was an act, I suspect," Lou said. "Alicia threw a tantrum after we gave suggestions. We tag-teamed her. Told her she should add somethin' with dolman sleeves, you know, batwings." She waved the bandana.

"Or white smocking," Cozette added. "Something in ghost-chic."

"We used fashion slang to get her dander up."

Cozette rolled her eyes. "Boy, did we ever."

"Yeah, when she got that seam ripper and came at us—"

"Who else witnessed this?" I asked.

"Pauline."

"She got a kick out of it—"

I held up a hand. "Never mind. Where could Alicia be?"

"She's stayin' off-ship in the Island House," Lou said. "She's probably cryin' in her eye-of-newt-soup."

I glanced between them. "The two of you get on your brooms, get over there, and apologize. A stage manager can run the show, but someone needs to represent the brand and give the curtain speech. *Get her back here.*"

As soon as they left, I realized my mistake. Sending the Inspectresses Clouseau to Alicia's guest residence was a bad idea. Not only because of the weather. A man had been killed and a detective was missing.

Lou and Cozette could walk into danger. It wasn't good that Alicia was there alone, either.

I texted Lou:

> Don't go inside. Apologize. Ask her to return with you. Then ALL OF YOU get back here!

Before leaving the passage, I waited a minute to ensure the text went through. No delivery failure emoji.

I also checked for a message from Cole. Nothing. He must be driving.

My phone tinged. Lou wrote back:

> Don't worry, cuz. We'll hogtie her and drag her back like a runaway calf if we have to. Sorry for messing up the show. Snowy out here—can barely see my broom, LOL. Can't wait to see ya in that dress. Break a leg, Mel!

The devil doesn't wear Prada.

He wears a slim-fit suit with an orange carnation pinned to the lapel.

Nathan Gould stalked the hallway. He wanted to come backstage, but I stopped him. Gould was new to the industry and didn't know models were changing, probably.

It didn't matter.

Decades ago, it enraged me when outsiders attempted to get backstage before the women were dressed.

I'd had no control over it then.

Now? Not on my watch!

I wore the gigantic orange dress. It took a prayer to the Zipper Gods and two dressers to get me into it.

"Where's Alicia?" Gould demanded. "We need her. This show has to go on!"

"Calm down," I said. "The stage manager knows the order-of-go. The polka band is ready. The models have practiced. Hank Leigel stepped in as emcee. We're great given the circumstances."

"Ichabod is dead. This show is cursed. The brand is cursed!" He pulled a flask from his coat pocket. "We never should have come here. The clothes should have walked in Chicago. They have cell phone service there, at least!" He gulped from the flask.

"It is *not* cursed. It's a heritage collection with an audience that will respond. Give it time—"

"Do you understand private equity? Time is money!" He stopped walking. "Look at what you're wearing. Who would buy that?"

I fluffed the skirt. It rippled like an orange ocean. "Do you understand editorial fashion? It's not meant for purchase. It's for attention."

"Attention from who? The Coast Guard? *Pumpkin Patch Bazaar?*"

Why was he so angry?

I evaluated Gould's body language, comparing it to his behavior before Ichabod died and Bruce DuWayne disappeared. His forehead dripped sweat. He paced the floor—*clap, clap, clap*. The man's footfalls sounded flat. A hard *slap!* to the concrete as though his feet lacked arches.

Fern Bubble was in PR, like Nathan Gould.

I recalled what she said about horses' movement: "Prized show animals don't make noise as they move around the arena. They're silent as cats. You never hear them coming. They sneak up and float right past."

Someone snuck up on Ichabod Hall.

A toxicology report was due on the designer. Yes, he'd sampled the buffet—but he hadn't died from tainted cheese curds, by being "breaded." The earth would crack like peanut brittle, and the mountains would fall into the fondue before anyone sabotaged Louella Jingle's snack bar.

Someone snuck up on Ichabod Hall.

I watched Nathan Gould.

He wasn't silent. Or cat-like. He was tense, loud, and a drinker.

Why was he so angry?

That emotion was different. Nerves, probably.

Or was it something else?

27

THE CATWALK

Through a slit in the curtain, I peeked at the audience.

The ballroom buzzed, and the polka band tooted "Hexenhaus." In English, "Hex House," a spooky oompah perfect for the moment.

The house lights flickered, then died. The crowd *oohed*.

The pumpkin globes hanging from the ceiling still twinkled because they were battery-powered. Same for the tall candelabras in the corners and the running lights along the catwalk. The ballroom glowed orange for about a minute.

The chandeliers re-lit quickly, thank goodness.

The moment proved thundersnow was unpredictable.

Showtime was in a few minutes.

I saw Captain Rand and Pauline in the crowd. He was a head taller than anyone else, his handsome face a friendly island in a silver sea.

Nathan Gould paced in the back, still upset, obviously. He moved between the wide entrance to the room and a door for the service workers, passing Tony G., who stood near the entrance, monitoring the crowd.

Todd Morgan sat near the runway, looking authoritative, like a ship's captain. Like he owned the show, which he did.

Eden Hoff was near him, still in disguise.

It was a relief to see her. It was surreal that the famous editor would see me on a runway in Cinnamon—ironic.

She'd been hiding in plain sight all along. Swan had claimed he'd been residing in the suite on the Gold Deck, but it had to be Eden. He'd fibbed; it was the only *time I'd ever known him to lie. He did it to protect her. Probably because he knew someone was setting her up.*

Swan was loyal that way.

Where he'd stayed was still a mystery to me. Did he even need a room?

Perhaps, like Prospero, he'd used magic to solve the issue.

Sheriff Cole hadn't arrived yet, from what I could see. And Alicia Cliff was still missing.

The house lights flickered. On purpose, this time.

"Places, everyone!" The stage manager called out. "Time for final makeup and hair. Put your cell phones away. We're walking in five minutes!"

Securing valuables was a problem during shows. Models carry personal items like everyone else. Wallets, phones, IDs, and subway cards.

Shows were put on in a tent or temporary venue, usually. Lockers were rarely available.

I'd heard plenty of horror stories: Personal items didn't just "walk" away. Designer bags, jewelry, and shoes disappeared, too.

That was another reason I'd worn vintage, understated clothes when I'd worked in New York. No one wanted my Plain-Jane attire.

In my model bag were car keys and a wallet. There was a small

room where our things would be locked up. It had been Ichabod's—
and then Alicia's—working space, too.

I waited for other models to store their items. Then, I entered the
room. Given the poofy tent I wore, only one of me could fit at a time.

I placed my bag under the desk. Despite my misgivings about the
orange dress, it had pockets, a place to hide my phone buried in the
layers of tulle. No one would see it, and Alicia Cliff wasn't present to
tell me I couldn't.

I checked for messages before tucking it by my hip. Cole wrote
that he was close:

> Roads are bad. Almost there!

Lou had written, too:

> Melanie, all is well. We'll be there shortly.
> Have an excellent show—break a leg.

THE BAND PLAYED NOTES FROM "THE ADDAMS FAMILY" THEME SONG, THE
cue we were seconds from walking.

Behind me was a row of models. Women from agencies in the
area. They were tall, short, all ages and sizes. Delightfully diverse.
Ichabod Hall's line of garments was perfect for such an audience.

The models' dresses were stylish, comfortable, and sewn with
natural fabrics. Mine was the exception—but as everyone knows,
there's one in every crowd.

I thought Pauline Pickle's sportswear line would blend seam-
lessly with the Hall Collection if she and White Owl Holdings could
form a partnership.

In front of me, the curtain was closed. The stage lights blazed,
and slivers of light seeped under the seams of the heavy drapes,

flowing like white water. It was so bright it looked like liquid set afire.

When the curtain parted, I'd be tempted to blink. My eyes would reflex at the contrast between the dark backstage and the hot stage lights.

It would sting, be painful, but models were experts in facial control.

Mel Tower would not blink.

She'd walk—*clack, clack, clack*—because the show must go on.

Then, she'd change out of a wacky editorial dress and solve a mystery.

A DRESSER FLOOFED MY SKIRT ONE LAST TIME AND SILENTLY STEPPED AWAY.

The curtain opened.

The stage manager spoke into the mic on her headset, then looked at me. "We're ready. Go!"

I waited a beat, allowing my eyes to adjust. The running lights along the catwalk twinkled; spots blazed down from above.

No blinking, Mel.

I dropped my shoulders, lifting the crown of my head as though pulled up by an invisible string.

Face neutral, no tension in the mouth or brow.

I focused on my core, where the power of my stride was; I engaged my lower back and rolled my pelvis forward, leading my body hips first toward the runway.

Clack, clack, clack.

The full skirt of the dress brushed my legs. A toe grazed fabric as my leg swung forward.

Don't get a heel caught—do not *break a leg!*

My arms fell to my sides, light and relaxed.

Breathe. Find a focal point.

Looking forward, I found someone to concentrate on, a person in the ballroom. Someone I knew was guilty.

I stared, my expression neutral. The show was about the clothes, not me—and the person who did it.

Clack, clack, clack.

Breathe, Mel.

Don't let anyone know *you* know.

Keep walking. Face forward, shoulders down.

Clack, clack, clack.

If there ever was a time to be a mannequin, the show in the Grand Salon was it. I couldn't reveal from the runway that I'd solved the crime of who killed Ichabod Hall.

28

FINAL LOOK

Other models had multiple looks.

I had one, the giant pumpkin dress, because getting in and out of it was a nightmare.

I completed my trip around the ballroom and returned to the back, entering via a side curtain like a plane dispatched on a mission and returning to base.

"Nice job," a dresser said. "Wait at the back for the Final Look, then we'll re-walk the entire collection. Alicia's coming to take a bow, but if she's not here soon, Todd Morgan will do it."

I nodded. "Fine."

I spied scissors on the dresser's folding table. When the dresser focused on the model after me, I swished over, grabbed the shears, and ... slipped them ... into a ... pocket.

Darn, it was hard to find in all the layers of fabric—it was like fighting a ghost!

I moved to the back of the room. The lights were dim, and no one watched me because they looked at the models, the front curtain, and the show.

There was a door I sought. A secret exit—*there!*

I gathered the voluminous skirt in an arm, yanked open the portal, and disappeared.

Did you hear about the fashion show in a dark passage with only two people and no audience?

It was a *waist* of time.

I heard footsteps. *Clack, click, clack, click.*

Someone was coming.

I pulled out the shears and cut the tulle, freeing my legs. "I know you did it!—I'm going to the police!" I yelled.

Clack … click.

The person stopped.

I had a head start. But the person would gain on me *fast*. I had to draw them away from the show and the ballroom. What if they had a gun?

I moved quick as possible. An editorial garment was *not* built for speed. I turned around once but couldn't see. The *clack, click* footballs began again, echoing in the desolate hallway.

There was an exit I sought. It opened out to the atrium, a place to draw them out, where I could fight back. Someone would see us, too, and I could yell for help.

Clack, click.

They were getting closer.

I found a staircase and scurried down—had Cole arrived? I hoped so!

There—a door!

I pushed on the metal bar. Wind slapped my face.

Agh! Wrong door!

I was outside by the pool. The muumuu swirled, tangling my legs. I stepped on the hem. Got a heel stuck. I was going down—*grab something!*

The pool deck was dark except for decor: pumpkins, light strings, ghosts on lawn furniture. I reached for a tree for balance. No, it was fake—*crash!*

Down I went, plastic branches covering me, slamming my head.

I scrambled, fabric ripping, the flimsy tree cracking.

Get up, Mel! Run!

WHAT DOES A FORMER MANNEQUIN DO UNDER DURESS?

She plays one!

I had seconds before my pursuer emerged from the exit—I threw off the plastic branches and crawled to the nearest recliner. I flopped down next to a ghost, a fellow who, underneath his white sheet, felt like straw bales.

Not the dangerous ones that nearly squished me in Fern's barn, I hoped!

No matter. I cuddled with the "guy" like I'd awakened from a nightmare. The reclining chair was cold plastic—*brrr!*

I prayed it didn't snap with my added weight and crash to the concrete.

Snow fell, and thunder rumbled in the distance.

The door clanged open, and my pursuer emerged. I froze, posing against Ghost Man like a photographer had asked for a still shot. As though demanding no expression and no tension—*or fear!*—in my muscles.

I wanted to inhale—*to breathe!*—because running the passages, falling, and then scrambling to the chair made me want to huff and puff.

My head ached—I felt a cough coming on!

Shut. It. Down. Use your training, Mel. Don't move. Control your airflow. Keep it slow. Eyes still, but take in your surroundings. Do. Not. Move.

My pursuer, a woman, scanned the pool area. She looked at the hut with its flashing disco ball and the meadow beyond. Lightning flashed.

She looked at the chairs, studying the silly scene of Ghouls by the Pool.

Be still, Mel!

I pressed against the bale, trying to be the best mannequin that ever lived.

I had to—*otherwise, I'd die.*

SHE SKIRTED PAST THE HUT—I LOST SIGHT OF HER FOR A SECOND. THEN, I saw a dark form dash down a meadow path, moving toward the untamed area beyond the pool deck.

"It's been great, but I've gotta *bale*," I whispered to my chunky companion.

I sat up and ripped away the rest of the underskirt. I ditched the heels, too. The concrete felt like ice on my feet, but I didn't care. I'd modeled swimsuits in the snow and winter parkas in stifling heat. I'd posed for hours with pins needling my skin. I'd been under blazing hot lights and leaped like an acrobat while wearing a gown and heels.

This model could jump, run, pose on a dime—she could do anything!

I was a supermodel!

Adrenaline pulsed; I felt its boost as though I'd ingested a drug. I ran toward the meadow path, my feet thunking heel-first on the hard surface around the pool—*thunk, thunk, thunk.*

I hit the soft mulch of the path—warmer to my feet. I moved faster.

Where did Ichabod's killer go?

Lightning flashed—*there!* I saw her standing in the flat area where the pickleball courts were proposed.

She saw me, too. We were the length of two courts, about thirty yards apart.

"I'll get you, Mel Tower!" she yelled and ran toward me.

"Help!" I screamed. "Help, someone! Come quick—Ichabod's killer is in the meadow!"

I moved to my right, scrambling up a mound of dirt, clawing the soil, spraying it toward her. She'd closed the distance between us *fast*. Below me was an abyss, the hole dug for the perc test.

I prayed she didn't bring a gun to a dirt fight.

"Help!" I screamed.

"Mel, if you know what's good for you—stop!" she ordered.

I quit clawing, then grabbed my calf. "I'm stuck. I think I broke my ankle!"

I spit dirt from my mouth—*phew!*

She attacked the mound, moving toward me on my island as though climbing a steep hill. She pushed away clods, grunting with effort. The dirt was loose; it slowed her down.

"Arghh!" she yelled.

Lightning flashed. I saw the woman's enraged face—*Alicia Cliff!*

She wanted the House of Hall to herself, just like Eden said!

"I've hurt myself!" I yelled. "Give me your hand." I reached down and tried to grab her arm—*I'd snap her scrawny wrist if I could get it.*

She kept climbing, pushing away soil. She got within striking distance of my feet.

I waited, then—*BAM!* I jabbed a heel to her nose with all the strength I had—a stiletto heel would have stabbed out her eye!

"Owww!" she cried.

She curled into a ball—*the pose I needed!*

I shoved her coiled body with my feet. Not easy from my position above her.

I started sliding!

I braced my arms to stop myself, then shoved mightily again.

She screamed and clawed the soil. Her nails scratched my calf—*ouch!*

Again, I pushed: "Ugh!"

She rolled down, down, down.

Once she started, momentum kept her going. I heard her hit the frigid water at the bottom of the hole—*splash!*

"Oh, no—help me!" she screamed.

29

A Hole in One

Cozette posed near the hole, holding her walkie-talkie like a gun. Snow fell harder, making it hard to see.

She pointed it down at the woman caught in the water. "Stop right there, or I'll shoot! Don't move a muscle!"

"Get me out of here!" Alicia screamed. "My leg—I think it's broken!"

"STOP RIGHT THERE!" Cozette repeated.

She convinced me, for sure. I froze on the dirt mound like a mermaid on a rock, my head pounding.

The resort's exterior lights powered on—whoa, they were bright! It was like a cruise ship lighting up after someone fell overboard.

Cozette yelled from below me. "Are you okay, Mel?"

"Y-yes."

My teeth chattered. The adrenaline boost was wearing off.

The soil suddenly felt like ice, and the thundersnow air chilled my bones.

"Help is on the way," Cozette said. "Gee whiz, I love solving mysteries!"

THE NEXT PERSON TO HELP WAS COLE.

The exterior lights of the GP flooded the area like a football stadium. Snow drifted down, looking like swirling crystals. Lightning flashed.

A pickup with a red bubble light on its roof barreled up the boulevard, turned toward the pool, then drove down the service lane to the pool bar.

Whee-oh, Whee-oh.

Other police vehicles followed, their lights cutting through the darkness, their sirens bouncing off the building.

Someone, thankfully, had called nine-one-one.

Cole jumped from his truck—I saw him from my position on the atoll about fifty yards away. He glanced around, weapon drawn, the truck's headlights lighting the path and our section of the meadow.

He pressed his back against the building, spinning and looking, trying to gain his bearings. For a second, he scanned the skeleton bartenders and ghost customers—for safety, I was sure.

He had to check if anyone was real or a threat.

I cupped my dirty hands around my mouth. "Cole, h-here! We're back here!"

Cozette held her ground, pointing her radio "weapon" at the hole, and yelled, "Yah, back here—we got her!"

He roared, "Mel, is that you?"

"It's me—we got her, Cole!"

He sprinted down the path, moving fast as a running back. "I'm coming!"

I pushed down the dirt hill, back end first.

Cole scrambled up, meeting me halfway. He scooped me in his arms. "You're safe, Mel, you're safe. *I love you.*"

He pressed me against his chest—so warm!

Alicia screamed from below ground. "Get me out of here!"

"Alicia Cliff is in that hole," I said. "She killed Ichabod—and she's got Bruce DuWayne somewhere. Lou, too, I think. Get her out, then call someone to find him."

He released me, removed his jacket, and wrapped me in it. He stepped toward the hole, tilting his head and evaluating what he saw.

Cozette holstered her radio, looking around the area lit by the truck's headlights and the blazing orbs of the Promenade. "The heck with pickleball. We could put an outdoor mini-golf course here—and Alicia would be our first hole-in-one!"

In the guard's office, I asked about Lou. "Is s-she okay?" Even though I was wrapped in a blanket, I still shivered.

Cozette was with me. "She's mad as a hornet but fine. Alicia ambushed us soon as we got there. Locked us in the walk-in pantry in that house's kitchen. Took our phones but forced Lou to text ya first."

I nodded. "That's how I knew. Lou *never* calls me Melanie."

"It was a mistake to lock us in that pantry. If there ever was a place Lou would escape from, it would be a kitchen pantry."

"H-how?"

"Rolling pin to the door knob. In Lou's hands, rolling pins are registered weapons."

"Where is she?"

"The ballroom, probably. She covered the inside; I took the outside." Cozette stepped back to stare at my dress. Ruined now, of course. "What are you wearin'?"

"It was what they call an editorial garment. The First Look of the show." I touched it. "Every fashion collection has multiple aspects: editorial, ready-to-wear. Hero Pieces. Those are—"

"I don't care what they call it! That's a Hero Piece if I ever saw one," Cozette said.

30
SUNDAY MORNING

Bruce DuWayne was found unconscious but alive.

He was tied up in a closet in the service building at the municipal airport, the lone building at the grass airfield, an island of sorts.

He'd showed up to question Alicia at her rental. At gunpoint, she'd driven him over, forced him into a closet, and locked it. She'd used his phone to text people, pretending he was still on the case.

DuWayne was discovered *before* she confessed.

White Owl Holdings' private jet was due over the weekend. While the catwalk was going on, the village's maintenance fellow went to the field to check it because of the weather. *He* found Bruce.

The charges against Alicia will be worse for not 'fessing up when she could have, according to Cole.

My fella stayed up all night, making sure his gal didn't have a concussion. Max helped, too. His Aunt Fern brought him when she'd heard about the show.

I rested on the couch, Cole was nearby in a chair, and Max guarded the doors, moving from the front to the back, sniffing the air flowing through their narrow gaps, remaining vigilant.

Animals know.

When the Tool & Rye opened in the morning, Cole got breakfast and brought it back.

Max stayed with me.

Between Cole and Max, I'd never felt so safe.

Cole made phone calls., then revealed what he could about Ichabod's murder.

"Alicia wanted the House of Hall to herself," he said. "Simple as that. Greed."

"What did she do?" I asked. "I found him. There were differing clues: the cheese curds, the scarf, the broken inhaler. What did she use to ... kill him?"

I still had trouble saying it.

"She'd planned it for a while, it seems. I can't say officially. But she may have given him medication to weaken him, and then snuck up and used his scarf to, ah, dispatch him."

"Just for control—greed?"

Cole sighed. "It will come out during the investigation. She had *designs* on things for a while, apparently."

Gruesome.

I didn't want to know more; the tragedy was too recent.

I didn't want to "burden my remembrance" of Ichabod Hall with a heavy heart.

Lou being Lou, and Wisconsin being Wisconsin, after the murder was solved, a tailgate party broke out at my house.

I heard the rumble of a truck's engine in the driveway about mid-morning.

A door slammed, then voices followed.

Max barked. *Woof!*

Cole walked to the front door, squinting through the sidelight. "Your cousin and Cozette Gallagher are here."

Lou barged in—she *always* barged—carrying a roaster with trays of buns balanced on top.

Cozette followed with a crockpot and shopping bags hanging from her arms.

I smelled onions, meat, and spices. Lou's homemade chili, probably.

Max noticed, too, as his nose twitched mile-a-minute.

Lou marched to the kitchen. "Hiya, folks. Figured you'd be stayin' awhile, Cole. So we brought food. Can you put up the tent in the backyard?"

From the couch, I looked toward the French doors. "What tent?"

Lou plugged in the roaster, then rubbed her hands together. "Hank Leigel's bringin' it, along with a sound system. He had so much fun with the Cheesehead quiz show, he's doin' another one."

"No, please—"

"Snow's already meltin'," she said. "Warm today. It's fine, Mel. It won't be a datin' game this time, just Wisconsin trivia. No bachelors or bachelorettes. We're gonna save that for this winter, February. We're callin' it 'Love Bash,' and it's gonna be great. Hold it out at the Promenade again. A week of fun, just like on the TV show *The Love Boat.*"

February was too far in the future to worry about! Cole and I were already on our own cruise, it seemed. I enjoyed every second with the man, even with a sore head.

My house soon flooded with neighbors. Someone turned on the Packers football game.

Fern Bubble arrived, looking much happier—it was wonderful to see her.

Hank Leigel came from Main Street. He threw open the backyard gate, and my vendors from the mall showed up. They sampled hot sandwiches, chili, and salads, gave well wishes to me, and then sat down on lawn chairs to be quizzed about Cinnamon and the Dairy State.

The sun broke through the clouds for the first time all week. Light glinted off the golden leaves on the trees, making them glisten. They looked like holiday trees except with orange and gold ornaments.

After encouragement, Cole volunteered for a round of questions.

Hank warmed him up with easy ones: "What's our state's favorite holiday?" *Packers' Sunday.*

Then: "What mythical beast haunts the Northwoods?" *A hodag.*

After that, it was a hard-hitter: "This former model from Wisconsin struggled with isolation and worried about her relationships. Ironically, because of a fashion show—a career she'd given up —she found herself again."

Okay, yes, I made that up.

The third question was: "This famous spirit is painted on a water tower in southwest Wisconsin."

Cole pondered the answer. After a few seconds, he said, "The Ridgeway Ghost." He winked at me.

Correct!

Hank gave him a prize, an apron that said, "Licensed to Grill." Lou had something to do with the awards, I suspected.

The Ridgeway Ghost was much better than the one I came up with—*Model Ghost.*

I'd have become a ghost if Alicia Cliff had caught me. I smiled, looking at Cole.

An island didn't have to be a place of fear or isolation. It could be one of safety, even inspiration.

I sat in my backyard, looking at my beloved home, seeing my place filled with the family, friends, and man I loved.

Max nudged against me, leaning against my legs, keeping me warm.

I didn't feel alone anymore.

31

THE TEMPEST

The Reader's Theater event at the library was canceled.

After a murder, a disastrous fashion show, and thundersnow, it was the best decision.

Boo Bash had been affected by a tempest. No sense in tempting the gods further.

All's well that end's well, folks.

A few weeks later, for Thanksgiving, Max and I traveled north.

Cole bought tickets for *The Tempest*. We watched the play at the community theater in Minocqua, then strolled to his truck, the night clear, stars bright.

The Northern Lights were even on display.

Or, it may have been a plane painted a delightful green and blue, a swirl on its tail.

I think it was Rand. I'm pretty sure I saw a wing wave in the sky.

Godspeed, my friend.

Later that evening, at Cole's place, we sat in front of the fire.

"Next summer, let's go to Mackinac and Washington islands," he said. "In February, let's try something tropical."

I laughed. "Sure."

"I love you, Mel Tower."

"I love you, too, Cole Lawrence."

Max looked between the two of us, his nose twitching, black eyes shining.

He agreed, I could tell.

Animals know.

32

MODEL RESCUE

A SNEAK PEEK

"Trust is like water," Chandler Weston declared, his amber eyes glowing. "It's necessary for life. A mother trusts the doctor to deliver her child. A horse, her rider."

He wore a green leather jacket and a sly grin. He leaned toward me. It was like watching an alligator slip into a pond. "A philanthropist must believe in his inner circle."

Other folks mingled in the foyer of the billionaire cowboy's log cabin palace (think Versailles but stick-built).

Still, Weston stared at me, Mel Tower.

I felt offended. As a former fashion model, I was no slouch in the trustworthiness department.

For two decades during New York Fashion Week, I'd kept my mouth shut for Big Name Designers during sneak-peek try-ons. Thus, I was rehired year after year.

I wasn't a walking bank vault but hardly an open book.

Weston didn't have confidence in me.

Why not?

Six board members had gathered at Pipestone, the man's ranch, on a blustery December weekend to establish a horse rescue organization.

I was a worker bee among pooh-bahs, a friend's plus-one who'd been hired to write public relations strategy.

Two board members ignored me, the hired help.

They didn't ignore me, exactly. Mrs. Chanel Suit asked about the powder room, and Mr. Ferragamo Loafers dumped their coats into my arms.

She may have ended up in the closet, and the coats in the bathroom, I don't recall—*they were the untrustworthy ones!*

Back to Chandler Weston, who looked stressed. A crease had formed over his brow as he watched people arrive. He shook his glass, jingling the ice, alerting the butler to refresh it.

Well, Mel Tower believes, besides cheese curds, Midwest Food of the Gods, humor alleviates worry and shortens the distance between people, even rich and poor ones.

I told Weston a joke: "Love all, trust few, do wrong to animal abusers. Shakespeare posted that on Instagram, I read."

He laughed, his neon eyes softening.

He may not trust me yet, but he knew I was funny.

###

WISCOCOA

A requested recipe among readers is Wiscocoa. Louella Jingle's advice is to drink it with friends because that's when it tastes best.

- Gather chairs, any number works, just enough to sit around a campfire in a backyard.
- Light up one campfire, preferably under bright stars. (Water nearby, just in case).
- Make cocoa. Any kind works. Powdered, or made on a stove in a pan with 1/3 c. unsweetened cocoa powder, 3/4 c. granulated sugar, a pinch of salt, and 1/3 c. boiling water. Pour the water over the dry ingredients, whisk continually until smooth. Stir about two minutes.
- Stir in 3 1/2 c. milk. Whisk on stove to near-boil. Don't boil! Watch carefully to prevent scorching.
- Remove from heat. Add 1 t. vanilla extract. (Or peppermint extract, if preferred).
- Into four heavy mugs, preferably made by a local artist, add cream, 1-2 T., and then whiskey to taste. Pour in the hot chocolate. Stir with a cinnamon stick.
- Add jokes, puns, love, and prayer to individual taste.

Serve among friends, cowboys, and cowgirls. Tell 'em Lou sent ya.

ABOUT TK SHEFFIELD, MA

TK Sheffield is a second-career author advocating for those who've dreamed of writing novels but had other obligations. In her late forties, she returned to school, acquired a master's degree, and taught college writing to share the love of the written word with students. Now, she writes novels and screenplays for readers who seek to laugh and escape, and she encourages older authors to get into the game of writing.

Her funny, family-friendly books and screenplays earned recognition from Killer Nashville, Eric Hoffer, Romance Writers of America, and many other organizations. She is a member of the Wisconsin Writers Association, Sisters in Crime, the Blackbird Writers, SCBWI, and Mystery Writers of America.

When not writing, she can be found in her Wisconsin backyard or cruising on a pontoon boat in the Northwoods.

Please join her on social media including Instagram and Substack, where she shares stories and encouragement with readers and writers. (Photo: Udo Spreitzenbarth)

9 798990 563131